I CAN SEE
CLEARLY
NOW

I CAN SEE CLEARLY NOW

A NOVEL

BRENDAN HALPIN

VILLARD

NEW YORK

A Villard Books Trade Paperback Original

Copyright © 2009 by Brendan Halpin

Published in the United States by Villard Books,
an imprint of The Random House Publishing Group,
a division of Random House, Inc., New York.

VILLARD BOOKS, VILLARD, and "V" CIRCLED Design are registered
trademarks of Random House, Inc.

ISBN 978-0-8129-7703-5

Printed in the United States of America

www.villard.com

246897531

Book design by Jo Anne Metsch

For the Seven Hills Bowling Team,
'85–'86

I CAN SEE CLEARLY NOW

CAROLYN

WHERE THE HELL was Jackie? Carolyn shifted in her chair and sipped her appletini. Jackie was off dancing with some shockingly hot guy, and, as so often happened, Carolyn was holding down the table alone.

Oh no. The only thing worse than holding down the table alone was what was about to happen. Some guy who had to be forty if he was a day came over and said, "Is it okay if I join you for a minute?"

"Well," Carolyn said, "my friend's just gone to the bathroom and . . ."

"Oh. Okay, then," he said. "Listen, let me just tell you that you have beautiful eyes and wish you a good evening, then."

Beautiful eyes. That was nice and unusual. Carolyn hated her brown eyes. Well, what the hell. Who knew when Jackie would be back. "Hey, listen, my friend is kind of—she tends not to make it back for a while if there's music playing. So, I mean, if you want to sit down just until she gets back . . ." So it had come to this. Well, it kind of always came to this. Jackie had all these hot, shaggy-haired boys throwing themselves at her, and Carolyn always ended up talking with the guys old enough to be her dad who usually had a little bit of a gut. Jackie got invited to art openings and poetry readings and rock-and-roll shows. Carolyn got invited to come over for coffee when the wife who didn't understand him was out of town so we can talk about Foucault. As if, after taking one class on Foucault in college, she ever wanted to talk about Foucault again, much less with some married professor.

Jackie told Carolyn it was her glasses and her whole bookworm appearance. She figured she just had that professorial trophy-wife look—like the kind of girl who was young enough to be scandalous, but who looked like she could actually talk about the contents of the *Times* on the Sunday morning after.

So tonight she was wearing Jackie's clothes, but her stupid contacts hadn't come in yet, so she was stuck with the bookworm glasses, and here was the old guy. "So what do you do?" he asked.

Carolyn thought about pulling out the kind of elaborate lie that just always fell off Jackie's tongue in situations like this. Jackie called them "bar lies" and felt that they were different from regular lies. But such things weren't Carolyn's forte.

"I'm a production assistant at ATV," Carolyn said.

"Yeah? What show do you work on?"

"Well, I'm actually—working on this big DVD set of this weird thing from the '70's called *Pop Goes the Classroom.*"

The guy's face lit up. "Oh my God! *Pop Goes the Classroom*! I love that! Funky solah systemmmmmmm . . . yeah!" he started to sing. He was all the way to Uranus when Carolyn caught a glimpse of Jackie. She drained her appletini and said, "Oh, my friend's coming back. But you know what, you keep the seat, and I'll just go with her."

The guy was faced, and he was so busy singing "Nine's Magic Multiples" as she walked away that she didn't even have to tell him there was no way he was getting her number.

"What the hell was that?" Jackie said.

"*Pop Goes the Classroom.* I don't know what it is about that thing. I don't get it at all."

Jackie, who'd watched the whole DVD with Carolyn out of loyalty, just shrugged. "Must be a '70s thing," she said.

THE NEXT MORNING at work, Carolyn thought about that. She'd had no trouble at all lining up a bunch of current celebrities to talk about the genius of *Pop Goes the Classroom* for the "Lasting Impact" mini doc that was going to be a special feature. In fact, she'd had such success that the folks over at ATV Records were deciding whether they wanted to release a tribute CD filled with tracks that so many musicians over thirty-five were practically begging them to be allowed to record.

She made calls to the hotel, the car service, and the airlines, just to make sure everything was in place. She annoyed Jim in studio 4-G by asking him yet again if everything was ready to record a commentary track tomorrow.

"Yes, Carolyn. You know, I think you're just looking for excuses to call me."

Ew. As if.

Still no word from Pamela Sanchez. Not one returned phone call. Well, fine, she'd miss the party. Carolyn hoped the boss wouldn't be too mad that the only semi-marquee name involved in the original project wasn't going to participate in the commentary track.

She figured she should tell the boss that she'd struck out with Pamela Sanchez. She could probably wait until the end of the day, but if she was going to get fired for being a failure, she wanted it to happen sooner rather than later.

She knocked tentatively on the boss's door. "Yes?" the boss said.

"Uh, hi," Carolyn said, reminding herself to look the boss in the eyes and not stare at her shoes. "So, uh, everything's all set for tomorrow. Except I still haven't heard from Pamela Sanchez. I even went downtown and pounded on her door."

"What did she say?"

Carolyn did her best impersonation of a staticky building intercom. "Leave now or I'm calling the police. And tell those bksshhhh at ATN that they can shhhkkkssshht with their wshhhhkkkkktttt."

The boss laughed. This seemed like a good sign.

"Okay," the boss said, and then her face shifted slightly. "I didn't really expect anything different. And I do appreciate your doing it. I can't imagine what kind of abuse she would have heaped on me if I'd been the one to call." She took a deep breath. "Wow. I'm really nervous."

Carolyn did not fall over at hearing the boss make this admission, but it took some effort. "Everything's all set, I've called the car service and the hotel and—"

"I'm not nervous about the logistics. I know you're capable in that area. It's just that . . . you know, I haven't seen these people in thirty-five years."

Wow. Apparently the boss was human. Who would have guessed?

Carolyn decided to push it just a little.

"Can I ask you something?"

"Sure, of course."

"Why—I mean, what do you think . . . why isn't Pamela Sanchez coming? I mean, she's very well respected, but she's not exactly burning up the charts. You'd think she'd want the exposure and the paycheck. What's she still so mad about thirty-five years later?"

"Well," the boss said. "It's actually a really long story."

1

DINGO

HE DIDN'T EVEN want to do the encore. The idea of staring at a half-empty theater for even five more minutes was just depressing. But the pathetic little crowd that had shown up had to hear "Shadows in the Twilight," and Dingo was enough of a professional to know that they owed it to them.

So he stared at his crash cymbal while Pamela sang her heart out. In her way, she was a professional too. The song ended soon enough, and the applause was enthusiastic; it only sounded pathetic when compared with the sound of a full house applauding.

They walked offstage, and Pamela seemed to be as elated as she always was after a show. She floated backstage, held aloft by the adoration of the crowd.

Dingo looked at Alec and Keith. They all just shook their heads. They'd been in the business long enough to know that this was the end of the line of the Pamela Sanchez gravy train. First she'd been dropped from her label due to what she insisted was the "crypto-fascism" of the head of the label. The label stiffed her on distribution of her latest album and made no effort to get it onto the radio, so without the sales and the airplay, the crowds just weren't big enough anymore for her to justify paying them. Especially not when she could tour around college campuses with no more expenses than gas and guitar strings and play little coffeehouses surrounded by worshipful eighteen-year-olds. She'd tell *Rolling Stone*, if they asked, if they cared anymore, that she had decided that the full electrified band experiment wasn't really working, and that she'd decided to go back to her roots and really connect with her fans.

They got backstage, and Dingo went to change clothes. When he emerged, Pamela was holding court with the usual crowd of girls dressed in peasant blouses like the one Pamela was spilling out of on the *Shadows in the Twilight* album cover and boys with big beards. After an hour or so of hearing about how far out the show was, how it really blew their minds, man, Pamela would leave with one of the boys, and, since this was a special night, last night of the tour and all, probably one of the girls as well. Alec and Keith would take whichever of the unshaven, disappointed girls didn't get to go worship more intimately at the altar of Pamela.

Alec, who was English, was particularly bitter about this end of the arrangement. He claimed to have gone to high school with members of Foghat, and he would periodically complain about how he could be shagging groupies far more attractive and less hairy if he'd only gone along when those blokes begged him to join their band.

Dingo found Alec tiresome. Actually, this being the end of the tour, he found everyone tiresome. He just wanted to be home. The hotel was only two blocks away, so he decided to walk while everybody else was deciding who'd get to ride the limo back to the hotel. Well, no more limos, Dingo thought. He'd better get used to walking.

As he walked, he tried not to worry, but he didn't succeed. When he got home tomorrow, he'd have to think about exactly how they were going to pay the mortgage once the money from this tour ran out. Would Cass's job at the doctor's office be enough? Why had he listened to her? If they'd stayed in the city, paying next to nothing in their rent-controlled building, they would have plenty of extra money to get through times like this. But no, Davey and Jenny deserved a yard, and Cass wanted a real house to take care of while he was on the road, she wanted to be a Jersey mom like all her friends, so she was a Jersey mom, which meant she needed a car, because you couldn't walk to anything, so that was more money, and all of this was fine as long as Pamela was still selling records and selling out concerts, but what about now? What the hell were they going to do?

Back at the hotel, Dingo kicked off his shoes and flopped on the bed. He reached over to the phone and called home. Running up hotel long-distance bills was another perk of being on the road with Pamela that he would have to get used to doing without. Then again, if he wasn't on the road, he wouldn't need to make long-distance calls. Cass picked up on the first ring.

"Hey, sweetie," he said.

"Hi, baby! How was the show tonight?"

"Depressing. Half empty."

"I'm sorry, honey."

"Yeah. Thanks. I guess I'll call Tony when I get home and see if I can get some commercial work." Dingo didn't really want to go lay down some drum part for a song about the joys of extra-soft toilet paper, but he had a family to support.

"Okay, honey. We don't have to worry about that right now. Let's just talk about how we're gonna celebrate you getting home. Davey is going to be thrilled. He's got a game at three tomorrow, by the way—do you think you'll be home by then?"

"Well, I mean, it's going to depend on how late Pamela sleeps. I sure as hell hope so."

"Well, you can take a train. It's only an hour and a half."

"You know what? I will. If she's not up by eleven, I'll just go take a train. I can't wait to see you. I miss you so much." Alec and Keith both had girlfriends they said the same thing to, sometimes while a groupie was down on her hairy knees in front of them, but Dingo really meant it.

"I miss you too. Now, I thought we were going to talk about how we were going to celebrate."

Dingo unbuttoned his pants and smiled. "Yeah. I'd like that."

DINGO WOKE AT eight, showered, packed, had a disgustingly huge breakfast in the hotel restaurant, and was not even all the way through *The Philadelphia Inquirer* when Pamela appeared in the lobby. Dingo was shocked and delighted. He'd be home in time for Davey's game.

"You're up early," he said.

"I have to meet someone," Pamela said. "Oh, there he is now." She was looking across the lobby at a man in a suit. Suits. That couldn't be good news. And yet, as Dingo took the guy in, he thought he didn't look sleazy enough to be a record company suit, so this wasn't about Pamela's career getting a new lease on life with a new record company. The guy was tall, blond, and good looking, but not stoned, adoring, or young enough to be Pamela's type. So what the hell was this?

It was mysterious. As Pamela walked over to meet with the suit, she said, "I left wake-up calls, but we're pulling out in half an hour, so maybe you want to go pound on Keith and Alec's door. Or maybe you don't. We'll go either way."

Dingo smiled, just imagining Davey fielding grounders, and imagining what Cass was going to do after Davey went to bed. He didn't particularly feel like facing Keith and Alec hung over and tired if he didn't have to. She'd left them wake-up calls; they'd have to pretend they were grown-ups and fend for themselves.

As it turned out, Keith staggered onto the bus with ten minutes to spare, reeking of sex, booze, and stomach acid. Dingo
wondered idly if the spots on Keith's shirt were his own vomit or
someone else's. Alec was left in the hotel in Philadelphia, and
would probably wake up in a couple of hours bitching about how
Foghat never would have left him behind at the end of a tour.
Good riddance.

Pamela huddled with the suit for the whole ride back to the
city. The bus pulled up at Penn Station, and the suit got out, as
did Keith, who gave a visibly repulsed Pamela a big hug. Dingo
headed to the front of the bus, and Pamela said, "Wait, David."
(When Dingo's mother had died two years earlier, she'd left
Pamela as the only person on earth who called him David.) "We'll
drive you home. I want to discuss something with you."

Well, Dingo thought, he did appreciate the fact that she was
going to give him a ride home when firing him. It showed professionalism and a certain amount of consideration for all he'd
done for her.

"Okay," he said, already mentally preparing his burn-no-
bridges speech, something about how much he'd enjoyed working with her, how she was a real professional and an artist as well,
and how he hoped if things changed in the future she'd keep him
in mind. He would probably leave out the part about how he
didn't really mind her screwing him out of a producing credit on
the albums she supposedly produced herself. Not fighting that
one had been a conscious choice—Cass had been furious, but
Pamela had already had a number one single under her belt at
that point, and Dingo figured that not making waves and sticking
with her would be better for maintaining the kind of steady in-
come that pays your Jersey mortgage than winning the credit and
then not being able to work because he was "difficult."

"So, David, that man I was speaking with was Clark Payson."

Dingo looked at Pamela blankly.

"Briggs Payson's son. We've been in touch since I co-hosted Mike Douglas. Of course that was NBC, but Clark took me to lunch and told me to look him up if I had a yen to perform on the boob tube again. I thought my falling-out with the fascists at Antigone Records might provide an opportunity to branch out."

"Well sure, of course." The ATN Paysons. All of a sudden, things were looking very different. Were they going to give her a variety show? It seemed unlikely—Pamela, despite having held her own on Mike Douglas, wasn't exactly Sonny and Cher, and Dingo had a very hard time picturing her cracking jokes with Special Guest Star Joey Heatherton on a weekly basis. Still, maybe they'd tape six or eight episodes before they canceled it, and that would be a nice chunk of change.

"He's given me the opportunity to guide a group of young songwriters through the creative process as they work on an educational project—educational songs to run between cartoons on ATN Saturday mornings."

So he was getting fired after all. Well, the TV show had been a nice, momentary dream.

"I see," he said.

"So I will be needing a drummer for this project, and they've asked me to produce the recordings as well. And, well, I've really appreciated everything you've brought to the recording process, so I was hoping you would work with me on this. They'll expect the first results on the air in a few months, but it's a yearlong project, and Mr. Payson said he'd pay you twenty thousand dollars."

Twenty thousand dollars! More money than Dingo ever could have hoped to make in a year of commercial gigs. They could pay off the Ford Torino station wagon. Hell, they could trade it in and upgrade to a Gran Torino. Actually if he was going to work in the city, Dingo would need a car, and that beautiful five-year-old GTO over at the used-car lot could actually be his if he was making this kind of money.

A year of steady work, a regular paycheck, and enough money that they could actually put some away for leaner times. If Cass didn't decide she needed to do some big home improvement projects. He'd probably tell her it was fifteen just so she didn't start planning a new kitchen or something.

Sure, he'd be doing producing work that Pamela would take credit for, but Davey would have back-to-school clothes, they'd keep the car running, and maybe they'd even take a nice family vacation.

"I'm in," Dingo said, and when the bus pulled up outside his house, it was all he could do not to kick up his heels as he ran off the bus and picked up Davey in a big, joyful hug.

TWO WEEKS LATER, Dingo climbed behind the wheel of his GTO and fired up the engine. Well, he actually coaxed the engine to life. Pamela hadn't wanted his input as she and the ATN guy chose the young songwriters to work on the project. Which was fine with him. He'd gotten reacquainted with his family (with a special stab of regret at how big Jenny had gotten, all the things she was able to do now that she hadn't been able to do when he'd left on tour). He'd then spent most of the last two weeks making the GTO look shiny and beautiful—cleaning the seats with a toothbrush, shampooing the floors, filling in scratches with the paint he'd gotten from the Pontiac dealer, and washing, waxing, and buffing the exterior. He'd neglected the mechanical side because everything had been running fine. But today the GTO seemed to be deciding that it needed a new starter.

Traffic was so heavy that Dingo never really got a chance to open the GTO up, which just seemed like a shame. He pulled into the ATN garage and showed his pass to the guard, who smiled and waved him through. It was surreal—most of Dingo's encounters with guys like that involved them kicking him out of places.

Inside the building he asked another uniformed guy for directions, then took the elevator up to Clark Payson's office. He checked his watch. He was five minutes early.

Sitting in the office were four kids who must have been the songwriters—they all looked really nervous, and the mousy girl with the brown hair really looked like she might actually vomit. Dingo was nervous too—you don't spend fifteen years in the music business without developing a fear of suits. Dingo's heart was in the garage rather than the coffeehouse, so he didn't really like most of the music Pamela listened to (or, for that matter, played) on the bus, but when she'd been in her fourth or fifth Woody Guthrie revival, Dingo had been struck by the line "Some will rob you with a six gun, and some with a fountain pen." Meeting with the suits almost always led to getting screwed.

Still, he was the elder statesman here, so he felt like he should try to put the terrified kids at ease. "Hi, everybody," he said as the secretary behind the desk glared at him. "I'm Dingo Donovan. I've been Pamela's drummer for the last three years, and I'm here to play drums and help on the production side." He grinned as broadly as he possibly could.

The first one to stand was a tall, thin blonde. "Julie Waterston," she said, extending her hand. Dingo shook it and turned to the person next to her since they were all standing now. "Peter Terpin," said a young white guy who really should have shaved this morning. The mousy white girl mumbled something and gave a weak handshake.

"I'm sorry?" Dingo said. "You've gotta forgive me, because I'm old and I've spent most of the last fifteen years sitting in front of a drum kit and next to a stack of amps, so I can't hear for beans."

This got a smile out of the timid girl. "Sarah Stein," she said.

The last one to shake his hand was the black guy. "Levon Hayes," he said, and shook Dingo's hand firmly. Dingo looked at him for a minute.

"I think I know you. You look really familiar," Dingo said. He paused. "Did you play with the Soul Starrs?"

"Nahh," Levon said, smiling, "Supersonic Funketeers."

"Right!" Dingo said. "I knew it was one of Calvin's bands! I saw you guys last year—that was one tight band! You were, what, Captain Butthole or something, right?"

Levon looked embarrassed. "Uh, that was actually Apollo Von Funkenburg."

"Huh. I could have sworn there was a butt thing there."

"Nah, it was a planet thing. My full title was Apollo Von Funkenburg, Duke of Uranus."

Dingo laughed aloud. "Right! I knew it! That's fantastic. Say hi to Calvin for me, will you?"

"Yeah, if I ever see him again. They left on a big national tour."

"And you stayed here?"

"Yeah. I . . . well, yeah, it's a long story."

"Smart move. Touring sucks." The kids looked like they were relaxing a little bit, and Dingo looked around to see them all hanging on his every word. He thought he might elaborate on how much touring sucked, but just then Pamela made her entrance.

"Good morning, everyone!" she said. She was wearing a peasant skirt with a purple blouse, and she had feathers randomly sprinkled through her black hair.

The kids left Dingo and crowded around Pamela. "Today is the first day of our—" she began, but the secretary interrupted her.

"Mr. Payson will see you now," she said.

"Well—we'll have more time later," Pamela said as she led the way into Clark Payson's office.

CLARK PAYSON, THOUGH he was older and better dressed than any of the kids, looked just as nervous as they were.

"Why don't you all have a seat . . . oh," he said. "There aren't enough chairs, are there. All right, I'll tell you what. Let's just meet Dr. Andrews, and then we'll go downstairs and I'll show you around your work space, and we'll talk down there."

They walked down the hall and into an office that surely must have begun life as a closet. Sitting at a desk surrounded by bookshelves on all the walls, a short, bespectacled man with graying hair and a Vandyke beard scribbled in a notebook. He didn't look up despite all the people standing in the hallway staring at him.

"Uh, Dr. Andrews?" Clark Payson said.

"Geh!" Dr. Andrews, startled, jumped back from his desk. "Oh, Mr. Payson, I'm sorry, you startled me. I was so deep into the project."

Clark Payson smiled. "That's perfectly fine. Dr. Andrews, I just wanted to re-introduce you to all of the young songwriters we'll have working on this project. Guys, you probably remember Dr. Andrews from the auditions. We're very lucky to have Dr. Andrews here on loan from the Early Childhood Education Department over at Teachers College. He's been busy putting together guidelines for your work, and . . . well, Dr. Andrews, perhaps you can explain?"

"Of course. Thank you. As you are all probably aware, the PBS people have pioneered educational television with *Sesame Street*. There's no point in our developing a similar project with puppets and such, especially given that our target audience here is actually in a different Piagetian stage than theirs. So, briefly, we'll be operating in what the Russian theorist Lev Vygotsky, whose works are not widely available in English but have, fortunately, been translated into French, which of course you have to learn if you're going to study Piaget . . . I'm sorry, where was I? Ah, yes, Vygotsky calls this the zone of proximal development."

Dr. Andrews gave a satisfied smile as though he had actually said something. Dingo stole a glance at the kids, who all looked as dumbfounded as he felt.

"Yes, well, thanks, Dr. Andrews," Clark Payson said, smiling. "Dr. Andrews is producing a series of curriculum guides hitting specific points you should be addressing in your songs. They're all in binders downstairs, and he continues to add to them, but for the moment, there's quite a collection of material for you to use when you're getting started. And now, without further ado, let's see where you'll be working!"

He led them down the hallway in silence that Pamela quickly filled. "Now, don't be shocked to find that we're actually in a basement. I've done some energy work down there with a shaman friend of mine, and I'm confident that we will be focused on our art, and that the somewhat . . . unconventional work space may actually help us to work outside the narrow conventions of this medium." Pamela was more coherent than Dr. Andrews had been, but only barely. He could feel the kids looking at him, checking his face to see if he thought Pamela was full of shit. He tried to erase any trace of expression from his face.

"Okay!" Clark said. "So this is the booth, and through that window, the studio. They've both been in continuous use in this building since it was ARN, the American Radio Network."

Dingo looked at the setup and his heart sank. They were going to have to use recording equipment that had been designed for 1940s radio shows. This stuff predated stereo. After *Sgt. Pepper's*, all the studios had been racing to keep up, to provide every would-be Fab Four that walked through the door the ability to do all kinds of studio magic. The studio arms race had begun five years ago, and this place wasn't even at the starting line. Well, so the equipment wasn't up to 1972 standards. He'd seen Sun Studios, and this was at least better than that. Still, he was going to have to rethink everything about how the recording was going to work if there wasn't going to be any multitrack recording.

Clark Payson led them down a long hallway past the practice rooms and back into the kitchenette/lounge, which had chairs, a new couch, a metal bookcase holding four big plastic binders, and the elevator that led to the outside world. It reeked of some kind of incense or something.

"As you can probably tell," Pamela piped up, "I burned some sage in here just to purify the space."

"Hey, that's great," Clark said. "So if you can all sit down, I just want to talk to you for a few minutes about the project."

Everybody found seats. Julie and Levon sat in the hard chairs that went with the table, and each took out a notebook and pen. Peter, Sarah, and Dingo slouched on the couch, and Pamela sat cross-legged on the floor.

"So as you may know," Clark began, "my father got reamed out on Capitol Hill several weeks ago. One of the complaints they hammered him about was that ATN's educational offerings have been pretty much nonexistent.

"Now, of course, my dad was furious, and he called me in to scream at me—" Dingo saw slightly fearful expressions on all the songwriters except for Pamela, who actually had her eyes closed and was breathing deeply. "Don't worry—you'll never meet him. I go and get screamed at so other people don't have to. It's actually a big part of my job." He clearly expected a laugh, but all he got were a few polite grins.

"So even though Dad was really angry, I couldn't help thinking that the senators had a point. I mean, here we are with the most powerful medium in the history of the world at our disposal, and we've done nothing with it but clown around, show crime-solving animated motorcycles, and sell sugarcoated breakfast cereals.

"We can and should do better. And that's where you come in. You all know the power of television. You can probably all sing theme songs to your favorite shows, you can probably all sing commercial jingles. What if, instead of just planting the theme to *Cowboy Jim's Wild West Adventures* or Nestlé Quik in your brain, we had actually planted useful information? What if students arrived in school already knowing their parts of speech, what if they learned their times tables, what if they knew who Isaac Newton was before they were eight?

"You know, if you search your brains, that we have the power to do this. I don't know what all the implications will be, but I really don't think it's outrageous to say we'll make this a better country. Maybe some of the kids now dropping out of school and hanging out committing crimes would have stayed in school if they'd had just a little bit of a leg up, if school had been just a tiny bit easier for them. We can do this for them. And we must. And not to toot our own horn too much, I really think we have an opportunity to do this more effectively than PBS does. Kids aren't going to sit down in front of our cartoons and know they're educational—we're going to sneak it into the midst of the entertainment, just like we do with the Barbie commercials.

"So please don't just think of this as a job. You've all been chosen for this job after what was, believe you me, a grueling audition process, at least for us"—again he held for a laugh that never came—"because Pamela and I believe that your songs showed that you have the ability to be one of the people who change the world with your music. Thanks."

They all applauded, and Clark Payson beamed. Even though Dingo knew he was probably too old to get caught up in "let's change the world" stuff, he couldn't help feeling a little inspired.

Because what Clark Payson had said was true—Davey could sing every commercial on TV, and the kid was struggling with math. If they could make that better, that would be something that was actually important—not just playing music to sell soap, not just paying the bills, but actually doing something worthwhile. For the first time in a long time, Dingo was really excited about work.

2

PETER

AFTER CLARK PAYSON finished his speech, he went and got on the elevator, and Peter, like everybody else, looked to Pamela to see what would come next.

He really didn't understand how this was going to work. Apart from "Our George, Not Yours," the song he'd written about George Washington and King George III and performed for Pamela, Clark, and Dr. Andrews at the audition two weeks ago, he had always just written songs whenever the mood struck him. He would scribble in a notebook while he worked, or he would pull out his guitar first thing in the morning.

So he didn't know how to just write something on command. It was reassuring to know that he had a binder full of important things to write about in the basement, but still, being called on to suddenly write a song about, say, the Battle of Bunker Hill was an intimidating prospect.

This was the break he'd been waiting for—all the time he'd spent living with the roaches, banging out his songs in seven-eighths-empty clubs, he'd been dreaming of having someone recognize his talent and reward him financially for it. And yet now that he had what he'd wanted, he felt like a fraud in terrible danger of being found out. Clark Payson had, after all, asked him about his background in history in the interview that followed the audition, and he'd talked about how he knew so much from being a history major.

But I really majored in songwriting, getting high, and getting laid, Peter thought, and only one of those things was going to prove useful here.

Well, probably only one. He'd never been under any illusion that he was the only guy who'd heated up a dorm room with Pamela after a college performance, and now it was years ago, but he had harbored what he realized was a pretty stupid hope that he'd get some glimmer of recognition from her, some secret smile that said, *Yes, I remember that night, and yes, it was about as good as sex with a nineteen-year-old boy could have been.* Through the auditions and interviews and into today, though, he'd never seen any sign from Pamela that she remembered him at all.

The room was silent as everyone looked to Pamela for some direction. She was dressed in a long skirt, and she was still sporting a peasant blouse that billowed and gapped and offered glances of her breasts, bare under the blouse. Peter peered at a nipple and felt slightly put out. That nipple was once in my mouth, he thought, and now I'm trying to sneak a peek at it like some sixteen-year-old.

Pamela grabbed a large bag and started pulling out candles. As everybody watched, she placed a candle on nearly every horizontal surface in the room—the arms of the couch, the table, the floor—and lit them. "I can't stand these lights," she said, flipping a switch and turning off the fluorescents overhead. Floor lamps in two corners and the candles provided the only light. Pamela drew two paisley scarves from her bag and threw them over the lamp shades, turning their white light dim, red, and warm.

Finally, she withdrew a stick of incense, lit it, and set it in a jade holder on the floor.

"Well," she said, "that's more like it. Now, I want to put your minds at ease about a few things. First of all, I have never come into an office and banged out songs. It simply isn't the way my creative process works. I'm not really sure that sitting down at the same time and place every day and trying to make yourself create is really creativity at all. It seems to me that that kind of songwriting has the same relationship to real songwriting as prostitution does to real sex. If you're just expected to start secreting the creative juices on demand, sometimes you're just necessarily going to find yourself dry and faking your way through it."

Peter laughed along with everybody else in the room except for the tall girl.

"So," Pamela continued. "I want to let you know that this is not going to be a job like the jobs some of you may have done before coming here. There is obviously no time clock here, and I'm certainly not going to be breathing down your neck about the progress you're making. My role here is to create an atmosphere that nurtures your creativity, and I'm confident that given the right atmosphere, your creativity will flourish, and we will create music that, as Clark says, changes the world.

"I know, and you know, that all artists thrive when they are in conversation with other artists. So if you want to just hang out in this room and talk to each other, or play each other's songs, you should feel free to do that. But you should also feel free to spend the day at the Met, go for a walk in the park, go to MOMA, go to a concert. I don't want this basement to be some island, isolated from the rest of the world; I want it to be a home base, a place from which we venture out to interact with the world and then return to make music.

"Finally, I know the muse strikes at unpredictable times, so I want you to feel that you can come in here at any time. If you have an inspiration at two AM, by all means come in and record something—we've got reel-to-reels in every room here, and of course if any of you are interested in learning more about working behind the board, Dingo and I can help you out with that.

"Now, of course, if we are working together, we need to get to know each other. We'll be having dinner at my place tonight. At that time we can really get to know each other in a more relaxed, informal social setting, and don't worry—I've got plenty of grass, so all you need to bring is yourselves.

"Well, no, not just yourselves. Yourselves after you've gone on a pilgrimage to one of this city's musical shrines. I have prepared an assignment for each of you—" Pamela began handing out pieces of paper that smelled like her perfume. Peter found himself kind of aroused by the smell.

He looked at his piece of paper:

New York City was the epicenter of folk music. Your assignment is to go down to Greenwich Village and visit the following sites:

There followed a list of sites Peter already knew by heart, and directions to Pamela's apartment. Peter had mixed feelings about the whole thing. On the one hand, it was a cool idea, sending them out to draw some musical inspiration from their surroundings. It did show that she understood the creative process and that she was trying to nurture them as artists.

On the other hand, Peter had been living in New York for three years, and the first place he'd gone to visit was where the cover of *The Freewheelin' Bob Dylan* was shot. He'd been to every important folk club, passing out demo tapes, playing open-mike nights, and never getting beyond a Tuesday-night opening slot. He'd been kicked out of his rat-infested apartment in the

Village for nonpayment of rent, and if this job hadn't come along, he would have had to return home to Ohio and admit he was a failure. Either that or go to Vietnam. He'd felt incredibly lucky to have gotten a high lottery number that allowed him to spend three years working in a comic-book store and not dying in the jungle, but he had a nagging fear that with the draft about to end, he'd pay for his good luck by being one of the last people called up, and he'd step on a mine on the day the last U.S. troops left, tails between their legs. This was how he imagined it, anyway.

Knowing the alternatives were Cincinnati and the jungle, Peter was happy to be in Midtown and getting paid for his music. He didn't really want to go back down to the Village and revisit the sites of his failures.

"Of course," Pamela said, "I know that my creativity is helped along by the use of mind-expanding substances. Natural ones, anyway. Speed kills, you know. In the kitchen, you'll find a Chock full o' Nuts coffee can that does not contain coffee. You should help yourself to its contents whenever it feels like the right thing to do.

"I will see you all at my place at six tonight. Come refreshed, inspired, and ready to talk about your musical walkabouts. Oh, and here," she said, producing a bunch of subway tokens from her bag. "You are working for ATN now, and your travel for this project will of course be reimbursed. There is a stack of taxi vouchers in the cabinet as well. You should feel free to travel whichever way feels best to you." She walked out of the room with a flourish and swept into the elevator, which seemed to have been waiting for her.

Peter stared at the list in his hand. Well, it was early in the day, and he didn't really have anything else to do. He'd head down and walk around the Village and then get as much of his stuff as he could carry out of the locker at the Port Authority and then be back here shortly after lunch to move in. He hoped nobody would care—if anybody questioned him, he'd just say he'd had an attack of inspiration at one in the morning and then he'd accidentally fallen asleep. He'd blown most of his money on a room at the Y for the last week, and he couldn't afford to both stay there and eat until his first paycheck from ATN came through. So it was either crash in the basement or find a convenient Dumpster, and Peter much preferred this basement.

His stomach growled, and he silently told it to shut up. Since he'd be getting a free meal at dinnertime, he didn't feel like he should spend any of the little money he had on food today.

3

JULIE

JULIE WAS FURIOUS, but one thing she'd learned from her mother was that such emotions weren't revealed in situations like this. They were more powerful when you forced them inside to emerge as little pointed remarks than if you spent them all in an explosion.

She took a deep breath, tried to forget the whole "whore" thing. No, she couldn't. Since Clark had hired her, Julie didn't know if Pamela Sanchez knew about her three years at McMahon & Tate writing jingles for floor wax and antacids and ATN. ("ATN's the place for me / for news and sports and comedy," she heard in her mind.)

So it might have been inadvertent, but Pamela Sanchez had essentially called Julie a whore for writing songs on the clock. And though Julie really wanted to, she hadn't said you have some nerve calling anybody else a whore with your boobs falling out of your shirt, building a career on looking easy and writing messy, self-indulgent songs with no musical literacy, no craft at all. It's a real stretch to call what you do songwriting at all, so how dare you call me a whore for being a professional?

She must have known. Why else would she give Julie this assignment:

The Brill Building was the center of the songwriting universe for many years. Go, wander around, and soak up the atmosphere that Carole King, Neil Diamond, Neil Sedaka, and Leiber and Stoller turned to for inspiration. Greatness can emerge even in a very commercial setting.

It was tantamount to saying, *Here, you whore, go see the other famous songwriting whorehouse.* As if Julie hadn't been there before. As if she needed to soak up any atmosphere to understand how to be creative in a tiny room with the clock running.

That prostitute remark was really galling. But then again, when she was getting ready to crack at McMahon & Tate, when the call from fellow Princeton alum Clark Payson had felt like a life preserver, hadn't Julie been working on a song where she'd called herself a whore? "Miracle Wax / shines your floor / I'm a no good stinking whore." She'd laughed to herself at the time about the mental image of a pearl-clad housewife in a commercial singing that. But she hadn't been putting down the housewife who would sing the song, she'd been putting down the songwriter. Well, maybe. But it's one thing for me to call myself a whore, she thought, and quite another for some hippie has-been to do it.

Then again, maybe Pamela didn't know about her past. Julie had, after all, mentioned Brill Building alumna Carole King at the audition in order to explain why she needed a piano, why she was the only person there not toting a battered acoustic guitar.

She looked at her assignment again. Brill Building. Total waste of time. She'd much rather go home and take Simone for a walk. Well, she was going to get this cleared up.

Without a word to her fellow songwriters (at McMahon & Tate, her fellow songwriters had been the competition, and there was no reason to believe it would be otherwise here), Julie went to the elevator and rode it all the way up to Clark Payson's office.

The secretary looked up at Julie with a look of hostility masked as friendliness that would have done Julie's mother proud. Julie felt an instant affinity with her. You and me, she thought, we come from the same culture.

"May I help you?" the secretary said, smiling. Julie understood that what she meant was *Go away*.

"Julie Waterston to see Clark Payson," Julie said, knowing that the secretary—KARA, her nameplate said—would understand that Julie's failure to acknowledge her with so much as a hello was a sign of Julie's importance. Had Julie said, *Uh, yeah, good morning, I was wondering if Mr. Payson was in,* she would have found him out for the day.

"One moment, I'll see if he's in," Kara said, and buzzed the intercom. A moment later, she said, "Go right in, Miss Waterston."

Having been acknowledged as a superior, Julie might have let it go, but, Elizabeth Waterston style, she decided to twist the knife just because she could. "Thank you"—and here she made a show of glancing at the nameplate—"Kara," she said, and breezed into Clark Payson's office.

Clark Payson stood up and said, "Julie, hi! Have a seat!"

"So, do you know what's going on down there? She's got a coffee can full—"

"Uh uh uh—Julie. I knew when I hired a rock musician that things down there weren't going to be business as usual. Business as usual is what got my dad grilled like a steak in Washington. But I don't need to know all the details of what goes on."

"But—"

"But, I also want to make sure that actual work gets done,

which is part of the reason I hired you. That and the fact that you've done great work for ATN in the past. So you are my undercover professional down there, which means I want you to set an example for those kids of how a professional writes songs. If we get a month into this thing and no work has gotten done, then, yes, by all means, come up here and tell me how I can be on really solid ground when I fire people. But for now, I want to give the experiment a little room to breathe."

Julie bit back her anger and summoned all the cool and professionalism she could.

"All right. I understand what you're saying. Everyone is bringing different skills to bear on the project. But I don't really need to go walk around the Brill Building and soak up the energy, do I?"

Clark smiled. "Well, I did the entire Manhattan Musical Walkabout with Pamela last week in order to soak up the vibrations, but I don't see why you should have to suffer through the same thing. No. Go ahead and write songs, work whatever way works for you, and by all means, skip soaking up the energy if that's what you need to do."

Julie felt her shoulders relax. "Okay. Thank you."

Clark stood, dismissing her. "You're welcome. Come on up anytime. My door is always open to you," he said, and though Clark's father was somewhat more rough-hewn than Julie's parents, Clark had gone to Princeton and learned to speak the language. She understood very well that this meant, Don't bother me again unless it's really important.

"Thank you," Julie said, "I appreciate that," which meant, Don't worry, I'll stay out of your hair. She walked by Kara without acknowledging her existence, took the elevator down to the lobby, and headed home to walk Simone.

She took an uncrowded subway to 110th Street, and Simone, her boxer, contorted herself with joy at Julie's arrival. "Who's my good girl?" Julie asked. Simone responded by twisting around as though intending to bite her own butt.

Julie slipped the leash on and took Simone for a long walk in Riverside Park. The sun was shining, and, however frightening the park might become after dark, right now it was exactly what it had been designed to be—a refreshing, beautiful oasis of green that made Julie feel lucky to live in the best city on earth.

Back at home, Julie made a cup of coffee and sat in her window seat reading. She noticed that there was really nice light in here in the afternoon. When was the last time she'd been home in the afternoon? Probably a year and change ago, when she'd had the flu and it was either cloudy or else she'd just been throwing up too much to notice the quality of the light in here.

It was wonderful to be here curled up on the window seat with a book and a cup of coffee. So why had she read the same page three times? Because, she finally realized, she felt guilty about not working. She was on the clock, and even if her immediate supervisor had given her a stupid assignment she had no intention of completing, she felt like she ought to be doing something. She glanced at the clock. It was one o'clock. Well, she could get a few hours of work in before she had to leave for the mandatory socializing at night.

She'd been to a few of these compulsory leisure activities at McMahon & Tate, and she always hated them. They weren't really fun at all—even with the free booze, it was the employers' way of telling you they owned you at all times of the day.

Of course, Julie could have traveled the route so many of her classmates at Princeton had traveled—married at twenty-two, mothers by twenty-five, and by the time they hit Julie's mom's age, they'd be sitting in a beautiful empty house in Greenwich waiting for hubby's train from the city and trying to drink away the emptiness, either alone or with the other leathery emaciated women at the club.

No, it was better to work and put up with the annoyances of the working world than to transform into Elizabeth Waterston. And one way to thrive at work was to understand the culture. She changed into jeans and a T-shirt. They were normally her cleaning clothes, and they smelled vaguely of Endust, but she didn't think the hippies would really mind.

She returned to ATN, endured the skeptical glances of the security guard, and went down to the basement. When she walked off the elevator, she was reminded immediately that this was not like any other workplace she'd ever seen. The whole place was suffused with a red glow from the lights shining through Pamela's scarves, and the air was heavy with the smells of incense and pot. The other girl was nowhere to be seen, and the white guy and the black guy were sitting on the couch in a fog of marijuana smoke and giggling over something. She didn't even acknowledge them; she just grabbed the Language Arts binder off the shelf and went straight to the one practice room with a piano in it.

She shut the door and sat in front of the piano. It was a Brand X upright that was a complete piece of garbage, but at least, she thought as she coaxed a few chords from it, it was in tune. It probably wouldn't be for long, though. She'd have to invest in a dehumidifier. Or better yet, get Clark to invest in one.

She was annoyed that two of her co-workers were already getting high. On pot supplied by their supervisor. This place needed a grown-up in a bad way if any work was going to get done. Whatever bullshit Pamela said about the muse, Julie knew that when there was a deadline and a client who would have your head on a platter if you didn't deliver, you always found a way to write a song.

We need a grown-up around here

she began to sing.

If we're going to get anything done
'Cause the kids don't want to work
They just want to have fun.

Hmm. Not bad. The lyrics, obviously, were crap, but that was a pretty nice, pretty catchy melody. Catchy enough to sell soap. Catchy enough to stick in some little kid's mind and teach him about . . . what?

And then, just like that, the muse visited. This was a song about verbs! Because you can't *do* anything without a verb! Just substitute *verb* for *grown-up*, and she had her first line already!

Quickly she flipped open the Language Arts binder. One large section was labeled PARTS OF SPEECH, but it was no help at all. It was clear that the incomprehensible Dr. Andrews wanted her to write one song about each of the parts of speech, but beyond that, the document—all 150 pages of it—was an impenetrable forest of academic jargon. She figured she'd write her verb song first and try to figure out how it fit with the guidelines after it was done.

For the next two hours, Julie was lost in the blissful fugue of creativity, unaware of anything but the song that was out there somewhere that she was trying to pull through the piano and her brain so she could transcribe it correctly. Finally, she was confident that she had a nearly complete verb song. She looked with satisfaction at the music she'd written out sitting on the piano. She switched on the reel-to-reel and played her song through once.

She kicked off her shoes, stood up and stretched, and then lay on the floor. As much as she hated the other people in the class and the instructor and the whole thing, she had to admit that yoga had helped her tremendously with the pain in her back that came from sitting on a piano bench for hours.

As she stretched out on the floor, though, Julie could not get her mind into a serene, relaxed place. She wanted to run screaming into the hallway, taunting everybody else. *That's how you get inspiration!* she wanted to tell them. *It comes from discipline. You make yourself sit down at the piano, and you work until something comes. You don't get stoned and go to museums! I've got two songs done already! What have you got?*

4

LEVON

L EVON LOOKED AT his assignment with disbelief.

*Many of the greatest musicians of the twentieth century played
at the Cotton Club or the Apollo. Head up and walk around;
walk in the footsteps of musical giants, and feel yourself grow.*

Send the black guy up to Harlem. Of course. Then again, as
Levon looked around at his co-workers, he figured if somebody
had to go to Harlem, it might as well be him.

Levon knew white people—you didn't grow up black in
Ridgewood, New Jersey, without getting to know a lot of white
people. In fact, you didn't grow up black in Ridgewood, New Jersey, without growing comfortable among white people, since
they were ninety-nine of every hundred people in town. Levon
had applied to Morehouse in the hope of not being a fish out of
water anymore, but Dad wasn't going to let him out of Columbia
Engineering. Dad had cut Levon off from black social life on
campus when he mocked a group of Deltas when he was helping

Levon move in: "Look at those fools. Brands are for cattle and *slaves*. Dr. King didn't die for that nonsense. Malcolm didn't die for that nonsense."

It had only been a few months since they'd killed Dr. King at that point, and already Levon was tired as hell of hearing about everything that Dr. King didn't die for.

Dad had, of course, been overheard, thus ensuring that even if Levon had wanted to pledge, he'd have been, well, black-balled. And the black Greeks ran black social life. So he'd spent college as he'd spent high school—as one of the only black people he knew. Well, most of college, anyway.

He looked around the basement. The tall blond girl had already stormed out. And it definitely was storming. Levon wondered what her problem was—it wasn't like *she* got sent to Harlem. Hippie boy went for the taxi vouchers, looked around, and said, "Anybody else going downtown?"

Levon watched as the mousy girl's face lit up. "Me!" she said.

"Great," he said. "Wanna share a cab?"

"Sure," the girl said.

He walked over to Levon. "Hey," he said. "I'm Peter."

Levon extended his hand and shook. "Levon." He repeated the introduction process with the girl, whose name was Sarah.

"So," Peter said. "Where are you off to?"

Before he could check his impulse, Levon found himself bugging his eyes out and saying, "Ise gwine to Haaalem!"

Peter slapped his forehead. "Oh God, send the black guy to Harlem. I'm sorry. Do you want to switch?"

Levon smiled, imagining Peter wandering around Harlem. "It's all right, but thank you."

Sarah piped up with, "Well, we could all go together . . ." Levon imagined for a minute being the Official Black Tour Guide to Harlem with two white kids. It wasn't a pretty picture.

"Tell you what. I can do this stuff fairly quickly. You guys wanna meet back here for lunch?"

Peter and Sarah agreed, grabbed a taxi voucher, and left. Levon grabbed some subway tokens. He figured that a black man trying to get to Harlem from Midtown could probably get there and back on the subway before he'd find a taxi to pick him up.

As the subway train rumbled uptown, Levon tried not to think. He couldn't really keep this job secret from his parents forever. Could he? Well, it wasn't forever. It was just until something broke loose on the engineering front. Which might be never.

He was calling home less and less these days because he didn't want to have that conversation with Dad. Dad would imply that he was a lazy failure because he didn't have a job yet, and he would want to say the few jobs available to black men go to guys who were in fraternities, and you ruined that for me. But of course, he wouldn't say that, and then he'd have a stomachache for the rest of the day as his anger sat there and turned to acid.

At least he didn't have to worry about Vietnam. After many years of hating Joey Ruggeiro for the bloody beating he gave him in fifth grade, Levon had wanted to find Joey and kiss him after he'd left the induction center and found himself ineligible for military service due to foreign bodies lodged in the joint of the knee. That would be the right knee, the one that was bloody after his "fight" with Joey Ruggeiro. He'd characterized it as a fight when he got home, but it was a pretty one-sided beating that featured Levon being thrown to the ground with considerable force. Enough force, it seemed, to lodge a pebble inside his knee and prevent him from kneeling properly for the rest of his life. He'd hated Joey every time he'd tried to kneel and had to lift his right knee up to avoid sharp pain shooting up his leg, but there, outside the induction center, pain in the right knee seemed like a small price to pay to avoid a bullet in the head.

He'd actually looked up Joey Ruggeiro out of curiosity and found he'd died in Vietnam. To this day he was unsure if this was justice or cruel irony or both.

Levon emerged from the ground at 125th Street and headed toward the Apollo. He didn't even know why he was doing this, except that this was what the boss told him to do. It wasn't like he had never been up here before. And as he stood outside the Apollo, he tried to will himself to think about James Brown, to think about musical greatness. But being in Harlem, all he could think about was his last gig with the Supersonic Funketeers, sometimes known as Supersonic Calvin and the Horns of the Cuckold.

The Supersonic Funketeers had taken the stage at ten and did not relinquish it until one thirty, by which time everybody in the club was thoroughly funked up. As Apollo Von Funkenburg, purple-jumpsuited, platform-booted, colossal-Afroed bassist transformed back into Levon Hayes, engineering student, Calvin, who never really stopped being Captain Supersonic, came up and gave Levon a big hug.

"Once again, my brother, we have escaped the bonds of the gravity of this puny globe with the help of your bassy funkmanship." Calvin always talked like this, and Levon never really knew how to respond. On stage, he had no trouble responding to Calvin's insane patter and even joining in. But backstage it just felt weird.

"It was tight," Levon had said, figuring he couldn't go wrong with this.

"It was tight, it was loose, it was interstellar. So Levon. My man. Will you aid the Funketeers in conquering the universe?" Calvin had been after Levon about this for months. He was taking the Funketeers on a tour beginning in the summer. Small clubs all over the country, New York to Los Angeles in two months, hoping to get a following and a record deal.

And Levon had wanted to go. But . . . "I don't know, Cal, I mean, my dad, you know, he ain't—"

"Remember Icarus, my boy! Better get me some wax wings just like Daddy! Look where it got him! Deep in the Aegean, wishing he had kept playing his lute and getting some of that wood nymph booty! At some point, Levon, all of us are called on to lift off from the parental launching pad and become our own funky beings."

Levon hadn't remembered a whole lot about Greek mythology, since they'd studied it in the ninth grade, but he was pretty sure there were some inaccuracies in Calvin's version of the Icarus story. Still, he took the point. But could he do it? It was easy to talk about blasting off from the parental launching pad when you didn't have Levon's dad.

"I'm gonna have to think about it," Levon had said.

"My brother, the time for thinking has ended and the time for action has begun. Inform me of your choice by next week, for if you cannot propel us across this great nation with the interstellar low-end drive, I will have to find somebody else who can."

"Okay, Calvin, I get it. I'll let you know."

Calvin hugged him again. "I know you will come to the right decision. You are as funky as they come." This from Calvin was pretty much the equivalent of anybody in the Engineering Department telling him he was the second coming of Isaac Newton, and Levon had felt himself getting all choked up.

"Thanks man," he'd croaked out.

He hadn't been getting interviews, and he was tired of the hurt and humiliation of applying for jobs he had no chance of getting. He was confident that he'd make a good engineer, but nobody who actually hired engineers seemed to share that point of view. It had been very tempting to just join the circus with

Calvin and tour the country doing something he was good at, something that would make him feel good and important instead of small and worthless.

But then he had imagined the conversation with Dad in vivid detail:

"You're doing *what*?" Dad shouted.

"Uh, touring America as the bass player in a funk band," Levon said quietly.

He'd imagined Dad's face as he sputtered with rage. "Engineering degree and you want to . . . you want to join some . . . in my day, a black man couldn't even *dream* of being an engineer. And you want to throw that away?"

"But, Dad, I've been to a bunch of interviews, and they all tell me how surprisingly articulate I am, and how they can tell that I'm a hard worker, but they just don't have a position for me at this time, and every white boy on campus has two job offers already, and—"

"So you gonna give up because it just got *hard*? Boy, who told you life was easy? Huh? Who told you that? Where would you be if every black man gave up when life got hard? Huh? Where would you be? Not in Ridgewood, that's for damn sure. You think everybody on this block wanted a black family in their neighborhood? You think integrating this block was easy? You think what I went through down south was easy? I got this scar from a police dog in Selma when you were still a little kid. I faced down dogs and fire hoses and men with murder in their heart so you could make something of yourself, and this is what you want to do?"

Levon knew from talking to other parishioners at the First Unitarian Society of Ridgewood that Dad's front-line Selma stories were somewhat exaggerated. Certainly he'd taken his life in his hands going down there at the time, but he'd mostly done voter registration and had been surrounded by a phalanx of his fellow parishioners—white Protestants all—the entire time. And the scar had actually come from tripping over an open file drawer. But he knew that he could never point that out, just as he could never say what he really wanted to say: Doesn't true liberation for black people mean that they would be free to do whatever they wanted? Life, liberty, and the pursuit of happiness?

Well, maybe, but he couldn't be happy knowing that he'd broken his father's heart. He alone had the power to break that mighty man's spirit, just by saying he wanted to get on stage and shake his ass and make people dance.

So here he was on the street in Harlem, following instructions even though the instructions were stupid and kind of racist, because he knew damn well that the only black guy didn't get to be the one to break the rules.

He looked at the façade of the Apollo and tried to will it to speak to him. But all he could think of was how to come up with a convincing lie about what he was doing this summer while he waited for a job to come through.

It occurred to him that he should look for an apartment while he was up here. He wasn't sure his money would hold out until the first paycheck from ATN came through, and he was burning through a lot of it just to keep a roof over his head. His dorm room was far more expensive as a summer rental than it had been as an actual dorm room.

But getting an apartment would mean signing a lease, which would mean admitting that he'd failed to get an engineering job and he really was doing this music thing, and he wasn't ready to admit that yet.

He wandered around, not really seeing anything, certainly not getting any positive vibrations from any of his surroundings. He had painful pangs of regret that he hadn't gone on tour, anger and frustration that he couldn't get a job in his field, and anxiety about disappointing his dad.

The hell with this. He went back to the subway and rode back to ATN. He showed his ID and signed in for the security guards and went down to the basement.

Peter was all alone on the couch. "Thank God!" he said when he saw Levon. "You have to check this out!" He leapt to his feet and ran over to the kitchenette. He opened a drawer and pulled out a large Chock full o'Nuts coffee can.

Levon stood there. "Yeah? So?"

"So this is Pamela Sanchez's coffee can. You know, the one we were supposed to hit up for inspiration? Come take a look!"

Levon went over to the kitchen. He peeked into the coffee can and saw some rolling papers and a plastic bag with enough reefer inside to get the entire building lifted. "Whoa."

"Shall we?"

Levon thought for a moment. If security came down, it would be pretty difficult to conceal smoking a joint.

"Let's fire one up," he said.

"Deal," Peter said, and he rolled a joint quickly and expertly. He took a matchbook out of his pocket and offered the joint and the matches to Levon. "After you, sir."

Levon lit the joint, inhaled deeply, held it, exhaled, and smiled. "Oh, shit. That's some good shit. That's like the stuff Calvin gets from that Jamaican cat."

Peter had already inhaled, and he said, "Who's Calvin? And how does he get pot from a cat?"

Levon looked at Peter and rolled his eyes at the joke. "Calvin leads the band I used to be in."

They sat and smoked in silence for a few minutes. "So," Peter said. "Did you soak up any useful vibrations this morning?"

"Naah. I mostly just thought about how I don't have anywhere to live."

For some reason, this caused Peter to start giggling.

"What, man? Why is that funny?"

"Because," Peter said, his laugh turning into a cough, "I just found a place today."

"And?"

"And you're sittin' in it."

Levon inhaled, exhaled, and looked at Peter. "You gonna live here?"

"Why the hell not? There's a shower stall in the bathroom, we got a little kitchen here, and I can save the money I might be spending on rent."

"And pot," Levon said, holding the joint aloft.

"And pot. Exactly. Anyone would have to admit it's a brilliant plan," Peter said.

Levon laughed. "If you do say so yourself."

"And I do, my friend, I do." They sat for another moment in companionable silence. Levon had just inhaled deeply when he heard the *bong!* announcing that the elevator had arrived in the basement. Levon panicked. He threw the roach on the floor and ground it under his heel and dug his elbow into Peter's ribs and pointed at the elevator. The doors were opening, and he couldn't hold this smoke in forever. Shit. Fired on his first day.

The doors opened, and instead of a big security guard, the up-tight tall blond girl walked out. Levon exhaled in a fit of laughter, Peter was laughing, and as he caught his breath Levon thought this was probably the best job anyone could ever hope to get.

5

SARAH

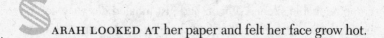ARAH LOOKED AT her paper and felt her face grow hot.

The Factory and Max's Kansas City have been great centers of musical and artistic creativity for years. Head down and soak up the vibrations. My name may or may not be enough to get you through the doors at the Factory. You can certainly give it a try, though I fell out of favor there a while ago.

She had no idea what the paper was saying. What kind of factory was this? She felt even more stupid and out of place than she had during the speech about how they were going to make the world a better place. She kept expecting Clark Payson to point at her and say, *Except for you, Sarah Stein! You puked from nervousness every time you tried to play an open-mike night! You lucked into this job with the one good song you ever wrote, and you'll be out of a job as soon as we know what a fraud you really are!*

He hadn't said that, but Sarah felt it was only a matter of time.

She looked at it again. The note said, "Head down." So the factory she was supposed to visit was downtown. Probably. Or else in Brooklyn. Or Queens. But nobody ever headed "down" to Brooklyn or Queens. They went "out" or "over" there.

So when Peter Terpin asked if anyone else was going downtown, Sarah said "Me!" in a really loud embarrassing voice. But she was excited. She'd seen Peter perform at a couple of the open-mike nights when she'd been sitting there too nauseous with fear to play "Loveless," which was her own Pamela Sanchez ripoff. She liked his songs and thought he was cute. And now she got to share a cab with him!

They met Levon, and she was a little embarrassed that Pamela had sent him to Harlem. She had hoped they could hit all of their destinations together—she'd never been to Harlem and she was curious, but she was still glad Pamela hadn't sent her to the Apollo. But Levon said they should all meet back here for lunch. That would be good. Still, what was she going to do about finding the right factory? Well, maybe she could get the right information out of Peter in the cab, and if not, she'd go to the library and research the factory so she could fake her way through and pretend she'd actually gone and soaked up the vibrations.

She would hate to do that, though. Pamela was a great artist, and she wouldn't have sent Sarah to check this place out if she didn't think it would help Sarah's art. And Sarah's art could certainly use some help.

So when they were waiting for a cab, Peter said, "Where are you headed?"

Sarah said, "The Factory," as if she knew what the hell she was talking about.

Peter nodded. "Okay. Union Square. You're the first stop."

Sarah sighed with relief. They climbed into the cab and sat awkwardly next to each other. Sarah wished she had a joint. Then she'd have the courage to reach out and just take his hand. But she hadn't smoked in days, not since Brian's good-bye party, when she was determined that he wasn't leaving for Boston without sleeping with her.

So instead she just thought of what to say and felt the silence growing bigger and stronger. Finally she couldn't stand it anymore, and she blurted out, "You know, I saw you perform a couple of times. I really like your songs."

She felt thirteen. It didn't feel good. She'd hated being thirteen.

But Peter turned to her and smiled. "Hey, thanks! I think you're the one!"

Flustered, Sarah felt herself blushing, and she said, "Well, I, uh, I, uh, um, uh . . ."

"I mean the one person who likes my music." Sarah wanted to sink through the seat and onto the road and have the rear wheels of the cab put her out of her misery.

Instead she said, "Oh. Heh. Well, I guess Pamela liked it. I mean, you got this gig, right?"

"Yeah. But I was having a hard time getting gigs before that. I was about three days away from getting on the bus back to Cincinnati when the phone call came through. I was writing a song about it called 'Failure-Bound on the Hound.'"

Sarah laughed. "I like that. I mean, that's a cool image. Because probably a lot of people head out of New York going back to those places they were trying to escape . . . I mean, oh, I've never been to Cincinnati, I'm sure it's nice . . ."

"It's nice. I just—James Brown recorded 'Please, Please, Please' and 'Cold Sweat' there, but since then not much has happened there musically. I mean, it's not the place to make it as a musician." There was a pause. "Oh yeah. The Lemon Pipers. 'Green Tambourine.' Remember that one?"

"Uh, nope."

"Okay, well, they were from Cincinnati. Or, anyway, Hamilton. Not far away."

"Mmm." Sarah felt the conversation sinking, and, desperate, she threw it a lifeline. "So where are you headed today?"

"Ahh. Well. Promise not to tell anybody?"

"Cross my heart."

"Well, I'm supposed to go to all these Dylan hot spots, but, I mean, I've been in New York for three years, and those places were like the first things I did when I got off the bus."

"When you were glory-bound on the hound," Sarah said, then cursed herself. He was going to think she was making fun of him.

But he didn't. He smiled. "Yeah. Exactly. So anyway, soaking up the vibes down in the Village where Dylan used to hang out didn't exactly bring me creative or commercial success."

"I don't know. I thought that Monkees parody was really good. I mean, whatever, the one that you sang to the tune of 'Gonna Buy Me a Dog.' "

Peter smiled. " 'Gonna Kill Me Some Cong.' You really liked that one? I thought it was kind of a cheap joke."

"No, I mean, I thought it was—I mean, maybe I was reading too much into it, but I thought it was about how mass media and the military-industrial complex conspire to sell the war. Like the war is just this prefab commodity they've sold us. Like the Monkees."

Peter looked surprised. "Yeah. That is exactly what I meant by that."

They both laughed. "And," Sarah continued, "don't tell Pamela, but I love the Monkees."

Peter leaned in to whisper in her ear. "Me too."

"So what are you doing instead of soaking up Dylan vibes?"

"I was gonna go get some of my stuff and try to find a safe place to store it."

"Oh," Sarah said. She wanted to kick herself. Her disappointment showed in her voice. She didn't want to seem desperate and clingy. She'd lost too many guys that way. Enough guys, in fact, that she'd stopped being able to say that men were afraid of intimacy with any conviction. Maybe the problem was her.

"But . . . I mean," Peter said, "we've got all day, and . . ."

Well, they had already shared a shameful secret about the Monkees. "It's just that . . . you have to promise not to laugh."

"I promise."

"I can read the words on this piece of paper, but I have no idea what they mean." She showed the paper to Peter.

"The Factory. Okay, that's where Andy Warhol does his thing. Paintings, prints, happenings, weird movies about guys sitting around, the Velvet Underground, stuff like that."

He hadn't spoken to her like she was an idiot. She appreciated that. "I really—I mean, you have to understand, I guess I lived a pretty sheltered life, and it was really only a couple of years ago that I started to understand that there was stuff going on besides like what was on TV and stuff. You know?"

Peter laughed. "Yeah. I do. I mean, the west side of Cincinnati isn't exactly a cultural hot spot. And I used to . . . I was like in plays in high school. Musicals." He was blushing! That was so cute! "All right. So let's go see the Factory together. And then I'll go get my stuff after."

Sarah exhaled. "Oh, thank you. I was just so . . . you know, Pamela Sanchez is the whole reason I picked up a guitar in the first place, and I'm really intimidated, and I don't want to let her down."

So they both got out of the cab at Union Square and walked over to the Factory. She tried to get Peter to tell her a little more about the Factory, but he said that was about all he remembered from stuff he'd read in *Rolling Stone*.

When they arrived, they just stood on the street for a few minutes staring up at the building. It didn't look like much. Finally, embarrassed, she turned to Peter. "Well. I know I need to trust Pamela, I mean, *Shadows in the Twilight*, right? She obviously knows what she's doing. But I'm really not sure what I'm supposed to be getting out of this. I'm not like picking up any sensations or anything."

"Yeah. Well, let's ring the bell and see if they let us in."

"What? Oh my God, no! I can't! I couldn't possibly!"

Peter just looked at her and grinned. "Why not? Come on!" He ran across the street and pushed a button on the intercom. Sarah tried without success to melt into the sidewalk.

"Hello?" a voice said. Sarah couldn't even tell if it was male or female.

"Yeah, hi," Peter said. "My name is Peter Terpin, and I'm here with Sarah . . ."

"Stein!" Sarah stage-whispered.

"Sarah Stein, and we're working on a new project with Pamela Sanchez, and she told us we should stop by and just kind of see what's going on in here!"

This was met with silence. Peter tried the door—Sarah certainly hadn't heard a buzzer, but Peter had been living in actual apartments in New York, not just a dorm room, so maybe he had a sense for these things. No such luck.

They looked at each other. The moment of silence became a full minute of silence, and then two.

"I guess that's a no," Sarah said.

"Apparently," Peter said.

"Well," Sarah said, "now what?"

"Well," Peter said, "I should get my stuff together. I can't really ask you to do that because it's boring, and, also, if you saw the conditions I've been living in, you might never want to hang out with me again."

"I doubt that," Sarah said before she had the time to consider whether she should say something like that. Sounds clingy! Don't drive him away!

There was a moment where neither one of them said anything, but it didn't feel awkward. And for the first time today, Sarah was picking up some energy, some vibrations. It was like she and Peter were standing at the very beginning of what might be something, and all the energy they might put into whatever might happen between them was just there, hanging in the air, waiting.

For the second time today, it occurred to Sarah to take Peter's hand, but she didn't want to. Not yet. Once they'd clasped hands, one way or another, whatever was going to happen between them would be on the way to becoming whatever it was. Right now it could still be anything.

"Okay," Peter said. "Well, I'm off. I'll see you back in the basement for lunch?"

"Count on it," Sarah said.

Peter had that look in his eye like he wanted to kiss her good-bye, but instead he just turned and started running away down the block. "I will!" he yelled out, and Sarah smiled.

Now she was alone in Union Square with no idea what she was going to say when it was time to report back to Pamela Sanchez tonight. She really couldn't go and just say, *Yeah, I stood on the street and felt the vibes that I'm really attracted to Peter, but otherwise I got nothing. It was just a building. I walked around the streets, and they were just streets with busy people on them. I didn't get anything out of this.* No, that would never do.

She hailed a cab and rode up to the library. She went straight for the *Readers' Guide to Periodical Literature* and looked up Andy Warhol. She read a lot of old magazines and learned enough about the Factory that she hoped she'd have something to say tonight. It was actually pretty interesting stuff. So interesting, in fact, that when Sarah finally looked at her watch, it was already quarter to one. Shit! She'd miss lunch with Peter!

Leaving her magazines strewn over the tabletop, she ran from the library and hailed the first cab she saw.

6

JULIE

STILL LYING SUPINE on the floor of the practice room thinking contemptuous thoughts about her co-"workers," Julie heard a knock on the not-fully-closed door.

She hopped to her feet. "Yes?"

The little mousy girl poked her head in. Her eyes were blood-shot and the smell of pot smoke followed her head into the room. "Hi," she said.

Julie mustered all of the politeness at her disposal. One wasn't overtly rude to people, even if they were tiresome. And few people were as tiresome when you were sober as people who were high. "Hello," Julie said.

"I'm Sarah, by the way," the girl said.

"Hi, Sarah," Julie said, repeating the name to make sure it stuck in her mind, "I'm Julie." She extended a hand and Sarah gave it a weak, tentative shake.

"Hey, we're about to go down to Pamela's place for dinner, and I just wanted to invite you to go with us, I mean that was why I came walking down the hall, but then I heard, well, I hope you won't be too mad or insulted or anything, but I heard the song you were writing, and it was just, I mean, wow, so far out, I mean, I'm sitting there wondering how I'm going to write songs and you're just in here doing it, and I just wanted to tell you that I feel really lucky to be working with you and I hope that I can learn how to be a better songwriter by hanging out with you."

Julie found herself unable to maintain her WASPy cool in the face of this. Yes, it was babbling from somebody who was high as a kite, but still, she'd just been given a really sincere compliment. When was the last time that had happened at McMahon & Tate? There it was only condemnation if you screwed up—never any praise for doing anything right. And you especially never got praise from a fellow songwriter unless they were trying to get inside your head and mess you up so they'd get the song for the next account.

"Well, thank you!" Julie said. "That's really very kind. I appreciate it." She thought for a moment. If she was going to be working here for a year, it would be a lot more fun if she could at least be friendly with her co-workers. Perhaps they could actually collaborate instead of competing. What the hell. "So, you're all going together?"

"Yeah, I guess we're gonna share a cab."

"Okay. But I am not sitting with the driver."

Sarah smiled. "I am so with you." Then her face darkened. "Except . . . well, okay."

"What?"

"Well, I . . . Jesus, I'm really stoned, I'm sorry. It's just that I was looking forward to sitting next to Peter . . ."

"Okay." Julie smiled. There was something disarming about Sarah's being so up-front about her little office crush.

"But . . . but then . . ."

"What?"

"Well, you, I mean in a situation like this . . . I mean, you can't say oh, the black guy has to ride with the driver."

"Ah. I see your problem. Well, I think we can solve this very easily. I'll hail the cab, and just as I'm getting in, you can slap your forehead and say 'Oh, I'm so stupid, I forgot my purse,' or something like this. Then Peter will gallantly offer to stay with you, you will tell me not to wait, you'll get another cab. Problem solved!"

Sarah thought for a minute. "But what if he doesn't gallantly offer to stay with me?"

"Then you've got a crush on the wrong guy."

"Whoa! That is so deep! I mean, it's so obvious, but I've just never . . . well, I've had a crush on the wrong guy before, but I've never really been able to sum it up like that."

"Yeah, I've got some bitter experience behind that. I'm always really wise about other people's bad decisions." Maybe it was just working in advertising, or maybe it was her twisted upbringing, but Julie felt like she almost never met anyone who was just what they appeared to be. She didn't get the feeling that Sarah was hiding anything—she really was a starstruck, kind of naïve kid. It was charming. "Anyway, let me just grab my purse and I'm ready to go."

JULIE'S PLAN WORKED flawlessly, and she ended up riding downtown in a taxi with The Black Guy. Of course she had to stop thinking of him as The Black Guy, so Julie extended her hand and said, "I'm Julie, by the way."

The Black Guy extended his hand and gave her a heavy-lidded, slightly stoned smile and said, "I'm Levon."

Having exhausted their conversational options, they rode in silence for several blocks until Levon said, "Can I ask you something?"

"Okay," Julie said.

"Did you . . . I mean, we have to report on this assignment thing, and I . . . I mean, I did it, but I didn't soak up any vibrations or anything, and to be honest it kind of pissed me off, sending the black guy up to Harlem."

"Oh God, she sent you to Harlem?"

"Yeah."

"That's *tacky*. But anyway, the good thing about talking about what vibrations you soaked up is that you can just make it up. She sent me to the Brill Building, and I didn't even go."

Levon looked at her with awe. "Wow! Really?"

"Yeah. I stayed in the basement and wrote a song instead. I felt like that was a better use of my time."

"Wow. That must be nice."

"What?"

"Well, I mean . . . let's just say I don't feel quite that comfortable disregarding the boss's instructions, even if they do seem kind of . . ."

"Stupid?"

"Yeah."

Julie thought about that for a second. "Well, I mean, I know it's not the same thing, but I was the only woman where I used to work, and I definitely felt like the men got to mess up without it being because they were male, but if I ever got upset in a meeting or couldn't meet a deadline or anything, there would have been all this talk about how flighty and emotional I was." She glanced at Levon nervously.

She suddenly felt an obligation to keep the conversation moving. "So what I plan to say—she sent me to the Brill Building, by the way—I plan to say that I felt a lot of positive energy from all the creativity that flowed through that place, but also that the pressure people were under might have been what was making me feel uneasy."

Levon smiled. "That's good! So maybe I'll talk about the neg-ative vibes of racism and oppression and how us black folks likes to dance and sing our troubles away. And then eats us some fried chicken and watermelon."

Julie gave a nervous, tentative "heh heh" and saw Levon smil-ing.

"I might go with something more along the lines of how great art is liberating. I think maybe you should try to work Mahalia Jackson or Leontyne Price in there too."

"Why them?"

"Well, for one thing, they're women, hear them roar, so that will probably make a good impression. And, for another, they're just . . . I think they're . . ."

"Not as scary as James Brown or Sly Stone?"

"Yes, I mean, I know Pamela's Mexican and everything, and I don't know how that works, but I would just . . ."

"Yeah, I don't get that California stuff. Around here it's not a big love-in between us and the Puerto Ricans, so I was just gonna assume she was white until she proved otherwise."

Julie smiled. "I think that's smart."

Soon they were outside Pamela's loft. They both decided they'd wait until Sarah and Peter arrived before ringing the bell. This led to an awkward ten minutes on the sidewalk. Finally an-other taxi rolled up, and Peter and Sarah got out of the back. Julie shot Sarah a quizzical look, and Sarah gave her a big grin that she quickly stifled. She would have to ask what happened. Perhaps they'd held hands in the taxi or something.

PETER PRESSED THE buzzer, and Pamela's voice, distorted by the intercom speaker, said, "Welcome, everyone! Please come up!"

Everybody spilled into Pamela's loft. It was large and beautiful.

Marimekko prints covered the walls, there were guitars everywhere, and Pamela's bed, low to the ground, sat on a wooden platform in the middle of the room. It completely dominated the room. Her red sheets were mussed, and atop them were at least a dozen pillows. This, combined with the musky incense smell that pervaded the place, made it almost frighteningly sexy.

Pamela ran around turning on lamps, all of which emitted the reddish glow she seemed to favor.

Everybody found their way to couches and chairs on the periphery of the room, and nobody, Julie noticed, could take their eyes off the bed. It seemed to be sending waves of horniness through the room. Even Julie, who hadn't had a thing to drink or smoke, was not immune.

"Well," Pamela said, "I've prepared a feast of delights that will help to purify our bodies and hopefully our minds. Everyone please grab a plate and help yourselves."

Everybody mumbled assent, still spellbound by the bed. Peter was absentmindedly stroking the neck of a guitar that was propped next to him on the couch.

They all went to Pamela's kitchen counter, plates in hand, and beheld a dazzling array of unappetizing food.

"I have brown rice and millet . . . and some steamed vegetables, a seaweed salad, and a homemade nut loaf," Pamela said, grinning broadly.

Julie worked her way down the line, taking tiny portions of each dish—the least she thought she could take while still being polite.

Levon whispered in her ear, "I'm going to need to smoke a lot more before this shit looks appetizing."

Julie suppressed a giggle.

"Of course you'll find no salt and pepper—I don't have to tell you about the dangers of salt, and pepper of course excites the system terribly—worse even than garlic. There are no members of the nightshade family, like tomatoes and eggplants, so you don't need to worry about that. I do have a canister of kombu flakes, and you should feel free to sprinkle some on anything here."

Wonderful. Unsalted grains and vegetables. Julie thought wistfully of the Chinese leftovers sitting in her fridge and wondered how soon she could possibly leave here so she could eat a real meal.

Once they all had plates, everyone sat down, and Pamela fired up a colossal bong. "And a crucial ingredient," Pamela said, "is just the right amount of grass. This will help sharpen your gustatory perceptions."

Julie looked around at her already stoned co-workers and thought that if their gustatory perceptions got any sharper, they might actually be comatose.

Once the bong reached her, Julie inhaled deeply. She soon found that she was having what she classified as Marijuana Reaction B—her mind felt clear as a bell, but her limbs felt relaxed and light, like the air was water that was holding her up as she floated in the room. This was preferable to both Marijuana Reaction A (nothing at all) and Marijuana Reaction D (paranoid freakout), though she might have preferred Marijuana Reaction C (light-headed and giggly) tonight.

Perhaps to stop himself from continuing his unconscious masturbation mime on its neck, Peter picked up a guitar and began strumming absentmindedly. Soon there were guitars in everyone's hands, everyone but Julie, who couldn't play a note on the guitar.

"Wonderful," Pamela said. "There's no better way for us to get to know each other than to play music together. In fact, if this didn't happen organically, I was going to insist on it. So here's what I'd like you to do. I'd like you to introduce yourself, tell us your specialty on this project, tell us what you got out of your assignment today, tell us when and where you lost your virginity, and play the song that brought you here."

Julie felt her buzz being killed. The loss of her virginity— awkward fumbling in the back of Brad Davenport's father's S-Class after a drunken cotillion—was not a subject she enjoyed discussing. Not that it was traumatic or anything. It was just none of anyone's business, and though this was a fairly with-it crowd, she still didn't want to say aloud that she had been sixteen and have everyone assume she was some kind of slut. And Julie couldn't play her song here, because there was no piano.

Peter spoke up. "Okay. My name is Peter Terpin. I went down to the Village today and walked in Bob Dylan's footsteps. What I got out of this was just this realization—I walked in these same spots and saw the same things as he had seen. I guess I've been used to thinking of Dylan as some kind of god, but being in those places just reminded me that he's a human being. And since I'm a human being too, maybe everything he accomplished isn't out of my reach. I was a history major at Antioch, so I'm working on the history songs. This is one I wrote called 'Our George, Not Yours.' "

"Virginity!" Sarah yelled out, and then collapsed in a fit of giggles.

"Oh, yeah. Um, I was nineteen, and it was in my dorm room late at night after a concert." He looked embarrassed, and then quickly started to play.

> Years ago in a town by the ocean
> A bunch of guys had a funny notion
> It was really pretty rare in its day
> That when people are governed they should have a say
>
> See they lived under a tyrannical king
> Named George who taxed them on everything

Took their money and made them mad
Said if you don't like it, well that's just too bad

This is what the colonists said
We don't want your taxes and coats of red
We'll choose our leaders that's for sure
We'll take our George, not yours
Our George, not yours

When the war they fought was finally won
They called up General Washington
They said George will you lead our land
We're new at this and we need a strong hand

But only for a couple of years
See tyranny is one of our biggest fears
Will you take the job and then leave it too
'Cause you work for us, we don't work for you

This is what the colonists said
You don't keep the job until you're dead
We'll choose our leaders in a way that's fair
So be our George, not theirs
Our George, not theirs

And still today when votes are cast
We throw off the shackles of the past
From the president to the mayor of your town
The leaders work for you and not the other way around.

Despite her nervousness about what she was going to do, Julie smiled and joined in the riotous applause. The bong came around again, and she took another deep hit.

"Okay." Sarah spoke up. "My name is Sarah Stein. I studied math and elementary education, and much to my mom's horror, I'm not teaching kindergarten right now. I went to the Factory today, and what I got was not just the thrill from the creative energy that ran through there, but a really strong feeling of unease and anxiety. I felt like there was a lot of negative energy there."

"So true, so true," Pamela said, nodding. Julie was proud of Sarah. She'd been set up by Pamela—who else was supposed to pick up negative energy anyway? But Sarah was too guileless to be a good ass-kisser, so she'd just said what she thought, and it turned out to be exactly what Pamela had been looking for. "Anyway, I have a song—"

Peter cleared his throat loudly, and Sarah began to laugh.

"I lost my virginity when I was seventeen in the basement of Temple Beth-El after my cousin Jacob's bar mitzvah. But not, you know, with my cousin Jacob or anything. Not with any blood relative. 'Cause that would be gross."

Everyone applauded. "Anyway, my song is called 'Nine's Magic Multiples.'" She strummed a few chords and began to sing.

With nine's magic multiples
It works out every time
The digits of the multiple of nine
Add up to nine

Nine times one is nine, that's simple to do
Nine times two is eighteen, one plus eight is nine too
Nine times three is twenty-seven, two plus seven's nine
Nine times four is thirty-six, three plus six you're doing fine

With Nine's magic multiples
It works out every time
The digits of the multiple of nine
Add up to nine

Nine times five is forty-five, and four plus five equals your
    friend (nine!)
Nine times six is fifty-four, and there's five plus four again
Nine times seven is sixty-three, and you know what six plus
    three is
Nine times eight is seventy-two, and seven plus two as you can
    see is one of
Nine's magic multiples
It works out every time
The digits of the multiple of nine
Add up to nine

Nine times nine is eighty-one, and nine is eight plus one
Nine times ten is ninety; nine plus zero and we're done.

Everyone applauded again. Julie was really impressed. She
wouldn't have guessed that Sarah had such a good song in her.

Levon spoke up. "All right, all right, I was nineteen, okay, and
it was backstage at the Apollo. So you can imagine what kind of
vibes I was soaking up today." Everyone laughed. "I was an engineering major, so I'm doing the science songs. This one's called
'Funky Solar System.' "

Levon began making some weird chords way up on the neck
of the guitar, bringing some distinctly un-folky sounds out of it.

I saw a spaceship land
And a little green man
Came and told me
That I should come along 'cause he had a lot of things
To show me

In the funky solar system
Funky solar system yeah

Funky solar system
Funky solar system yeah

Well we started at the sun it was such hot fun
That we went off to Mercury
Then we landed on Venus with thick clouds above
He said you know this planet's named for the goddess of love

In the funky solar system
Funky solar system yeah
Funky solar system
Funky solar system yeah

Well Earth I knew already
Red Mars was rockin' steady
Jupiter was bigger than any of the others
Saturn had rings even nicer than my mother's

In the funky solar system
Funky solar system yeah
Funky solar system
Funky solar system yeah

Uranus, Neptune, Pluto
So cold it was outta sight
I said get me home little green man
I want to sleep on Earth tonight

But it's a funky solar system
Funky solar system yeah
Funky solar system
Funky solar system yeah

More applause, and Julie felt awful. Because now it was her turn, and she had no way to play her song. And she didn't want to talk about her virginity. She had lost her virginity at a younger age than everyone else who'd spoken so far, which was embarrassing, but, more than that, such things simply weren't anyone's business.

"Well, I went to the Brill Building today, and I really felt impressed that professionalism and creativity could go hand in hand," Julie said. She was tweaking Pamela's nose, and she didn't care. "And I am writing the grammar songs for this project. Uh, I was, uh . . . after a dance in the fall of my senior year of high school"—*when I was sixteen, but you'll probably assume I was eighteen, and I won't do anything to correct that impression*—"in the back of a Mercedes."

There was an appreciative "oooooh" from the crowd.

"And now, I'm afraid I can't play my song because I play piano, and it's not—"

"Just tell us the chords," Levon called out. "We'll follow along!"

"Yeah!" Sarah said.

"Okay," Julie said, tentatively. She told them the progression and waited for a few minutes until everyone seemed like they had it. Then she began to sing:

> *In, out, up and down*
> *Above, below, and all around*
> *Polly Preposition came to town*
>
> *When you need to know just how to state*
> *How two nouns or pronouns relate*
> *Don't panic, help is on the way*
> *It's Polly Preposition to save the day*
>
> *She'll help get your ice cream into the cone*
> *Or be with your friend so you're not alone*

She'll get your book up on the shelf
And put shoes on your feet that you can tie yourself

Over, under, with and through
Polly Preposition's here to help you
Above, below, and all around
Polly Preposition came to town.

If you're feeling under the weather
Polly's here to help you put your nouns together
Put your heart in your throat when you're out with Chris
Put your lips together and give him a kiss.

Over, under, with and through
Polly Preposition's here to help you
Above, below, and all around
Polly Preposition came to town.

Now that Polly's here to stay
We all know she'll never go away
Because without prepositions our team would never win
Because they couldn't drive the winning run in!

Over, under, with and through
Polly Preposition's here to help you
Above, below, and all around
Polly Preposition came to town.

Everyone applauded, but it just hadn't sounded right. Julie sat down and sulked while Pamela spoke.

"Well, I am thrilled to be working with all of you, and I'm just so excited by all of your talent. Now I believe I owe you a story." And Julie sat there in disbelief as Pamela spun a tale straight out of a paperback romance novel of how she'd been a poor Mexican migrant worker in Cah-lee-fodrr-knee-yha, and how when she was a precocious fourteen, the son of the man who owned the farm where she was working took her to his room where she thrilled to the experience of a soft bed with luxurious sheets as he, as she put it, initiated her into the mysteries of womanhood. When her father found she'd lain with a gringo, he called her a whore and disowned her, and of course the young gringo wanted nothing to do with a dirty Mexican.

"And the pain of that experience eventually gave birth to this song," Pamela said, and she sang "Shadows in the Twilight." And as much as Julie was annoyed by Pamela, by her ridiculous, probably fictional story, and by this whole scene, she had to admit that Pamela was a gifted performer with a fantastic voice. While everyone else had been nervous and tentative, no one more than Julie herself, Pamela took command of the room and brought them all into the world of her song.

MORE POT WAS smoked and more songs were played. At some point, bottles of wine were opened. The kind of thing you might expect at a hippie campfire: Peter and Levon dueting on that moronic Dylan song about everybody getting stoned; Sarah doing "One Tin Soldier"; Pamela doing her greatest hits and covering the weakness of her songwriting with the strength of her performance. Even Levon, who Julie hoped would play some old Motown or Stax songs (was that racist? She didn't know), played "The Lonesome Death of Hattie Carroll." Well, at least Levon could sing, which made his version slightly less grating than the Dylan version.

Julie sat and fumed, feeling her limbs regain their normal density. Why had she even come here? This was like junior high—trying to be something you weren't in order to fit in with people you didn't really like and ending up hating them for rejecting you and yourself for selling yourself out in the attempt.

She ground her teeth and thought of how to excuse herself. She couldn't think of anything, so she got up to pour herself some wine.

All the bottles were empty, so Julie grabbed a full bottle and called out, "Hey Pamela. Where do you keep your corkscrew?"

"Oh," Pamela said with a heavy-lidded smile, "the screw could really be anywhere in the apartment. The floor, the table . . . of course usually it's in the same place. Top left drawer."

Julie turned away and rolled her eyes. Pamela appeared to be that rare woman who was even sluttier than the way she dressed. She found the corkscrew and turned back to the crowd as she opened the bottle. Unable to find a wineglass and unwilling to provide Pamela with another opening for a cheesy seduction line (Julie wasn't sure how Pamela would turn the question about wineglasses into something sexual—maybe something about putting liquid into a receptacle?—but she was sure she'd make the attempt), she poured the wine into an empty jelly jar with Betty and Veronica on the side.

She looked up from the glass and over to the room where Pamela was busy being Veronica, raven-haired, wealthy, and seductive, while Sarah's Betty—the nice girl, even if Julie was the blond one (and who was she? That ugly girl who went out with Moose?)—sat on the couch watching Peter and Levon be enthralled by Pamela.

"Hey, Julie, why don't you sing another song?" Sarah called out. "You've got a fantastic voice!"

Julie smiled. "Thank you, Sarah. But, you know, without a piano . . ." She gulped some wine down and was surprised to hear Peter say, "Come on—go a cappella then! Or start something and we'll follow along! Right, Levon?"

With difficulty, Levon tore his gaze away from Pamela and said, "Yeah. Definitely."

"Come on," Peter said. "We promise not to screw it up as badly as the last one." Julie noticed that Pamela's voice was absent from those clamoring for her to give them another song. This, and one more gulp of wine, made up Julie's mind. She'd give them a song as far from the folky crap they'd been singing as she possibly could. As long as she was feeling like she didn't fit in, she might as well *go all the way*, as Pamela might have said. She racked her brains for the least folky song she could think of.

For no reason in particular, her mind, after flying through the top forty of the last few years, lit on Tony Orlando and Dawn's "Knock Three Times." Tony Orlando, with his cheesy mustache and tuxedo and backup singers in evening gowns, was about as close to the anti-Dylan as Julie could imagine.

"Okay," she said, grabbing a spoon from a kitchen drawer, "here goes!" She heard the opening horn blasts in her mind and decided to sing them aloud.

"Bap-ba-badada! Bap ba-badadadada dad a!" she sang, and went right into the first verse.

She expected everybody to react with horrified silence, to just sit there slack-jawed as she committed a folk music faux pas.

She certainly didn't expect what happened, which was this: She was still in the first verse when Peter's face broke into a big grin and he began to play along. Sarah followed along, and Levon began adding these little flamenco-ish leads.

When she reached the chorus, Julie went ahead with her cheesy plan, even though she wasn't succeeding in pissing anybody off. When she got to "Knock three times," she knocked three times on the countertop, and at "Twice on the pipes," she clink-clinked the spoon on the kitchen faucet.

Smiling now, forgetting all her anger and resentment, Julie really poured it on as the song continued, singing this slice of pop cheese as though it were the most beautiful song on earth, which, at that moment, it was. Now as she sang "Knock three times" everybody knocked on their guitars, and at "Twice on the pipes," Pamela, who Julie assumed had gotten up from the couch to go pout in the corner, actually beat a crescent wrench against the exposed pipes in the corner.

They wound up with several more choruses than Tony Orlando had, turning the three-minute original into an extended five-minute jam. Five minutes of musical perfection, with everybody smiling and laughing and singing and making something wonderful together.

7

SARAH

SARAH HAD TO PEE. With some difficulty, she got Peter's arm off her and got up off the couch. Peter remained asleep, mouth open. Levon was also asleep in a chair. Pamela was asleep in her bed. Sarah's watch told her it was one thirty in the morning. As she reached the bathroom door, she heard a flushing sound, and Julie emerged. Sarah felt all blurry, like her whole body was covered in moss, but Julie looked as fantastic as she always did. Looking at her, you'd never know that it was one thirty and she'd been drinking and smoking all day.

Wait, Sarah thought. That was actually me. Julie had worked at least part of the day. It had been long enough since Sarah's last toke and glass of wine that she was starting to hate herself for having wasted so many hours being drunk and high. Then again, it had been really really fun.

Julie smiled as she saw Sarah. "Hey," she said. "Do you wanna . . . well, forget it, I'll ask you when you get out of the bathroom."

When Sarah emerged from the bathroom, Julie said, "Hey, I wonder if . . . I would really like to go sleep in my own bed, but

I'm a little leery about getting a cab in this neighborhood at this hour. Do you think you'd like to share a cab? I mean"—Julie was blushing—"I know it's dumb, I can stand behind the door down there and just run into the cab, but I'd just feel better if . . . you know, I wasn't all alone."

Sarah hesitated, and Julie jumped back in with, "I mean, listen, I . . . I'm sorry, I shouldn't ask you that. If I was interested in either of those guys, I wouldn't leave them here, either. I'm sorry. I'm just being neurotic, and . . ."

"What are you talking about?" Sarah asked. "No, I mean, I was just thinking about how the place I'm staying until we get our first paycheck is a lot dirtier and more menacing than this place, and I was kind of looking forward to crashing in a place that's not, you know, a scary hellhole."

Julie's face brightened. "Oh, well, you can crash at my pad if you want to. I can offer you your own couch."

Sarah looked around—there was no comfortable place to sleep here, and Peter would be passed out for hours, and it's not like you could get any privacy here anyway, so maybe crashing at Julie's place would be okay. "Yeah, okay. That sounds nice."

Julie looked relieved. "Great. I'll call us a cab." She went to the phone and called a cab while Sarah wrote a note.

Dear Party Poopers,

It's only 1:30, and the night is young, but you are all asleep. We're going out to a club near Julie's house. See you tomorrow!

She showed it to Julie, who laughed and happily signed her name. "Wonderful. I love it."

Sarah smiled. "I figure it's better for me to look wild and exciting. More alluring, you know, than just, *I wanted a couch to myself.*"

"Got it," Julie said. "I think that's a good plan."

"You really think so?" Sarah said.

"Well." Julie paused and looked around the room. "There's a lot of wild on display here, if you know what I mean. I think it's a good idea not to cede that territory."

Sarah didn't get exactly what that meant, but she was already sobering up enough that she felt awkward asking Julie to explain it.

When they got into the cab, Julie gave an Upper West Side address. That was surprising. Not really a starving-artist neighborhood. They rode in tired silence for several blocks with Sarah turning over what Julie had said and trying to make herself either understand it or stop thinking about it. But neither one was working, and she knew she was going to have to ask or else she'd just churn it in her mind all night and never be able to sleep.

"Um, can I ask you something?" she said, and she felt her face getting hot. She hated that. Now Julie was going to think she was some pathetic, idiotic kid.

"Sure," Julie said.

"Why . . . um, what made you say that you wouldn't want to leave the guys there if you were interested in them?"

Julie looked slightly taken aback. "Oh. I, uh, it's probably nothing. It seemed to me like Pamela was kind of sending out some signals tonight."

"Really?"

Julie hesitated for a second. "Well, I don't know. It looked from where I was sitting like she was being kind of flirty with Levon, but maybe I'm just a catty bitch."

"You don't think . . . I mean, did you think Peter was . . ."

"Oh no! Not at all. Actually, to be honest, I didn't even really see Levon getting too into it. It's probably nothing. Like I said. When I was in high school, my best friend stole my boyfriend, so I've been kind of paranoid about stuff like that ever since."

"Got it," Sarah said, but she didn't get it, not really. Maybe Julie and Pamela both lived in this alternate pretty-girl universe.

Maybe that's why Julie was tuned in to this stuff. Sarah had been jealous before, but it wasn't like she ever really had to keep a close eye on her guys because, let's face it, they weren't exactly the kind of guys that a lot of other girls wanted. Some of them had been very sweet, but they were not the kind of guys that she ever had to worry about the pretty girls stealing away.

This was actually one of Sarah's favorite things about college. Everybody understood that there was a two-tiered system, and people who weren't on the top tier stopped trying to get people too good looking for them and kept to their own tier, where it turned out there was a lot of fun and companionship and good sex to be had.

Sarah brooded all the way uptown. Because she did like Peter, but he was in the top tier, and so was Julie, and so, for that matter, was Pamela. But Pamela wouldn't want to sleep with him, right? She was practically their boss.

Finally the cab arrived at Julie's place, and Sarah was able to get her mind off the track to dumpsville. Could you actually go to dumpsville if you hadn't ever actually gone out with someone? Well, a mystery for another night.

A doorman held open the door for them and said, "Good evening, Miss Julie."

Julie smiled at him and said, "I think it's actually good morning at this point, William, but thanks just the same."

Miss Julie? Sarah had done some student teaching and had been called "Miss Sarah" by her students, but she couldn't really imagine being called "Miss Sarah" by anybody over the age of six.

Off the elevator, Julie opened her door and Sarah couldn't help gasping. "Oh my God," she said. "This is a nice place. I mean a really nice place. I've been apartment hunting, and you just don't find a place like this . . ." The neighborhood, the high ceilings, the fact that it was a one bedroom rather than the horrible studios and efficiencies Sarah had been looking at . . . .it was literally breathtaking. As was Julie's huge, slobbery dog, who jumped and licked wildly until Julie got her calmed down.

Julie looked sheepish. "Yeah, well, I'll let you in on a secret. I actually worked in advertising for the last few years. Writing jingles and stuff. Being a whore who wrote songs on the clock, as Pamela would say."

"Oh, I don't think Pamela really meant—"

"Well, in any case, I made enough money to live somewhere nice."

Sarah looked around and forced her jaw closed. "It is really, really nice. Wow. You're so lucky."

"Listen, you . . . you won't tell anybody, will you?" Julie had that same slightly embarrassed look on her face she'd had when admitting that she was afraid to take a cab alone. "I already feel kind of like I don't fit in, and I don't want people hating me."

"Oh, geez, Julie, nobody's going to hate you. I mean, we're all a team, you know, we're all in this together, making music. It doesn't matter what you did before."

"Well, it doesn't matter to you, but I bet it would to Pamela."

"I don't think so, but I won't tell anybody if you don't want me to."

"Thanks."

"You know, you're really talented. Your song is great. I can't wait to hear the next one."

"Well, it sounded like shit tonight, but thank you. I do think it's a pretty good song. Just not as good as yours."

Sarah was shocked. "Really? I mean, really? I didn't think mine was . . ."

"You've got a great melody, a great chorus, and you actually taught me something. I never realized that about multiples of nine."

"Really? Well, thanks! Glad I could help! Next time you have a third-grade multiplication quiz, you can thank me if you pass it!"

They both laughed. Then Julie said, "You're laughing, but there will be kids who will thank you for that. Think about that."

As she snuggled under a blanket on the couch in the darkness ten minutes later, Sarah did think about it. She didn't think about Peter, asleep in Pamela's apartment, with Pamela on the bed bra-less and probably not wearing underwear under her skirt. No, she didn't think about that. Instead, she thought about a little girl with glasses and pigtails going into school and humming "Nine's Magic Multiples" under her breath and getting a gold star and a big hug and a kiss from her dad, and then she was the girl and they were serving dolphin in the cafeteria and Joan Baez was the lunch lady, and Melanie was her teacher and kept saying, "Are you ready? Are you ready for the test? Are you ready?"

SARAH WOKE UP to the sound of coffee percolating. Her head felt like it could barely contain her swollen brain, her legs ached like she'd run a marathon, and her stomach . . . she couldn't even bear to think about her stomach.

She raised her head, which rewarded her by radiating throb-bing pain through her skull. Through half-closed eyes, she could see Julie, awake, dressed, and bustling in the kitchen.

"Hey!" Julie called out. "Ready to go change the world?"

"Um, if that's a synonym for barfing, then yes. Otherwise, no. Jesus, I've never been hung over from grass before."

"There was wine too," Julie said.

"Was there? Really? I wonder why I don't . . . oh, yeah." Ten-tatively, Sarah raised her body. "Ugh. Oh." Slowly, she stood up.

"Want some eggs?" Julie said. This was all it took to send the contents of Sarah's stomach screaming for the exit. She ran to the bathroom and vomited red wine and half-chewed bits of brown rice and steamed vegetables into the toilet. She finished, splashed cold water on her face, then repeated the process.

After an hour of slowly sipping tea and watching Julie read the paper and wishing she could focus enough to read the paper, Sarah started to feel human again. She showered, borrowed clothes from Julie, and was ready to go to work.

"God, our first real day of work, and we're not getting in until ten," Sarah said as they rode a taxi to the ATN tower.

"I will give you ten dollars if any of the other people are there before noon," Julie said.

When they got out of the elevator, they peeked their heads into the studio and saw no one.

They peeked into all the other rooms: empty.

"So will you play me your songs?" Sarah asked, hoping she wasn't being annoying. But what Pamela had said was really true—Sarah definitely found her own work inspired by other people's work. In fact, thinking about it, she realized she'd had some inspiration last night brought about by Julie's performance of "Knock Three Times." What the hell was it? Something about three . . . had she written it down somewhere in Pamela's apartment? She thought maybe she had.

"Hey! Somebody there?" a male voice called out from the direction of the kitchen/lounge. Startled, Sarah and Julie instinctively grabbed each other's arms, then laughed.

"Yeah," Julie said. "It's us."

"Well, that clears things up," the man said. He walked into the lounge, and Sarah saw it was the guy from yesterday who had been there at the beginning and then not for the rest of the day. He had some kind of weird name. Dippy? He was a tall guy with a kind of big gut, blond hair down to his waist, and a beard that went down to his chest. She hoped Pamela went for the Gregg Allman type—that might keep her away from Peter.

The guy gave a big friendly grin. "Hey there! It's Sarah and Julie!"

Sarah panicked—she had no idea what his name was. All she could think was "Dildo," but she was pretty sure that wasn't right.

"Dingo," Julie said, bailing Sarah out. "Good to see you again."

They all shook hands, and Dingo said, "So how was the dinner party last night? I was going to come, but then my daughter got sick, and my wife had to work, so I had to go home and clean up vomit."

"Yeah, there appears to be a lot of that going around," Julie said, and Sarah was mortified—she'd puked all over Julie's hospitality, and now Julie was mad at her. She'd wrecked whatever chance she had to make a good impression. But then she glanced at Julie and saw that she was smiling.

"I figured it would be that kind of party. So I guess we shouldn't expect Pamela for at least another hour."

"I guess," Sarah said. " Julie and I left at about one, and everybody else was passed out."

"Who's everybody else?"

"Oh, you know, just Peter and Levon and Pamela," Sarah said.

"Peter *and* Levon, huh? Pamela usually starts with just one. Must've been a big night."

"What do you mean?" Sarah said, maybe a little too breathlessly. "I mean, they were just . . . we were all together . . . it wasn't like . . . ."

Dingo smiled. "Okay," he said. He had this look on his face like a parent who's just had a kid argue that there is too a Santa Claus. "So you guys want to make some music, or what? I haven't played a lick since we got off the road a month ago, and I'm rusty as hell and jonesing for some music. So who's got a song?"

"Julie does," Sarah said. "She was just about to play it for me."

"Okay then," Dingo said. "Let's hear it."

They trooped into what Sarah already thought of as Julie's room, and Julie played them "We Need a Verb." By the end of it,

Dingo was so excited he was practically jumping up and down. "That was great! You!" he said, pointing to Sarah, "what do you play?"

"Uh, guitar," she said.

"Okay. Think you can follow Julie's chords?"

"Uh, I guess," Sarah said. No, actually no way could she follow those chords. F minor was about the most complicated chord she knew. But if she was here working as a professional musician she'd have to get beyond G–C–D7 sometime.

"What about singing? You sing?"

"Yeah," Sarah said, more confidently this time.

"Great, let's focus on that first. Let's put some harmonies on the chorus, and I'd love it if we could do some Supremes stuff in the last verse—you know . . . Julie, can you play it?" Julie played her last verse, and Dingo, singing falsetto, came in with "Do it do it do it dooooooooo" behind Julie's vocals.

Sarah laughed. She never would have thought of it, but it sounded perfect. God, she had so much to learn.

Dingo and Julie got everything set up in the studio, and Sarah sat there in a stew of nerves. She'd finally gotten her stomach to calm down, and now she felt like she might puke again. There was no way Pamela had seduced Peter. Right? But where were they? They couldn't all still be asleep. Could they?

And now this nice but gigantic guy was expecting her to sing on a recording, which was terrifying. She knew she could sing, but deep down she also knew that she was a fraud, that she was nowhere near as talented as anyone else here. She'd lucked into this job, and she'd hoped to have some kind of training period or something to write some songs and build up her confidence before she'd be called on to produce something. And now she was going to have to sing on a recording. While she was hung over! She'd be fired by tonight.

Finally, Dingo reappeared and saved Sarah from her own

thoughts. "All right, listen, we've gotta record everything in mono, like we're Buddy Holly or something, can't overdub anything, so we've gotta record live. Well, if Phil Spector did it, so can we. So can you play the guitar part and sing at the same time?"

Sarah wanted to say, *Yes, of course, I'm a professional,* but she couldn't. She didn't want to waste everybody else's time, she didn't want to ruin Julie's song, which was by far the best one she'd heard yet. "I . . . I don't think I'll be able to give a very good . . . I mean, I can definitely do the vocals, but I'd need more rehearsals to do the guitar . . ." Sarah looked at her shoes and waited for Dingo to yell at her. Maybe she'd even get fired right now—can't pull your weight on this project, better get back to elementary school. Except she'd already gone back on her word and pissed off a superintendent who pledged to blackball her, not to mention how pissed off her parents were, so what would she do after they fired her from her dream job?

Dingo didn't yell. He reached down from the clouds with a massive hand that he put on her shoulder. "Thank you, kid," he said. "You have no idea how many people would make us waste hours of time and miles of tape because they'd never admit they couldn't do something. That's real professionalism. I'm glad we're going to be working together."

Sarah gave a little laugh, she was so relieved that she wasn't getting the *it's just not going to work out, you're fired* speech. "Thanks," she managed. "Me too."

"Now we just need a guitar," Dingo said.

At that moment Sarah heard Peter say, "Hello?" He walked into the lounge. Alone. Sarah let out a long, slow breath she seemed to have been holding since she woke up and smiled. She looked at the clock on the wall. It was eleven fifty-two AM. "Hey Julie," she called out, "you owe me ten bucks!"

8

DINGO

"**R**OLLING!" DINGO said as he ran from the booth to the drum kit. He wasn't sure why they hadn't hired an engineer to sit in the booth, but it was a simple enough setup that Dingo didn't really need to man the board while they were recording. He sat and clicked his drumsticks together four times and Julie came in with her piano part. He wished that Julie had written something that wasn't in 4/4 time. Dingo could keep 4/4 time in his sleep—indeed, he often did, if Cass was to be believed when she woke him up yelling that she wasn't a goddamn bass drum, so stop kicking her in rhythm. Dingo's explanation that he'd actually been kicking her with his hi-hat foot didn't do anything but infuriate her.

Since he didn't have to concentrate on his drumming, Dingo was free to look around the studio hoping that he'd miked everything correctly, looking to see that the girls were the proper distance from the mikes, and listening for the inevitable wrong note he knew was coming. It did come, about two minutes into the song, from Peter. Otherwise, it was a pretty good take.

The kids all clustered around the board as Dingo played the recording back. Julie listened with her eyes closed, nodding. Sarah winced whenever her harmonies came in, even though they sounded perfect. Peter winced when his bad note came in. When it ended, before anybody else could say anything, Dingo said, "Okay, people, I'm sorry, but I'd really like to do another take. Drums are way too loud, and I don't want to blow out anybody's TV speakers. You ready?" Everybody nodded, Sarah and Peter looking at him like he'd just saved their lives. All part of the job.

THE SECOND TAKE was perfect, and everybody knew it. Well, everybody but Sarah, who was the only one not grinning from ear to ear when it was over. "Yes!" Julie called out. "Wow! That was fantastic!"

Dingo played it back and crossed his fingers, hoping the sound was okay. He'd love it if the guitar were a little louder, and the high end sounded a little weak, but there was nothing to do about that. Day one, take two, one song in the can. Dingo was beaming.

He sent the kids away with profuse thanks. They were all so happy it was contagious. Dingo had been a professional musician for so long that he'd forgotten what it was like to work with people like this who were actually thrilled by the act of making music. When he saw Peter's big grin during the playback, Dingo suddenly flashed back to practicing in his friend Karl's basement with Victor and Dan, playing "Come On Everybody" and thinking they were the coolest things in the world.

He looked at the clock. One fifteen PM. He'd already cut it too close. He popped the reel off of the recorder, boxed it, wrote DINGO TEST REEL #1 on it, and stuck it in the back of the bottom drawer of the file cabinet that stood in the corner of the booth. It was behind sheaves of paper that held the cast lists for all of ARN's old radio dramas. They might be of interest to historians someday, but Dingo felt confident that Pamela would never look in there.

Which was good, because there was no way Pamela was going to be able to stop herself from sabotaging a recording she had nothing to do with. Maybe they'd re-record Julie's song later anyway, but it felt good to have a decent take in the can, and he wasn't going to have Pamela wrecking it. He'd been in the studio with Pamela enough to know that, even without multitrack recording, she might take days to get a single song on tape. And after nearly endless dithering, Pamela would turn to Dingo for a quick fix, which he would deliver, and then Pamela would take the credit.

Now at least if they ever needed to come up with something quickly, Dingo had a song he could hand over at a moment's notice, and he wouldn't have to stay out late and not be able to kiss the kids good night.

He'd only been home a few weeks, and already the idea of missing the kids' bedtime was intolerable. He'd spent most of their lives on the road, and suddenly, knowing he was going to be around for a year, he no longer understood how he did it. He no longer understood how he'd thought any job was worth being away from his kids for so long. Jesus, he should have been pumping gas or something, anything to be around them. Certainly not laying down inoffensive drum parts behind self-indulgent folk rock in front of dwindling audiences. Certainly not letting Pamela steal his producing credit and getting only a session man's pay for it. If he'd actually gotten producing credit, he could be working as a producer on his own schedule—but that was pointless. Once you turned on the what-if machine, you could drive yourself crazy within about five minutes.

He told himself he was actually saving Pamela from herself, but she'd never see it that way. Record companies might put up with Pamela's idiosyncratic work habits, but Dingo had no idea if a TV network under pressure from Congress would. If Pamela spent as much time farting around as she usually did, they might all get fired. And Dingo liked being home. He wanted to hold on to this job as long as he could.

Dingo went out into the lounge as Peter was explaining how he'd woken up at nine and walked all the way up here from Pamela's place. Sarah was visibly relieved. Dingo knew Peter's story was bullshit, but he knew just as surely that it was none of his business. No way Pamela had two boys in her apartment and didn't sleep with either or both of them. She just didn't operate that way. But if Peter wanted to pretend otherwise, well, that was his decision.

"So who else has a song?" Dingo said, grabbing a reel-to-reel recorder. Peter volunteered immediately, and, after insisting that yes, he really did want to hear it, and if it had been good enough to get her hired, it was good enough to play while they sat around in the basement, he got Sarah to play hers. He started doing arrangements in his head as they played, and then he went back to the studio with the tape he'd just made to think some more.

He thought he'd probably be ready to record them tomorrow. He played the demos a few times in the booth and then spent a few minutes moving instruments around the studio and trying to decide how best to use the space.

An hour later, Pamela arrived with Levon in tow. The kids gushed to Pamela about how they'd already recorded a song, as Dingo knew they would, and a few minutes later Pamela demanded a private word, as Dingo knew she would.

"I just feel . . . I don't think it's going to be good for our art here to commit it to tape before it's ready. You know what I mean? Part of what I'm trying to accomplish here is to create a real sense of community, and I think the best songwriting and playing is going to emerge from this sense of community."

"I hear ya," Dingo said. He said this a lot with Pamela because it suggested that he agreed but wasn't technically a lie. "I just thought we'd give the kids a little taste of the recording process, you know, so they kind of know what the end point is."

Pamela paused, inhaled, and exhaled slowly. "But that's just what I'm trying to avoid. I don't want to mess up their creative process with any kind of goals. For right now, it just needs to be art for art's sake, you know? Pure creativity."

But it's not just for art's sake, Dingo thought. It's for cartoon's sake, it's for paycheck's sake, it's for covering Briggs Payson's ass's sake. "I gotcha," he said.

"So, if you don't mind," Pamela said, "I'd really like to hold on to today's master tape. Just so we can have everything together, and so the energy from that doesn't start taking over the process here."

"No problem," Dingo said. "Let me just get it." He walked into the control room with Pamela on his heels and pulled the reel with the recording of him hitting his snare drum in different corners of the studio and saying "No dice, son, you gotta work late" into all of the different mikes in many different locations. He felt pretty confident that Pamela would never listen to it, but if she did, he could just say he really thought it was that tape, he must have accidentally erased it, he'd been up all night with a sick kid, sorry, it won't happen again.

"Thank you, David," Pamela said warmly. "I really appreciate having you on board." She walked out, and Dingo sat in the booth for a minute trying to figure out what he was going to do until Pamela decided she could actually do some recording.

Since Dingo was here to play on, engineer, and covertly produce the recordings, he couldn't be seen to be working when

Pamela was around until she decided to allow recording to happen. So he wandered out to the lounge, where pot smoke hung thickly in the air and Peter and Levon and Pamela were strumming their guitars absentmindedly. Dingo looked at them all. Neither Peter nor Levon looked particularly sheepish around the other, which probably meant that they hadn't seen each other naked and grunting, or else they were just particularly shameless about that activity.

It was four thirty. Upstairs, underpaid twenty-two-year-olds were running around frantically making sure all the pages were typed and in the right order, makeup was being applied, cameras and sound equipment were being tested, and, in a dressing room, Walker Wallace was probably doing voice exercises, preparing to deliver tonight's news with appropriate gravitas. Meanwhile, down here, people were stoned on couches doing nothing.

He exchanged greetings with Peter and Levon and then turned to Pamela. "Well, if it's okay, I'm gonna head home and get Davey to the dentist. It never freakin' stops. I'll see you tomorrow."

"Okay, David," Pamela said absentmindedly. She was far too busy casting predatory gazes at the boys to care much about what Dingo did.

On his way out, he peeked into a room where Sarah and Julie were playing a song.

" . . . and it's all because of threeee . . . ," Sarah was singing.

Dingo applauded, and Sarah and Julie looked up at him. "Sounds great. Hey listen," he said, "I'm going home, but maybe we can record this tomorrow."

Both girls gave an enthusiastic "Great!" and Dingo pressed his palms down in the air to quiet them.

"So Pamela thinks it'll be disruptive to the energy or something to put this stuff on tape, but I've never recorded on this kind of setup before, so I can really use the practice. You think we could do this early in the morning and just keep it under our hats? I'd really appreciate it."

Both girls said, Sure, absolutely, but Julie looked a little more sure and absolute than Sarah.

"I'll be in nice and early, like eight o'clock, so you can show up anytime in the morning."

"Thanks, Dingo," Sarah said.

"Yeah, thanks. See you tomorrow," Julie said.

"Okay," Dingo said.

Dingo took the elevator up to the lobby, then took another elevator down into the ATN garage, then drove out and spent an hour in tunnel traffic on his way home. Good thing he didn't actually have to take Davey to the dentist. The regular paychecks and being home every night were definitely going to be good things about having a straight job, but this business of sealing yourself in a car and sitting in an underground chamber felt to Dingo uncomfortably like dying. No wonder so many of his neighbors were such tight-asses about the state of their lawns and cars: They enacted this little death ritual every day. Talk about creepy.

Still, instead of eating crappy greasy spoon (or worse yet, macrobiotic) food, he was eating Cass's lasagna and hearing about Davey and Jenny's days at school and feeling like a real, regular dad instead of some guy who got to visit this nice family in New Jersey sometimes.

The phone rang after dinner, and Cass handed it to Dingo. "Clark Payson," she mouthed.

Shit, Dingo thought. Was he fired already? Had Pamela figured out he'd given her the wrong tape and gotten Clark Payson to fire him?

"Hello, Mr. Payson," Dingo said.

"Hi, Mr. Donovan . . . Dingo. So, uh, listen, I know today is only your second day on the job, and I just wanted to just . . . we only met briefly, but I got a sense of professionalism from you, and I was just hoping you could tell me how you think things are going. I . . . uh . . . I stopped down there and the whole place reeked of pot smoke, and Pamela told me some long thing about the energy, and I just . . . I'm hoping . . . listen, I'll keep you on board for the year regardless, but do I need to pull the plug on this project? Am I throwing money and my career down the toilet here?"

It was kind of fun to hear the panic in Clark Payson's voice. Dingo's first feeling was one of triumph. Though he felt about a hundred years old compared with the kids in the ATN basement, he'd been a musician in the 1960s, he'd been to Woodstock (as a spectator, but still), and he could dig the idea of the inmates taking over the asylum, and he relished the idea of making somebody in a suit, that symbol that identified you as part of the establishment, pee his pants about where his money was going.

Jenny came and tugged on his sleeve and begged for a story, and Dingo held up one finger telling her to wait and thought about the situation. Clark Payson seemed okay, but he was, you know, The Man. If Dingo became Clark Payson's little spy in the basement, he'd be selling out a lot of what he'd thought he believed for the last eight years or so. He would also be allying himself with a powerful TV executive who might be able to get him work in a variety of situations, work that paid real money and didn't involve any more grungy clubs that he was too old for. Work that would keep him, God help him, in New Jersey where he belonged. If, on the other hand, he was loyal to Pamela, who had employed him for the last three years and gotten him this gig in the first place, he'd be doing the right thing, standing up for freedom and grooviness, and he'd be able to sleep at night. In a shitty motel room touring with God-knows-who, cursing himself for throwing in with a washed-up folkie who was touring solo without drums.

When he'd played "Come On Everybody" in the basement all those years ago, he'd pictured a life of cool rock-and-roll rebellion. He'd wanted to be Eddie Cochran, James Dean, and Elvis. But Eddie Cochran and James Dean were dead, and Elvis was in Vegas. Jenny was coming in again to ask for a story, and Dingo thought about her getting picked up for the prom and not having a dad to scare the shit out of her date. He glanced at the stack of bills on the table. He decided to throw in with the suit.

"Well, here's what I think," Dingo said. "You've got some really talented kids down there. And as much as Pamela's kind of a . . . loose cannon, she is convincing the ones who maybe need a little confidence boost that they can do this work. I think some great stuff is going to come out of this." He heard Clark Payson exhale.

"That's great. Because I thought, you know, I've just given these hippies a place to hang out, and . . ."

"Well, it's definitely that, but there is work getting done. I've got one song in the can already. Should have one or two more by tomorrow."

"Oh, wow, that's just great!"

"Yeah. Don't worry. We'll get it done."

"Well, thank you. I really appreciate it."

"Not a problem. Call me anytime."

"Okay, Dingo. Thanks again. And listen, my door is always open to you. Stop by anytime."

"Thanks. I will," Dingo said, and hung up the phone. Well, they used to say, "Never trust anyone over thirty," but maybe they should have said, "Never trust anyone with kids and a mortgage."

9

LEVON

EVON LOOKED AT the clock. He'd been on the couch for three hours. Two days at work, and all he'd done was get high. He giggled. Nice work if you can get it, he thought.

He knew he should get up, should do something, but he was just feeling too good on the couch to do anything but sit on the couch.

He hadn't even realized how exhausted he had been until he had stopped working. Four years of college, of busting his ass to get good grades and make his dad proud and uplift the race, and prove that Dad had done the right thing by moving them all to Ridgewood when they would have had a smaller mortgage and a higher comfort level somewhere else. And even though the music had been fun—had been really the only fun he'd had in the last eight years—it had also been exhausting to balance practices and gigs with studying.

And now all he had to do was sit on the couch and get high. And eventually write some more songs. But not now. He just felt like he could sleep for a hundred years. If he could ever get off the couch and get his ass back to the Y.

Which didn't seem likely.

Pamela got up at some point and said, "Well, the lack of windows here is really oppressive. I need to get myself into a place with better energy flow." She cast a glance at Levon but did not say anything.

He was half tempted to go with her, to say something about having the munchies, needing to go out and get some food, but something in the pit of his stomach was telling him it was a bad idea.

He'd woken up in Pamela's apartment feeling groggy but not especially hungover, since he'd only smoked the night before. Peter was nowhere to be seen, and Pamela emerged from the shower dripping wet and wrapped in a towel. "Good morning," she'd said as she made for the kitchen area.

"Hey," Levon had said. "Where is everybody?"

Pamela had looked around and shrugged. "Not here, apparently." She'd looked at him intently, then opened a cabinet, reached up, and got a mug. "Tea?" she said. "Something hot?"

He'd decided to play this the way he'd been playing it from the beginning. Like he was a total innocent who didn't get that Pamela was throwing herself at him. He wasn't really sure why he was doing this. Certainly he'd met his share of girls when he was Apollo Von Funkenburg, and if he'd been hesistant and shy with the first one, he certainly hadn't with the tenth, or the fifteenth, or the . . . he'd stopped counting. So why now? Well, this wasn't some groupie on her knees in the back of a club; it was somebody he was supposed to be working for, or with, or something. He didn't know what the implications would be of taking her up on her unspoken offer, and so maybe he was going to make her speak it.

"Uh, yeah, sure, a cup of tea would be nice," he said.

Pamela filled a kettle and turned on the stove. "So what did you say your stage name was again?"

"Uh, Apollo Von Funkenburg," he'd said.

"Wasn't there more to it?" Pamela said, smiling.

"Duke of Uranus," Levon said.

"Hmmm," Pamela had said. "Oh, dammit, I dropped my teabag." She'd bent over at the waist, offering Levon, aka Apollo Von Funkenburg, the Duke of Uranus, a clear and enticing view of his domain.

Levon was confused, angry, frustrated, and horny. Why was she doing this to him? And why didn't he just get up off the couch and give it to her right in the dukedom? It was obvious that was what she wanted. But there was something wrong here; until he figured out what exactly it was, Levon was keeping it in his pants.

He'd looked at his watch, feigned shock at the time, and said, "Oh, shit! My bass has been in a Port Authority locker for forty-seven hours! I gotta go get it!"

"They never enforce that forty-eight-hour rule," Pamela had said. "Brown rice syrup?" she asked as she stirred the tea. "It's got great natural sweetness."

Yeah, I've got your natural sweetness right here, Levon hadn't said. "No, thanks, I really gotta get up there and get my instrument."

"I once left a bag of grass in a locker there at the beginning of a tour. It was still there at the end. You really don't have to worry," Pamela had said with an amused smile on her face.

"I don't have to, but I guess I am anyway," Levon had said. "I'm sorry, but I'm not going to be able to think about anything else until I get my bass."

"Well, we couldn't have you distracted," Pamela said, smiling. "And I admire the fact that you're careful about where you put your instrument."

Levon had all but run from the loft, already exhausted by Pamela's barrage of come-ons, and it wasn't until he was nearly at the ATN building that he realized what the problem was, why he hadn't claimed his dukedom this morning.

Not surprisingly, it all came back to Dad again. While he was comfortable concealing the fact that he had taken a job in the entertainment industry from Dad, he still wanted to work, to feel like he was actually earning his money, to feel that he'd gotten the job because of his talent and not just because he was a mascot, a token, a sex object. When the showdown with Dad came, as it would eventually, Levon wanted to be able to point to some accomplishments, to say, Look, Dad, I am making my way in the world, nobody's handing me anything, and I'm making it because I'm good at this.

So until he felt like he had done something besides get high and sit on couches, he wasn't fucking the boss, no matter how sexy and obviously available she was.

And he was really glad about it when the huge white guy— Dingo—had reappeared, and a wave of paranoia had crashed over Levon. He still didn't know if Dingo and Pamela were together, but if they were, he was pretty sure that Dingo would not take kindly to her being with another guy. Dingo was colossal, and Levon had been convinced that he was going to flatten him just to send him a warning about staying away from Pamela.

But then Dingo had talked about taking a kid to the dentist, and Pamela hadn't acted like she cared one way or the other. So if they were together, neither one of them was really acting like it.

So Pamela left, cast Levon a meaningful glance, and Levon sat on the couch. And Peter sat on the other couch. Time passed. Levon wondered idly where his determination to work hard and make his mark and achieve something he could point to had gone. Up in smoke.

Suddenly, out of nowhere, Peter had turned to Levon and said, "So did you and Pamela . . . ?"

Levon looked over at Peter and kind of wished he had. Because he could see that Peter was trying to play it casual but was actually worried about the answer. Levon suddenly felt a surge of annoyance at Peter. He'd really thought they were becoming friends, but now Peter was getting all freaked out about the black man's sexuality. Or else he was just acting like a friend would act and asking if his friend got any last night.

"Did we what?" Levon said, still trying to figure out whether he was going to lie to Peter just to mess with his head.

"You know. I mean, did you . . . did she . . ."

Well, Levon decided the truth might mess with Peter's head enough. "She sure as hell tried. But I had to call bullshit on that."

"No kidding," Peter said. "Why?" Levon couldn't read Peter's tone of voice.

Either way, Levon couldn't resist the temptation to make a joke. "Why the hell would I want some old-ass bitch like that? Shit, if they're out of high school, I'm not interested. Junior high is even better." Levon could barely get the whole speech out before laughter erupted from his mouth.

Of course his laughter was contagious, and Peter laughed until he literally fell off the couch. "Oh, man," he finally said as he was catching his breath, "that's good stuff. Funny funny shit. Either that or I'm really stoned."

And suddenly Peter seemed tolerable and even likable again. "You hungry?" Levon asked him.

"Starving. But I'm too lazy to go get anything."

"Yeah," Levon said. "Damn sure can't see getting my ass back to the Y tonight. I was thinking I might take a page from your book."

Peter started to giggle. "I think there's probably a space for you at Pamela's place," he said.

"Yeah, I think I'll take my chances here. Unless, you know, you're gonna get nervous with me down here. Think I'm gonna steal your stuff or something."

Peter laughed. "If I get anything worth stealing, maybe. Until then, yeah, I think I can put up with it."

Levon smiled and was suddenly powerfully hungry. "All right," he said, rising from the couch and finding with some surprise that his legs still worked, "I want something to eat."

"Me too," Peter said. "Where are the girls?"

Levon just looked at Peter, and they both broke out laughing again, and it was a long time before Levon could gasp out, "Damn, Pete, I was talking about food! You horny motherfucker!"

"Hey, Sarah!" Peter said a little too loudly. "Julie! We were just talking about getting something to eat—"

"You know," Levon said, "I get—shit, I don't know, whichever one's younger. Ask 'em for some ID," Levon whispered, and he and Peter both started laughing again. Levon's stomach actually hurt from laughing too much.

"Deal," Peter whispered back. "Do you guys want to go get a bite?" This was too much for Levon, who ran snorting to the bathroom for fear he might actually piss himself as the girls came into the lounge. When he returned, Peter was alone. "Julie said she was tired from *working* all day," Peter said, rolling his eyes. "So I guess we're on our own."

Sarah immediately glued herself to Peter's side.

They wandered out of the ATN building, Peter telling the security guard that they had reels and reels of tape to edit, so they'd be back after dinner.

The last rays of the sun were still shining, and Levon found it kind of shocking. He felt like he'd just woken up. This was partly because his buzz was wearing off, but also because, apart from the transit time from Pamela's place to ATN, he'd spent the last full day half or completely asleep under dim red lights, and the yellow cast of the sunlight and the frantic activity of the New York streets were such a jarring change that Levon felt kind of dizzy.

The three of them walked around for a while, eventually finding a small, somewhat dirty pizzeria and ordering a large with mushrooms and onions. Sarah talked about the songs she and Julie had been working on, while Peter and Levon devoured the rest of the pizza before Sarah had even finished her first slice. They ordered another pizza, consumed it with a little more restraint than the first one, then waddled into the street.

They stood outside the pizzeria for a moment, contemplating their next move. Peter and Sarah were doing some kind of elaborate flirtation dance, obviously attracted to each other but pretending not to tip their hands, trying and failing to act casual, as though they didn't much care where they went or who they went with, when all they really wanted to do was ditch Levon and go fuck each other's brains out.

Levon spaced out and just looked around. Cars rolled down the street, neon shone from restaurants and storefronts, people walked down the streets—couples, groups of friends, guys in suits, hookers, junkies, whites, blacks, Puerto Ricans.

You could feel the excitement in the air. Levon had spent the last four years in Manhattan and had been here plenty of times before that on school field trips and special family outings, but this was different. For the first time he felt of the city, not just in it. Something was happening. Levon wished for just a moment that he could get his dad into his brain, just so he could experience this sense of possibility, this excitement. This, Dad, this is what you cut yourself on a file drawer in Selma for. So I could stand on the street, a black man, and feel like anything is possible. I can go back to my job at a television network, or I can go out on the town. If I want to, I can probably go downtown and fuck a folksinger in the ass. It was an exciting and wonderful feeling, and while Levon knew that most of Dad's stories were no more than a quarter true, he also knew that a sense of infinite possibility was not a feeling that had been available to Dad or to many black men his age.

The revolution, he realized, will be televised. The revolution will be little three-minute cartoons with songs by a brother who felt invincible. Songs about science, songs about guys who felt the same feeling—like they were standing on the threshold of a new age. Pioneers, discoverers. Newton, Einstein, Faraday, mother-fucking Archimedes in the bathtub shouting Eureka. Shit, he needed to go write some songs. Right now.

"Where to?" Sarah said, looking hopefully at Peter.

"I don't know about you guys," Levon said, "but I just sud-denly felt like I had to write some songs. Like I've got about four songs on deck, and I need to go get them done right now."

"Cool!" Peter said. "Let's go back to ATN!" Sarah looked dis-appointed, but accompanied them.

Once they were back in the basement, Levon ran to a practice room, grabbed a notebook and a curriculum binder, and started to write. He flipped open to a page that said FAMOUS SCIEN-TISTS AND INVENTORS at the top followed by a bunch of gob-bledygook that Dr. Education upstairs had written.

He tossed the binder aside and played, and wrote, and wrote and played, and "Newton's Apple" was followed by "Funky Franklin Had the Key," then "Eureka." Levon laughed aloud as "Eureka" came to him. It turned out he really did have a song about motherfuckin' Archimedes.

At some point, Levon wandered out to the kitchen for a glass of water. The clock on the wall told him it was three AM. He headed back to his own practice room, too wired with creativity to even think about sleeping (and, for that matter, he'd slept till noon the previous day and then had been half asleep on the couch for hours). On the way back, he passed the closed door of a room that definitely contained two people having sex. Levon assumed they were Peter and Sarah.

Finally. Now the rest of them wouldn't have to contend with those two pretending they didn't want each other all the time.

The only problem was that those noises made him horny. If Pamela had been here, Levon would have certainly ignored the protestations of his conscience and common sense and fucked her brains out. But Pamela wasn't here, so his hand would have to do.

It took very little time to release all his pent-up horniness, and he felt like he had just curled up on the floor to try to grab a couple of hours of sleep when he heard Dingo's voice bellowing down the hall. "Anybody here? We got work to do!"

10

PETER

PETER WOKE UP to the sound of Dingo bellowing. "Oh shit!" Sarah said, sitting up and patting the floor around her looking for her clothes. "We're supposed to record!"

"Uh, we are?" Peter said, as he turned on the light.

"Ack! Thanks. Ah, here we go," Sarah said as she located her shirt. "Yeah, Dingo said he needs some practice working on this kind of equipment, so we're just recording whatever songs we have now. We're not supposed to tell Pamela, though."

"Why not?"

"I don't know," Sarah said, flipping her hair around. Peter wondered for a second how women did that. She was wearing yesterday's clothes, she'd slept barely three hours, she had some serious rug burns (as did he), and yet she looked completely presentable with just a shake here and a fluff there. Whereas Peter, grabbing his jeans that were filthy yesterday, knew that he looked exactly like a guy wearing yesterday's—well, okay, two days ago's—clothes who had slept three hours on a hard floor. Maybe it had something to do with caring about your appearance as a lifelong habit. Well, something to think about.

"Hey," Sarah said, smiling. "You're staring at me."

"Hey yourself," Peter said, "you're beautiful."

Sarah blushed and was so adorable that the idea of moving from this room and having to be with other people suddenly struck Peter as really painful.

"You're sweet," she said. "Listen, I want to . . . I mean we should really talk about everything, but I guess later, after we record some songs and everything."

"Uh, okay," Peter said. Oh Christ, they had to talk. About everything. He wanted to talk, sure—he wanted to know what she was like as a little kid, he wanted to talk about some exciting places they could go together, he wanted to talk about how great her work was, but what he didn't want was to talk about everything. About where the relationship was going, about all that crap that women always assumed you wanted to talk about just because you played an acoustic guitar.

Sarah kissed him and smiled, and Peter instantly forgave her for her compulsion to talk. About everything. She was, after all, a prisoner of her genes, and she could no more not want to talk about everything than he could figure out how to look good sporting two-day-old clothes after having slept on the floor.

Sarah sprinted down the hall to the studio, while Peter shuffled down the hall. Another door opened, and Levon stumbled out, eyes red, Afro making irregular peaks and valleys on his head.

"Whoa," Peter said. "You look as bad as I feel."

"Fuck you," Levon said. "See, there's an important difference between us. I look like some sorry motherfucker who was up all night. You look like some sorry motherfucker who got some pussy and some sleep last night. So I look a lot worse than you do."

Peter looked at Levon again, and they both started laughing. "Why were you up all night?"

"Writing songs, my friend. You know, the whole reason we were hired?"

"Oh, yeah! We gonna record some?"

"Is that what Dingo was yelling about?"

"Yeah, Sarah says he needs practice with the equipment, so we're recording whatever we've got just to get some practice. But apparently we can't tell Pamela. I don't know why."

Levon backtracked to the room and brought out his bass. "Yeah, we're gonna record some of my songs. I wrote a song about Archimedes!"

"Who the hell is Archimedes?"

"They really don't teach you shit in those liberal arts courses, do they? You were a history major, and you have to ask me who Archimedes was?"

"Well, I'm guessing ancient Greek. What can I say, my concentration was American history. Hey, can you teach me to play some of those funk chords on the guitar?"

"Yeah," Levon said.

"I mean, we're recording live, so I guess you're gonna have to."

They arrived in the studio to find a clean, made-up Julie seated at the piano, a presentable Sarah standing in front of a microphone, and Dingo bustling around.

"Good morning, gentlemen!" Dingo said. "You ready to make some music?"

"Yes," Peter said. He was struck again by the fact that he was the luckiest man alive. He'd had sex and slept without fear of rats and rolled out of bed—well, okay, floor—and gotten to make music. Now if he only had something to eat.

"Doughnuts in the control room, if you want some," Dingo said. "I'm gonna need a couple more minutes to set up in here. Peter, this your guitar?" Peter nodded. "Okay. And Levon, why don't you just set your bass over here, and I'll get your amp all miked up."

Peter wandered into the control room and pondered the box

of doughnuts for a long time, unable to make a decision. Chocolate-frosted or glazed? After a long time, he settled on glazed and exited the control booth.

When he returned to the studio, everything was set up, and Julie played and sang "Tell Me How." Then she played it again, and again, and again, each time somebody joining in, Dingo making suggestions along the way, and after six times through the song, Dingo said they were ready to record.

Dingo ran into the booth to twiddle knobs and start the tape rolling, and then he counted off the beginning of "Tell Me How. "

Four takes and Julie's song was in the can, so they moved on to Sarah's "The Power of Three," which was done in three takes.

Everybody else appeared happy and in the groove. Though Peter had never really played with a band, he had done a number of those Friday-night jams in the dorm lounges, and he could feel this group coming together as musicians, getting a feel for what the others were going to play, anticipating the harmonies, feeling the rhythms from early on.

He guessed a lot of people would say the connection he was feeling with the others in the room was nothing special. The same thing was happening in garages and basements and re-hearsal studios all over the place all the time. So yeah, it wasn't unique. But that didn't mean it wasn't special.

"Okay," Dingo said. "Lunchtime. You guys did great. Sand-wiches are on me! Here—" He threw take-out menus from a deli at them, and Peter felt his stomach suddenly turn into a great gnawing void in his midsection. It had been fine as long as they were making music, but now, looking at the names of sand-wiches, seeing the food described in what seemed to him to be pornographic detail, Peter felt like he might actually faint.

"Uh, I'll have corned beef on light rye," Peter said, and just saying the words sent a surge of saliva into his mouth. "Thanks, Dingo."

"Happy to do it! Great work today. Okay, Sarah, what about you?"

Peter slumped down the hall to the practice room and lay on the floor, trying in vain to think about something other than food.

Fortunately, Sarah came in a moment later.

"Hi!" he said.

"Hi yourself. Are you okay?" Sarah said. She leaned down over him and gave him a kiss.

"Mmm. I'm better now. I'm just . . . well, I don't know if I really conveyed to you how incredibly broke I've been. I haven't eaten anything but that stuff at Pamela's in two days. I'm just freaking starving."

Sarah smiled. "So that's why your hip bones were digging into me. I'm gonna have bruises."

"Sorry," Peter said, smiling.

"I don't think you really are," she said. There was a pause where they just sat there and smiled at each other.

"Can I just ask you something?" Sarah said. Uh-oh. Here it was. The Big Talk. About Everything. And it had to come while he was starving. Well, at least it would give him something to think about besides food. How long until the sandwiches got here? Maybe twenty minutes? Well, this might actually be okay. This conversation would have a natural end point when the food got here, which was way better than having it late at night, when it could stretch out until dawn.

Willing his face not to grimace, Peter said, "Yeah?"

"I just . . . are we . . . I mean, either answer is okay, right, I'm not trying to lay some head trip on you or anything, but I just want you to be honest with me."

"Okay," Peter said.

"Are we . . . I mean, last night was really fun, but is that like . . .

I mean, is that gonna be it, or is there more to it? You know? I mean, you didn't make me any promises or anything, so like I said, I will be okay with either answer, I just want to know."

Jesus. Peter felt like he needed to tread carefully here, and he was just too hungry to choose his words carefully.

"I really like you and I guess I was hoping we would just see what happened with us. I mean, I'm not . . . I don't want to close any doors right now."

Sarah looked fretful. "Really? I mean, I don't want you to say that just to spare my feelings, because it'll hurt more later. You know? I will totally understand if you—"

"Do *you* want last night to be the end?"

"Oh God, no, not at all."

"So why are you so convinced that I do?"

"Promise not to laugh?"

"Promise."

"I just don't understand why you would want to spend time with me. Because you're so good looking and talented, and I'm not."

Peter looked at Sarah for a long moment and wondered how the hell she could think that. He'd found the feminists at college annoying, but maybe they'd had a point about growing up female. It seemed like every girl he'd ever had any kind of relationship with eventually revealed how little she thought of herself. He supposed there were probably girls who believed they were good looking and sexy and wonderful, but those were probably the ones who'd dumped him early on before the relationship got to the "showing our scars" stage. Either that or their scars were so deep and ugly that they always broke it off before they had to show them. Okay. How to reassure someone with a lifetime of self-hatred under her belt that she was desirable? Didn't the fact that we had sex last night count for something?

Well, though Peter himself had never done it, he knew plenty of guys who'd slept with girls while high that they wouldn't touch sober.

"Well, first of all, I'm too skinny and kind of funny looking. Second, you are good looking. And I'm not just saying that. I mean, it's not like Julie Christie is the only sexy woman in the world. You know? And you are very talented. I mean, it's really one of the things I like about you. You're really good, and you have no idea—it seems like you think you don't deserve to be here, but you really do. You're not here because anybody took pity on you. You're here because you're good at what you do."

Sarah was looking at him with tears in her eyes. "That's the nicest thing anybody's ever said to me," she said.

Peter sat up, held her, and whispered in her ear. "I'm sorry about that. You deserve to hear nice things all the time."

He kissed her, and she kissed him back hungrily. His stomach made a loud squelching sound, and Sarah broke off kissing so she could laugh.

"You weren't kidding about being hungry, huh?" she said.

"I told you!"

"Mmmm," she said, hugging him. "I really like you."

"I feel the same way," Peter said.

"Lunch everybody!" Dingo called from the hallway.

"But I really need a sandwich."

Sarah smiled, and they walked hand in hand to the lounge, where Dingo briefly raised an eyebrow at them. They sat at the table and Peter was lost in a haze of mustard and grease and pickles.

AFTER LUNCH, PETER sat on the couch in a food-induced stupor for a period of time that could have been anywhere between twenty minutes and an hour. Dingo strolled into the lounge with a big grin on his face. "Well, apparently Pamela's tied up at home and won't be able to make it in today. So"—he clapped his hands together—"who else has songs?"

"I do," Levon said.

"Great!" Dingo said. "Let's lay one down!"

Peter waddled to the studio, and Levon came over to Peter and took his guitar. "Okay, Pete, look at this." He studied Levon's fingers on the fretboard, and Levon handed the guitar back to him. He tried to form the same chord and gave a tentative strum. Not funky. Levon repositioned his fingers. "Try that," he said.

Peter gave a little strum. It sounded like the right chord. He kept strumming.

"Okay, Pete, you've got the chord, but you got to work on the rhythm. This isn't 'Masters of War.' Think more 'Cold Sweat.' "

Peter thought about "Cold Sweat" and tried to strum in a funkier fashion. If only the girls at Antioch had been a little more into R&B and a little less into Dylan, he thought, this would probably be a lot easier. Still, he kept at it, and eventually Levon nodded.

"Yes," Peter said, "make it funky now. Hot pants. Say it loud, I'm black and proud."

Levon laughed. "Okay, James Brown. You just slide that chord up and down and you are getting about as funky as your white folky ass can. Can you remember that?"

"Yeah," Peter said.

Peter played the James Brown chords, Dingo came in on the one, Julie and Sarah added some Ikette vocals, and Levon laid down the funky bottom and sang "Funky Franklin Had the Key." It was so much fun that Peter couldn't stop just because Dingo told them the tape had surely run out by now, and they ended up playing this thirty-minute extended funk jam that was about as far from anything Peter had ever played in his career as a Would-Be New Dylan as he could imagine.

"All right, all right, I gotta piss like a racehorse!" Dingo finally said, throwing his drumsticks down and running from the studio. Everybody laughed, and that broke up the party pretty decisively.

"I need a nap," Levon said.

"Me too," Sarah said. She came over to Peter and whispered in his ear, "A real nap. With sleeping. I'm exhausted."

Peter knew he was too, but the music had given him a serious buzz. He was flying high, and he was jealous of everybody else's songs. He wanted to have something to record too.

"I think I'm gonna hang out for a while," he said. "I think I have a song on the way."

"Wonderful!" she said. "I hope you'll play it for me when you're done."

"Absolutely," Peter said. He sat there alone for a few minutes, strumming chord progressions and thinking about the thrill of working with smart, talented people on something new and exciting. He wondered if this had been the way it felt when those brave men were starting a country here nearly two hundred years ago.

This thought led directly to "All Right Tonite (Bill of Rights)."

AFTER WRITING "All Right Tonite (Bill of Rights)," Peter staggered to the couch in the lounge and fell asleep. He was awakened by Sarah kissing him. "Hey," she said. "Julie and Levon and I are going up to the employee cafeteria for dinner. Do you want to come?"

Peter sat up and tried to clear the fog from his head. "Um. Yeah. Dinner. Yes. I do want to eat dinner. Let me just . . ."

Sarah smiled and tousled his hair. "Take a few minutes and wake up. We'll wait."

They all took the elevator upstairs and sat there eating their sloppy joes and whispering about all the faces they recognized from the other tables. Peter had absorbed Paul Candel's Vietnam coverage for years; and there he was, on the other side of the cafeteria, with orangey sloppy joe juice on his chin.

"Hey," Sarah said, twitching her head to the left, "isn't that Captain Sunshine over there?" They all looked, and sure enough, there was Captain Sunshine, ATN's morning puppeteer, pouring the contents of a flask into a carton of orange juice.

"Damn," Levon said, "I thought I was the only one who used to watch that show high."

"Speaking of which," Peter said.

"You guys, we're gonna burn through the supply," Julie said, smiling.

"Yeah, I hope so," Peter said.

11

LEVON

EVON AND JULIE sat alone in the lounge. They had all gotten high, again, and Peter and Sarah had disappeared, again.

"Can I just say something bitchy?" Julie said.

"By all means."

"I'm getting . . . I mean, those two . . . I mean, I'm happy for them and everything, but they just . . ."

"Make you want to vomit sometimes?"

"Yeah. Exactly. I'm sorry. I'm a terrible friend."

"Nah, I don't think so. It's only natural. They've started finishing each other's sentences. Have you noticed that?"

"Yeah."

"Still," Levon said, "it's . . . I mean, you cannot deny that the two of them have written some really good songs. I mean, so have you—"

"You too," Julie said, and Levon took a little bow, which made them both giggle.

"But I mean, you know, I think they've got like a Holland-

Dozier-Holland thing going on, or like Leiber and Stoller or whatever." Levon was actually a little jealous. He wasn't so jealous of the relationship—he liked Peter, but they hadn't been good enough friends for Levon to resent how much time Peter was spending with Sarah, and he found Sarah's insecurity more annoying than alluring—but he was jealous of their creative partnership.

They'd all been retreating to their practice rooms after dinner to write songs. Julie and Levon worked alone, and Peter and Sarah worked together. A couple of times Levon had poked his head into Peter and Sarah's room while he was on his way to the bathroom, and he was horribly jealous of what was happening in there. While Levon sat alone and wrestled with the muse or whoever wrote the songs he was trying to hear correctly, Peter and Sarah would be trading lines, adding to each other's melodies, swapping verses and choruses. It was fascinating to watch, but it wasn't too long before Levon would start feeling guilty about watching them. It was just amazing to see two people in this kind of creative zone, where they almost seemed to be sharing a brain. Levon had had that kind of experience playing music before—just knowing when Malachi was about to solo, feeling the change in the beat that Frankie was about to lay down before he did it—when you were connected to someone else through the music. But he'd never felt that in the actual songwriting. So it was cool. But to watch it—it felt like it was just something so intimate that outsiders shouldn't see it. It was funny—Peter and Sarah always kept the door closed while they were having sex, but they always had it slightly ajar when they were working. Levon felt like it probably should have been the other way around. After all, pretty much everybody has sex, but not many people have a creative connection like that.

After retiring to the practice rooms, everyone would emerge sometime after midnight and play each other their songs and add harmonies, figure out different parts, suggest changes, and then collapse near dawn and sleep for a couple of hours. Then Dingo would come in, and they'd do some recording, and everybody would sleep from lunch until dinner and do it all over again.

It was a weird way to live.

"Is this, like, day five?" he said to Julie.

"Um. I . . . let me think. I've walked Simone three times. I think. I mean, I can't really remember."

"It's weird. I hardly ever know if it's day or night anymore."

"Yeah," Julie said. "It's like how casinos don't have any windows so you'll never have any idea how much time has passed."

"I mean, the only reason I know it's daytime is because I see Dingo."

Julie laughed. "Some people have the sun, we have Dingo."

This led Levon to pick up a guitar and start playing and singing. "Dingo's the sun . . . Dingo's the sun, doot-n-doo doo . . ."

He broke up at that point, wondering if George Harrison knew he was singing about doo-doo, and then Julie broke up. When they calmed down, Julie said, "Let's write it. Let's write the whole song, and then we'll play it for him in the morning."

"Nah, let's go record it, and then we'll just tell him we want to hear the last thing we recorded yesterday, and then he'll hear it. It'll be far out."

"Great!" Julie said. It didn't take long at all to write the rest of it, and, with Levon on acoustic guitar and Julie on piano, they recorded "Dingo's the Sun."

"All right. That was a lot of fun. I've gotta get home before my dog completely destroys the apartment."

"Cool," Levon said. "Well, I'll see you tomorrow. Or whenever."

"In a few hours," Julie said, and then she was gone.

LEVON, SUDDENLY EXHAUSTED, lay down on the floor of the recording booth, promising himself he'd get up and go to his practice room to sleep in just a few minutes.

Dingo woke him up with a scream. "Jesus! Levon, you scared the shit out of me! What the hell—is this a comfortable place to sleep?"

Levon felt pain in his back and his neck. "Oh. Not at all. Not at all."

Dingo stretched a huge hand down and helped Levon to his feet.

Fifteen minutes later, Julie and Levon conned Dingo into playing back their tape. They stood behind him in the booth while "Dingo's the Sun" played back, and Levon was surprised to see Dingo actually wipe a tear from his eyes when the song was over.

AFTER ANOTHER RECORDING session, Levon lay down and tried to sleep. It occurred to him, though, that he really should call home. He'd been putting it off, but Mom would worry if she hadn't heard from him.

But he hated to lie. He couldn't say what he was really doing, and he certainly couldn't say, Yeah, the job hunt has come to a complete standstill because I've been sitting on my ass and getting high and writing songs. It was a funny kind of situation. He'd decided to tell his parents he was working as a waiter to make rent while he waited for an engineering job to come through. Which was a pretty innocuous lie, but how many people would have to tell their parents that they had a lower-paying job than the one they actually had? Strippers. Porn stars. And Levon Wilberforce Hayes.

He tried to sleep, but he realized he wasn't going to be able to rest until he made the call. Now, while everybody else was asleep, would be a great time to make the call from the phone in the booth.

He didn't think ATN would notice one extra long-distance call. He hated to call his parents collect. It just made him feel like a kid.

"Hello?" his mother said.

"Hey, Mom," Levon said.

"Oh my goodness! How are you? I was worried! You didn't leave us a number, and I don't even know if you're still at the YMCA . . ."

"I'm sorry, Mom. It's taken me a while to get myself together. But I've got a job—I'm working as a waiter at this new restaurant downtown, and I'm still sending out résumés, going on interviews, hoping something will break through."

"Oh thank the Lord. I was . . . well, you're going to laugh at me, but I thought you were using drugs."

"Me? Mom, you know me better than that." Levon felt a knife of ice slide between his ribs.

"Well, it was just that when we didn't hear from you for so long, I started to worry."

"Well, you don't have to worry. I'm doing fine, I'm not giving up, I've got a roof over my head, I'm making honest money, and I'm going to be fine."

Mom thanked the Lord again and then told him some scandal about cousin Elvin, and said she knew he'd be disappointed, but Dad wasn't home right now.

Levon said he had to go get ready for work, and Mom said she loved him, he said he loved her, and they hung up. Levon felt nauseous. He didn't have any idea why he thought that telling all kinds of lies to the one person on earth who loved him unconditionally (well, the one since Grandma passed) would actually help him get to sleep.

He went to the lounge, opened up the coffee can, and examined the contents. The reefer supply was growing dangerously low. At this rate, they might have to spend an entire day without getting high. That wouldn't do at all. Still, Levon needed a little something to help him sleep.

He rolled a joint and had just fired it up when he heard the toilet flush and the sound of someone approaching. He hoped it was Peter—maybe he could convince him to get high and sit for a while, and they could laugh about nothing and Levon could forget feeling like a piece of shit.

But it wasn't Peter. It was Julie. "Hey," she said sleepily.

"Hey. I thought you went home."

"Yeah. I should have, but I was just so worn out that the idea of going all the way upstairs to get a cab seemed unbearable. So I was going to take a nap in the practice room, but I'm . . . well, I'm just too used to sleeping in a real bed. I don't know how you guys sleep in there."

"Well, for me anyway, I just look at every pain in my neck and back as representing ten bucks I saved that night. You know?"

"I don't know, actually," she said.

Levon laughed aloud. "Yeah, me either. It's not the money, actually. I have money. It's just . . . ah, it's complicated and boring stuff having to do with my parents."

Julie was staring at the joint and gave no sign of having heard or appreciated what Levon felt at that moment was the great gift of his sincerity. "You gonna smoke that whole thing yourself, or you gonna share?" Julie said.

Levon smiled and passed the joint over, and Julie took a long inhale. "So," she said. "You seem to want to talk about your complicated family stuff, and you shared pot with me, so I owe you. Let it rip."

Levon looked at Julie, not sure if she was putting him on or not. Well, if she was putting him on, the best counter to that was honesty. "I just talked to my mom, and she . . . I . . . well, they wouldn't approve of this. Not at all. I have an engineering degree. So I had to tell her all kinds of lies about where I'm working and where I'm living and all the drugs I'm not doing."

Julie took another long hit from the joint. "Mmm," she said. "Parents you have to lie to? I know all about that. I mean, I don't actually lie to my mom, but she disapproves of me working at all. To the point where she just won't recognize that I actually do any work. I can't tell if this is for real or if this is a technique she uses on me, but she acts like my work is just a particularly wrongheaded husband search. Like I failed to find a husband at college like Meredith . . ."

"Meredith?" Levon tried not to laugh, but it was impossible.

Julie smiled. "My sister. She actually goes by Muffy. She has cocktails with my mom at the club every day at four."

Levon kept snorting and laughing. Muffy. Cocktails. It was just too much. At that moment it was the funniest thing he'd ever heard.

"Yeah, we're hilarious. Anyway, so she either thinks or pretends to think that the only reason I'm at work is to find a husband, so that's all she ever asks about."

"I think my dad will be satisfied when they make me the First Black Emperor of the World. Anything else is going to be a disappointment."

"I'm pretty well resigned to being a disappointment," Julie said, glancing at her watch. "Speaking of which, my dog is going to express her disappointment by destroying my couch if I don't get home. I'll see you later."

"You will," Levon said. "I'll probably be right here."

Julie left. Levon put out the joint and stretched out on the couch and let a cloud of smoke carry him off to sleep.

Some time later, he was awakened by what had become an unfamiliar sound—Pamela's voice. He pulled his eyelids open and saw Pamela there talking to Dingo. The fact that there was a conversation going on would explain why the dogs in his dream had been talking. Maybe.

"Hey," Levon said, sitting up.

"Levon!" Pamela said, walking over to him and giving him a big hug. Levon felt his morning erection poking into Pamela's midsection. She must have also, because her eyes briefly flitted down to his crotch before she said, "I have some wonderful, exciting news to share! Where are the others?"

"I guess everybody's asleep. You want me to go get them?"

"Yes, yes, please," Pamela said.

Julie had apparently slept at home, because she looked freshly showered and she was at the piano working. Levon opened the door to Peter and Sarah's room and called in, "Time to wake up!" without looking to see what was happening. "Pamela's here!" A few minutes later, Peter and Sarah walked into the lounge hand in hand.

"I'm so happy to see you all!" Pamela said. "And I'm really sorry to have abandoned you for so long. But I have something I have to share with you. Everybody sit down!"

There was a weird musical-chairs moment as everybody went to find seats, and Pamela ended up on the couch between Peter and Levon.

"I was absent for the only excusable reason," Pamela said. "Some songs found me. I'd love to play them for you and hear what you think."

And with that, she'd gotten her guitar and began to play. And just as everybody else did, Pamela would say things like, "I'm not sure about this bridge here—anybody have any ideas?" or "Do you guys hear a harmony on this chorus?" or "Julie and Sarah—do you think you can give me some doot-doots on this one?"

Levon had never really liked Pamela's music all that much—a heresy he would never speak aloud down here, except possibly to Julie—but he had to admit that these were really good songs.

12

JULIE

WHEN LEVON CAME into her room and announced that Pamela had decided to grace them with her presence, Julie had felt a strange twisting sense of dread that was weirdly familiar.

As she walked into the lounge, she remembered: She'd been sixteen, and she and Muffy had come home drunk and broken the antique clock that sat on the table in the sitting room where nobody ever sat. Julie had been on her knees picking glass up off the floor and still trying to figure out how they could convince Elizabeth that she was the one who'd come home drunk and broken a cherished antique, when she'd heard Muffy's voice, sounding resigned and tired, saying, "Mom's home."

There hadn't even been time to panic. Like Muffy, she had been immediately resigned to her fate, and though she dreaded the punishment (grounded for months, no swimming or tennis at the club, and a screaming lecture featuring words Julie wouldn't have guessed her mother even knew), she just had no time to worry. Well, that's it, she'd thought, the jig is up.

This was exactly how she felt now, walking into the lounge.

She'd had the best week of her life, professionally speaking, and she had really enjoyed feeling like the other songwriters down here were colleagues rather than competitors.

And now Pamela was here. Julie didn't think much of Pamela's songwriting skills, and she found her constant prattling about energy to be just annoying. She watched as Pamela maneuvered herself between Peter and Levon on the couch, and then used all the willpower she had available not to roll her eyes when Pamela said she'd been absent for the only excusable reason and then hadn't proclaimed a death in the family or serious illness.

But now, as Pamela was playing her songs, Julie felt herself softening. They were, for the most part, really tender songs of love and loss, and Julie especially liked it when Pamela turned to her and said, "Julie, I hear this song really crying out for a piano part. Do you think you could come up with something to fill in the spaces in the verses?"

When she was done, Pamela said, "Well, you've been kind enough to listen to my new songs. I'd love to hear what you've been working on." They all looked guiltily around at one another. They could all play all the songs, but if they all played together, then Pamela might know that they were recording, which she felt was bad for the energy. Julie thought the whole thing was ridiculous—it was stupid not to record the songs when they were ready, and Dingo was doing the right thing. Still, it wasn't clear who reported to whom here—was Pamela Dingo's boss? Was Pamela Julie's boss? Nobody knew, and Julie felt pretty sure that everybody else agreed with her that they didn't want to get Dingo in trouble.

So they all went into the studio, because they could fit in there and there was a piano there, and everybody played their songs, and it was all Julie could do not to do the "doot-doots" on "Funky Franklin Had the Key" or play her piano fills on "Emancipation Proclamation." She enjoyed hearing all the songs again, but it felt weird and unnatural to conceal her contributions to all these songs.

Pamela had her eyes closed and smiled and bobbed her head throughout the performances. When the last song was played, everyone looked to Pamela somewhat nervously. Julie knew she was twice the professional Pamela was, and yet she was nervous awaiting Pamela's verdict. Why? Maybe because they'd all had an incredibly productive week, and if Pamela was displeased by what they'd done, it would be demoralizing to everybody. And maybe, she thought, this was why Dingo had them record every-thing. After all, he knew Pamela better than anyone. Maybe he wanted to make sure they had a finished product so they wouldn't be too crushed when Pamela dismissed their work.

The seconds stretched out, each one feeling like a minute. Julie looked to Dingo, hoping to read something on his face. He shrugged. Finally, Pamela reached down to the floor into her macramé bag and pulled out a baggie of pot and some rolling pa-pers. Julie was relieved—if Pamela hadn't come to resupply them, they might have had to send somebody out to score today.

Still not speaking, Pamela rolled a joint, lit it with a paper match, inhaled deeply, and passed it to Peter. "Aaah. That's bet-ter. I thought this would help clarify my thought process."

Pot had never had anything but the opposite effect on Julie, but then she didn't smoke as much as Pamela. Well, she hadn't smoked as much as Pamela before this week. She had started noticing herself feeling agitated if it had been a whole day since she'd smoked.

"So," Pamela said, "I am just thrilled with what you all have done in my absence." Julie could see everyone else's shoulders slump slightly as they relaxed, and she realized that hers were doing the same thing. "You have all made a fantastic beginning on our journey together. I hardly know where to begin in prais-ing the work you've done. I just heard so many wonderful things—so many memorable melodies, so many clever turns of phrase—that I just know when you really get going, your art is going to be completely transcendent."

When we really get going? Lady, we've been going for ages! Where have you been?

"What I'd like is to get together with each one of you individually and really talk about your passion, really find out exactly what drew you to history, or math, or science, or English, to really get to the heart of your passion. What you've done so far is a fantastic first step, but in order to really speak to the children, we've got to find the child in each of you. We've got to explore what really turns you on about your subject area, we've got to get right to the heart of your passion, so that you can instill that same passion in the children who are going to be hearing your music on Saturday morning. We've really got an opportunity to do something really, really real. Parents will park their children in front of the set expecting them to be indoctrinated into little cereal customers, little consumers, little cannon fodder, little My Lai soldiers, and what they'll be indoctrinated with instead is a passion for beauty.

"It's my belief that what draws all of us to our passions is beauty. The beauty of a balanced equation, the beauty of a Shakespearean sonnet, the beauty of Newton's laws, the beauty of humanity as its history unfolds. If we can make children think about beauty instead of all the ugliness that surrounds them every day . . . I'm not talking just about the ghetto here. I sat down last Saturday and watched what the children are exposed to. Horrible, jerky, cheap animation, almost criminal stupidity . . . Everything on television aimed at children shows our contempt for them. We know they will accept ugliness, so we don't bother to give them beauty. Look at how much schools resemble prisons . . ."

Pamela droned on and on and Julie discreetly checked her

watch. It seemed like the pot was making Pamela chatty today. And yet, for the first time, Julie actually understood and kind of agreed with what Pamela was saying. Maybe they had an opportunity to make sure a kid knew more than parts of speech or times tables. Maybe they could make her see the world differently, to demand justice, because beauty means justice too.

Finally, Pamela wound up. "The other thing I would really like your help with is putting together some demos of the songs I've been writing. Hearing what you've done, I know your input would help me, and I hope that recording with me could serve as a kind of apprenticeship for you."

Julie looked at Pamela intently. Was Pamela cynically using them for their free labor, or did she really believe what she was saying? It was a mystery, and the pot was dulling her social radar so much that she couldn't solve it.

"But for now, we've all worked very hard for several hours—how about if I take you out for some food?" Everybody voiced their agreement, and half an hour later they were downtown in some dark vegetarian restaurant with a remarkably inefficient staff of true believers. They sat around a blond wood table and tried gamely to pretend that the tasteless, brown-rice-based dishes that were set in front of them were appetizing.

Julie found herself calling on her old push-food-around-the-plate-so-as-to-appear-to-have-eaten strategy she used to employ at home whenever something horrible was served for dinner. Now if she ate the garnish and moved some of the grains over to that side of the plate, it would look like she'd eaten more.

Julie turned to Sarah, hoping to share a joke about how awful the food was, and was surprised to see Sarah pick up a forkful, put it in her mouth, and chew deliberately with her eyes closed. So rather than saying How's the cardboard?—which is what she wanted to say—Julie opened with the more neutral, "What do you think of the food?"

"Well," Sarah said, "I think I'm not used to the taste yet. Pamela was telling me all about it on the way here. I think that my system is basically in shock. My taste buds have been so over-stimulated by everything I've been eating that they're just out of sync with my food. She said I should think about doing an herbal cleanse of my system. It would be great for my health."

"Are you feeling unhealthy?" Julie asked.

"Well, you know, I've been feeling tired lately," Sarah said.

"Do you think that has anything to do with staying up late and having sex all the time and barely sleeping?"

"Hey, it's not all the time," Sarah said, smiling. She looked over at Peter, who was laughing at something Pamela was saying.

"It's pretty frequent," Julie said.

"Yeah, it is," Sarah said, getting this dreamy, faraway look in her eyes.

After dinner, or whatever you called a meal that was eaten at three thirty in the afternoon, Pamela said, "Well, I'm going to take my leave. I will rejoin you early in the morning, and we'll begin the next stage of our journey."

They all thanked her for lunch, and Julie got in a cab and re-turned to her apartment. Simone jumped up and contorted her-self into a joyful circle when Julie got home, and Julie felt guilty about how much she'd neglected her. At first she'd slept at home every night, and then she'd made sure to come home twice in every twenty-four-hour period to walk and feed Simone, and then it was once. Simone was spending a lot of time alone. Which would explain the stuffing all over the living room and the chair that had been clawed and chewed into a complete mess.

"Oh, I'm sorry, baby, I've been a bad mom," Julie said. The apple doesn't fall far from the tree, she thought. Simone forgave her instantly, and after an hour-long walk in the park, they stopped by the butcher shop and Julie bought Simone a steak, which she devoured in seconds.

Julie brewed herself a cup of tea, grabbed off the shelf the copy of *The French Lieutenant's Woman* she'd been meaning to read for two years, and sat on the couch, her favorite reading chair having been transformed into a large and very expensive chew toy.

Simone lay contentedly at her feet, and Julie opened the book and started to read. She kept looking over the same page over and over again, unable to process what the words were saying. She was here alone with her dog, but back at ATN things were happening. She'd valued her solitude for as long as she could remember, and she still did love having a place to retreat to that was just hers. But back at ATN things were happening. There could be some tremendous creative breakthrough happening there, and if she was sitting here by herself sipping tea and reading an unsatisfying book, she'd miss it.

Well, Simone needed her. She'd stay here. She tried to read again and found her mind wandering. She remembered all the days at McMahon & Tate when she'd just dreamed of retreating to the sanctuary she'd paid for with commercial jingles, when just sitting here with Simone was all she wanted to do.

"Ugh, I'm sorry, sweetie, I've gotta go," she told Simone. She pulled a pig ear out of the pantry and tossed it to Simone and all but ran from the apartment so she wouldn't have to look at Simone's sad, droopy face and feel guilty.

When she arrived at ATN, Julie found Sarah, Peter, and Levon in the studio. They all greeted her enthusiastically.

"We're just working on a new song of mine," Sarah said. "I was just thinking about what Pamela said about what inspires us, you know? So I just always thought . . ." She trailed off and blushed.

"Thought what?" Julie asked.

"Sarah's got a crush on eleven," Peter said, and Levon laughed.

"Shut up," Sarah said, smiling. "It's not really a crush . . . it's just that I think eleven is really cool and I want to be friends!"

She and Levon and Peter laughed hysterically, leaving Julie standing there wondering what the hell was so funny.

"It's just . . . I'm sorry, Julie, we're a little giddy . . ."

"Pamela left us some good smoke to stoke the creativity," Levon added. "You want some?"

"Yeah," Julie said, "sure."

Levon dug under his seat and pulled out a makeshift bong made from what looked like parts from the back of a toilet.

"Do I even want to know about the origins of this thing?"

Levon giggled. "You do not. But let's just say Captain Sunshine may find it difficult to flush."

"You guys raided Captain Sunshine's bathroom to make a pipe?"

"It was Peter's idea!" Sarah said, pointing.

"No, it was my idea to cannibalize the toilets from the Misty Lee variety hour. But *somebody* was jealous of Misty Lee."

Julie took a deep drag off the toilet bong, exhaled, and said, "Misty Lee's a whore."

There was a moment's pause before the room erupted. "How do you know that?" Peter asked.

"See what I mean?" Sarah said, punching Peter in the arm. "He's just a little too interested."

"We . . ." Julie inhaled deeply again. "Mmm. I think this is even better than the stuff she gave us last year. Week. I mean week. Month. Whatever." She joined in the general laughter and completely forgot her train of thought until Peter demanded to know why Misty Lee was a whore. "Misty Lee sang on a couple of commercials I did, and she basically threw herself at any penis in sight. Especially if it was connected to a man who could help her career. Wouldn't be surprised if she climbed on top of Clark Payson to get that variety show."

Sarah had this cringing awkward face on. Peter and Levon just stared at her.

"You wrote commercials?" Peter said.

Oh boy. Well, given the amount she'd been smoking, she supposed she should be glad it had taken her a week to spill her deep dark secret. At least Simone would be happy: She'd be spending more time at home once she was ousted from the commune here.

"That is so far out!" Levon said, grinning. "What did you write? Anything we know?"

"Julie, you have to play us some. Come on, what did you write?" Sarah said with a big smile on her face.

Perhaps, Julie thought, she'd underestimated her friends. "I wrote a bunch of stuff. I don't know if you saw any of them or not."

"Play some!" Sarah said.

"All right, all right," Julie said, and sat down at the piano. She cleared her throat and began to sing.

> *Creamy nougat and caramel too*
> *Choco-logs are here for you*
> *Nuts and rich milk chocolate*
> *Choco-logs are what you've gotta get*
> *So when a snack attack hits you*
> *Choco-logs are the bars for you!*

"Oh yeah," Sarah said. "I think I remember those."

"Yeah, they came out a couple years ago, right?" Levon said. "Do they still sell them?"

"No," Julie said, "because *Choco-logs look just like poo!*" Everybody broke up at this.

"More!" Levon said. "More!"

"Okay, okay," Julie said. She played the ATN song, and everybody sang along. When she played the Burger Barn theme "Mom's Treat Tonight," everyone played and sang.

After Julie had finished her greatest hits, Levon reached

under his chair and pulled out a bottle. "This is why I suggested raiding Captain Sunshine's dressing room. He had some good liquor in that toilet tank. Fifteen-year-old scotch."

Well, scotch was Daddy's drink, and so Julie usually turned it down, but when the bottle came around she took a small swig, coughing as the liquid burned her throat.

"Ack. Never understood the appeal of this stuff," Julie said. "So, Sarah, you want to explain how you're in love with a number?"

Sarah rolled her eyes. "I just always thought it was cool that the multiples of eleven were all these double numbers, you know, twenty-two, thirty-three, whatever. I always really liked it when one of those came up on a quiz. So I wrote a song about it."

"Play it!" Julie said.

Sarah did, and Peter and Levon were already playing along, and it wasn't hard for Julie to follow on the piano.

An hour or so later, they felt like the song was complete. Maybe they'd be able to record it tomorrow. If Pamela allowed it.

At midnight, they all retired to the lounge and grabbed some snacks, and it wasn't long before Peter and Sarah pronounced themselves "tired" and went down the hall, leaving Julie sitting there with Levon.

The silence was awkward. Julie got up. "Well," she said, "I guess I'll go out and grab a cab home."

"Yeah," Levon said, standing and stretching. "Suppose I should get some sleep myself."

A moment passed, and they could hear Sarah moaning. They looked at each other and laughed. "Thought those rooms were supposed to be soundproof," Levon said.

"They are," Julie said. Sarah's moans increased in volume and frequency, and now they could hear a low grunting that could only be Peter. "I guess they were so eager to get to it that they forgot to shut the door."

More moaning. More grunting. Julie's skin was suddenly electric. Julie couldn't see why Pamela was always complaining about the energy down here, because right now it was practically crackling in the air.

"Yeah," Levon said. "I guess so." They looked at each other for a moment, and then they were kissing hard and fast and hungry, and Julie was electrified from head to toe.

13

SARAH

SARAH WOKE UP at eight. Peter was still asleep, and when she went to the lounge, she saw Levon asleep on the couch. Remembering what Pamela said about cleansing her system, Sarah decided she was done with coffee. She poured herself a big glass of water from the tap, hoping the noise of the glass filling wouldn't wake Levon. It didn't.

Sarah padded back down the hall. Leaving the door open a crack so she could see, she rooted around looking for clean clothes. She really needed to go to the Laundromat today. She found only her emergency backup underwear, the pair that was probably one washing away from needing to be thrown out. She grabbed them and the shirt and jeans she'd worn yesterday and headed to the shower.

When she was dry and dressed, she heard a timid knock at the door.

"Just a minute!" she said.

"Sarah?" She heard Julie's voice.

"Yeah?"

"Are you decent enough for me to come in?" Was she decent? Probably not. Last night had been particularly indecent.

"Come on in," Sarah said. Julie looked uncharacteristically haggard. "Whoa! Are you okay?"

"Yeah, yeah, I'm okay, I'm just kind of sort of freaked out."

"Why? Smoke too much?"

"No, not pot freaked out, like really freaked out. Levon and I . . . well, last night after you guys went to bed . . ."

Sarah smiled. "Far out!" she said. "That's great! How was it?"

"Ah, it was really nice, but it wasn't . . . I didn't mean to . . . it's your fault, you know, you guys were so loud."

"Nice try, Jules. The rooms are soundproof."

"Yeah, only if you shut the door, genius."

Sarah thought back to last night, realized that they'd been echoing through the basement. Oh well. Apparently it had done some good if it had helped Julie loosen up a little. "Sorry," she said, insincerely. "Jules, I'm sorry, I'm not trying to be insensitive here, but what's the problem? Is it because he's . . . you know . . ."

"No, no, that's not it. That just makes it even more complicated. It's just that I don't know what it means. I don't really understand everything now, and I . . . I mean, I don't think I really want a relationship right now, but I'm afraid if I tell him that I'll just look like some kind of sexual tourist, you know, and it wasn't . . . it wasn't like that at all, I mean, it wasn't because . . . I mean, he's good looking, and I like him, and . . . why the hell did you have to be so loud?"

Sarah laughed. "You know, I wonder that myself. I was never that vocal with anybody else. Anyway, I got you laid. You ought to be thanking me."

Julie cracked a smile. "Yeah, okay. Thank you. It had been a while. Way too long, actually. But now I don't know . . . I was just getting comfortable, and I was really happy with how things were here, and I feel like everything has changed now."

"Nothing's changed. Unless you want it to."

"That's the problem! I don't know what I want! I have no freaking idea!" Sarah pondered Julie. She was normally so poised and put-together and composed, and here she was completely going to pieces, completely not herself.

Sarah didn't feel at all like the person she'd been when she walked into ATN, but this was only a good thing as far as she was concerned. Pamela and Peter and Julie and Levon and Dingo had given her a self-assurance she'd never had before. And she realized that if she had gone into a classroom this year, the students would have eaten her timid former self alive. Even now, if she never had a music career after this year, Sarah knew she could walk into a classroom and act like she was someone who deserved to be listened to.

"Well, let's make some music, and maybe you'll figure it out. Did you have breakfast?"

"Yeah, I grabbed coffee and an egg sandwich on the street."

Poor Julie. It was no wonder she was such a disaster. She was pouring toxins into her body all the time. That can't help but affect how you feel. "Well, I'm going to go raid that fruit basket that Pamela brought by," Sarah said.

Julie looked strangely timid. "Uh, have you seen Levon?"

"Yeah. He's asleep on the couch."

"Okay, then, I'm going to just, uh, I'll meet you in the studio," Julie said, turning tail toward the studio.

Sarah grabbed her arm. "Hey, now. Is that how you were raised? What about all that stuff you told me about your mom's WASPy cool? What would Elizabeth do in this situation?"

Julie laughed. "If Elizabeth slept with a black guy? Probably douche with bleach before quietly hanging herself. It's one of the most considerate methods of suicide, you know, because it doesn't leave an unsightly mess. I expect she'd choose the pantry or somewhere where she could ensure she'd be found by the help."

Sarah looked at her, slack-jawed. "Whoa. Whereas my mom would run screaming to my father, 'See? See what happens when nobody pays attention to me? I go and sleep with a *schwartze*!'"

They giggled, and then Julie straightened up. "Okay. Elizabeth broke an engagement to Andrew Throckmorton in order to marry my father, and still runs into him at the club. This is what she looks like when she sees him." Sarah watched in awe as Julie contorted her face into an expression that communicated aloofness, superiority, and utter lack of interest all at the same time.

"Wow! How do you do that?"

"It's in the genes. But that's probably over the top. Oh, Jesus, let's just go." Julie softened her face and strode confidently into the lounge. Well, Sarah thought, she sure didn't need any help feeling confident. Is that what being born into money does for you?

Sarah decided she'd ditch Julie in the lounge and let her work it out with Levon on her own. She'd have to get her fruit later. She went back to her room, and Peter raised a sleepy head when she walked in.

"Hey, beautiful," he said. Love, or maybe sex, or some combination thereof, had made Peter blind, but Sarah was happy for it. She gave him a slow kiss, then looked back to see if the door was closed. It wasn't, so she got up and closed it.

"Guess what?" she said to Peter.

"I don't know. What?" Sarah told him about the door and Julie and Levon, and Peter laughed. "Good for them!" he said.

Just talking about it made Sarah want to do it again right now. And after all, she wasn't sure that Julie and Levon weren't going at it again too. Then again, it was daytime, and if that was the case, you never knew when Dingo might wander in.

When she and Peter came to the lounge, Julie and Levon were sitting on the couch together, looking relaxed but not holding hands or touching in any way. Sarah shot Julie a quizzical look, and Julie gave her a look that Sarah felt she was nowhere near WASPy enough to decipher.

Sarah got her fruit and drank another glass of water. She couldn't wait for Pamela to get here. She was really excited about working on Pamela's songs, and she wanted to play her eleven song for Pamela. It was nice that Peter and Julie and Levon liked it, and they'd certainly had fun playing it, but she wanted to know if Pamela thought she was really getting at the heart of what made her like math.

Pamela had really inspired her. Not just with her amazing songs, though those were also inspirational and made Sarah want to write a song even half that good, but also with what she'd said about changing the world. Wasn't that why Sarah had wanted to be a teacher in the first place? You can stage all the sit-ins and teach-ins and protests you want, but there's nothing as revolutionary as spending time with a bunch of little kids. Maybe they really did have the power to make the world a better place with their music. Maybe these little songs, repeated over and over and over, would help make kids into better adults.

It felt like an awesome responsibility, and as much as she loved all the time with Peter and Levon and Julie, she felt like they needed a grown-up to guide them through it. Certainly Dingo was a grown-up, and he was really helpful with all the sonic parts—getting the right harmony, miking up the instruments correctly, suggesting a change in the bass line—but Pamela was the visionary.

Fortunately, Pamela, guitar in hand, arrived even before Dingo.

"Good morning, everyone!" she said, sitting down. All conversation immediately stopped as everyone focused on her.

"So I thought we would begin today with recording a demo of 'Long Distance.' Do you guys remember that one?" She began to sing, "I hang up the phone and cry / watch the rain and wonder why / he's a long distance from me / and I'm a long distance from who I want to be."

"Yeah!" Sarah said, then looked around, embarrassed. Everybody else had just nodded coolly. But how could she possibly be cool? She was too excited. She used to listen to "Shadows in the Twilight" in her dorm room and wonder how Pamela Sanchez had seen into her heart, dreaming that she could one day write a song that would touch someone like that song had touched her, and now here she was, about to harmonize on the chorus of Pamela Sanchez's new song! Sure, it was just a demo, and she probably would never be on the final version, but she was singing with Pamela Sanchez. Maybe she could get Dingo to make her a copy just so she could prove to her kids that she had once sung with Pamela Sanchez. It was a big deal, and if she acted like a kid going to Disneyland, well, that's just because that was the way she felt.

And the feeling continued after Dingo arrived, and they did ten takes of "Long Distance" until Pamela was satisfied with everything. Even after ten takes, Sarah wasn't sick of it—it was simply a brilliant song. If there were any justice in the world, it would bring Pamela back to the top of the pop charts.

The only problem was, after playing Pamela's song ten times, Sarah felt far less confident in her own work. The idea of playing her eleven song for Pamela now just seemed humiliating. Pamela was drawing beauty from the universe, weaving these beautiful, complex webs of words and music that caught people's souls, and Sarah was writing songs that were nothing but playground chants at best.

"All right, everyone, thank you so much. That sounded just perfect," Pamela said.

Sarah heard Dingo whisper "Just like the last four takes" to Levon, who smiled. Sarah immediately felt protective of Pamela. Dingo was a craftsman, and a really good one, but Pamela was an artist, and she needed to be satisfied with her art.

"Sarah," Pamela said. "I've brought some brown rice and steamed vegetables. Maybe you'd like to have lunch with me, and then we can take a walk in the park and talk about your passion."

"I'd love that," Sarah said. She was relieved, because she wasn't really sure about what to eat and what not to eat to cleanse her system, and her confidence in her own ability was so shaken by her encounter with Pamela's genius that she didn't know if she could go back to writing this afternoon anyway.

PAMELA GRABBED SOME circular metal containers and motioned for Sarah to follow her to the elevator. "You can't keep your food in plastic," Pamela said. "You have no idea what kinds of toxins are leaching in from all the petrochemicals they use. Metal's not ideal either, of course, because it tends to alter the energy balance of the food, but what can you do? "

Sarah laughed like she had some idea what Pamela was talking about. She was humbled by all the things she didn't know. They walked out of the ATN building and onto the bustling Midtown street. Sarah paused involuntarily, shook her head, and kept walking.

"What is it?" Pamela asked.

"I . . . oh, nothing. It's just kind of jarring to go from this dark, cozy place out into this bright, busy street with everybody hurrying."

Pamela smiled warmly. "You really are attuned to the flow of energy in the world, aren't you? It's one of the things I like about you—you're very sensitive."

Sarah never would have said she was particularly attuned to the flow of energy in the world. Good at math, okay. Good with kids, yes. Maybe that was what allowed her to work with children so well, though. Maybe she was attuned to the changes in energy that flowed through groups of children like tides, and maybe that's what made her like teaching. "Well, thanks," Sarah said.

The crowded sidewalks were not conducive to conversation, so they walked in silence to the park, eventually finding a bench. Pamela opened the containers of food between them, handed Sarah a pair of chopsticks, and began to eat.

Sarah picked up a broccoli floret, which she thought would be big enough to pick up easily. She held it before her for a moment and looked at all of the hundreds of tiny buds on the end of it. She looked at its color—light green on the stalk, dark, rich green on the floret. It was a beautiful thing. She popped it in her mouth, closed her eyes, chewed, and tried to think of nothing but broccoli. It had a remarkable, complex flavor, with hints of sweet and bitter, but, overall, it just tasted green. She was actually tasting the color!

She opened her eyes and saw Pamela staring at her. "It's remarkable what happens when you really allow yourself to experience your food, isn't it?" she asked.

"Yeah," Sarah said as she swallowed the last bite. "I mean, I've had broccoli cooked to death or smothered in a salty cheese sauce, but I've never really taken the time to just concentrate on how it tastes." She laughed. "I know this sounds weird, but it tastes green."

"That doesn't sound all that weird to me," Pamela said. Sarah made an awkward grab for a piece of red pepper that flopped off her chopsticks. "Do you need some help with those?" Pamela asked.

"Well, I only ever really use them on Christmas," Sarah said.

"Here," Pamela said, taking the chopsticks, "hold your hand like this." She grabbed Sarah's hand and positioned it into a kind of relaxed handshake. "Now"—she was still holding Sarah's right hand with her left—"you slide this one in here," she said, sliding one chopstick into the crook between Sarah's thumb and index finger and resting it on her middle finger. "And then you squeeze this one between your thumb and forefinger like this." Sarah did it. "Now you have much more control—a lot of people try to hold it like a pencil, but that won't work. Go ahead. Pick up a grain of brown rice."

Sarah reached down and tried to grab a grain of rice, but she couldn't get it. She was very disappointed, but Pamela just smiled. "Like sex, it gets better with practice," she said.

They ate in silence, and once the food was gone, Sarah asked about how she might cleanse her body of the various poisons that had built up inside her.

"Oh, you're doing the right things," Pamela said. "Fruits, vegetables, maybe the occasional fish. Lots and lots of water. You may feel tired and headachy for a few days as the toxins your body has been storing begin to come out of your tissues and leave your body. It's a difficult process. But what you're aiming at—well, you'll know you've reached success by your bowel movements."

Sarah involuntarily looked around the bench to see if anyone had overheard. A businessman took a quick glance at them and arched an eyebrow, but then he scurried away to wherever he was going. Sarah was embarrassed at first, but then thought how great it would be to believe in yourself that much, to be so confident that you could talk out loud about shit in Central Park and simply not care what anybody thought of you.

Pamela continued, not noticing or caring about the looks she received from passersby. "It should emerge easily, without straining.

You shouldn't be sitting on the toilet fighting to get it out. Now, I'm not talking about diarrhea, here, but I'm just talking about a smooth, easy transition from colon to toilet bowl. It should emerge as one long, unbroken rope, ideally of a light brown color and very mild odor. Our horror and revulsion at our own excrement comes from the fact that we are excreting horrible chemicals and toxins all the time, and this is what causes the awful smell. If you don't put anything awful into your body, nothing awful will come out. Shall we walk?" Pamela said, packing up the food containers.

"Um, sure, yeah," Sarah said.

"Oh, yeah, also it should float," Pamela said as they started down the path.

"Float," Sarah said, still unable to believe that she was getting a poop lecture from Pamela Sanchez in the middle of Central Park.

"Right. If it sinks to the bottom of the bowl, that indicates that it's heavy with fats and oils, and you need to adjust your diet accordingly. I guess it goes without saying that it should have a uniform appearance. If you're chewing correctly, you won't see any identifiable chunks."

Sarah was unable to suppress a gag, and for a moment, she was afraid she would puke all over Pamela's sandals, and Pamela would critique her chewing technique if she saw an identifiable chunk of broccoli.

"Oh, I'm sorry," Pamela said, turning to Sarah. "I'm so deep into this that I forget about the denial most people live in with regard to what their body does. Your vaginal discharge, for example."

A young woman pushing a baby carriage stared, openmouthed, at Pamela at this last sentence, and Sarah had had all she could take of bodily functions. She wanted to discuss vaginal discharge even less than she wanted to discuss excrement. She needed to change the subject at all costs.

"So I wrote a new song yesterday," Sarah said, hoping Pamela would jump from the excrement and discharge train onto the music train. Sarah breathed a sigh of relief when Pamela did.

"Wonderful. Tell me about it," Pamela said. As they walked through the trees, the dappled light struck Pamela's black hair, her face, her body, lighting up tiny parts of her in turn. She looked completely at home here among the trees with tiny spotlights on her all the time. Though they were roughly the same height, Sarah felt hideous and small next to her.

"Well, uh, I just . . . I was thinking about what you said about our passions, and I just remembered how I really liked eleven when I was a kid."

"Eleven?" Pamela asked. She looked at Sarah like she was the most interesting person on earth at that moment, and this made Sarah feel slightly less hideous.

"Yeah," Sarah said, "I mean, I always enjoyed how if you multiply eleven by three, you get thirty-three, you know, all the multiples up to nine are just doubling the number you multiply it by. It's very satisfying."

Pamela didn't respond for a moment, and Sarah suddenly got afraid that she had said something wrong. Finally, after what seemed like ten minutes, Pamela turned to her with a smile. "Well, I think that's a wonderful place to start. Multiples of eleven. I get it, I get how seeing those numbers double is a beautiful thing. But what else is beautiful? What is it that makes you like math more than you like the other things you'd have to teach as a grade school teacher?"

"Beautiful? I don't know, I mean, there are so many things that seem so cool. Fibonacci numbers."

Pamela stopped. "Enlighten me. I have no idea what you're talking about."

Pamela looked genuinely interested. "It's a sequence of numbers starting with zero and one where you get the next number by adding the previous two. So it goes zero, one, one, two, three, five . . . and like that. So, I mean, so what, right? That's just a math trick, who cares? But it turns out that you find these numbers everywhere in nature! Like pinecones—flowers, the branching of trees . . . you can find Fibonacci numbers in all kinds of places that . . . I don't know, I'm not doing a good job of explaining it."

"No no no, you're doing a wonderful job, because your passion is bubbling over."

"I just think it's cool that something that just seems like a pointless exercise should actually describe all this real stuff."

"Wonderful!" Pamela said. "What else is cool?"

And Sarah was off, suddenly bubbling over with enthusiasm as she remembered how a professor had told them that if humans had eight fingers, they'd probably have base-eight math. She talked about infinity, prime numbers, and everything she'd ever found mind blowing or satisfying in her study of math.

When Sarah finally came up for breath, she noticed Pamela beaming at her. "Uh, I'm sorry, I guess I kind of went on and on."

"No no no—it's wonderful! What I want you to do now is go right back to ATN and try to harness some of this passion. You've really—I can see your aura brighten as you discuss this stuff, and if you can channel some of your love, your excitement, into your work, you'll produce works of genius."

"Well, I don't know about . . ."

"Uh uh uh! Don't doubt yourself. You are by far the most talented songwriter we have on this project, and I don't even think I've heard the best you're capable of."

Sarah suddenly felt like she was walking on air. She couldn't stop smiling, and it was starting to hurt her cheeks.

"But I do need to . . . just a note of caution before you go back to the lair."

"Yeah?" Sarah felt a shadow cross her elation.

"I just . . . I notice that you and Peter have been spending a lot of time together."

"Well, yeah, sure."

"I just want to . . . I just want you to . . . when someone is as talented as you are, people who don't have your gift may try to get close to you in order to leech off you. I'm certainly not saying that's the case here, but as you go through life, it is something that a real artist like you needs to watch out for."

Sarah dismissed this. "Well, thank you, but Peter's very good too, you know."

Pamela gave her a smile. "Yes he is, dear. But he's not as good as you. I'll see you tomorrow!" Pamela turned and walked into the heart of the park, leaving Sarah alone.

She walked back to ATN slowly, not really attuned to her surroundings, lost in thoughts of Fibonacci numbers. There was definitely a song in there. Fibonacci's tree, something like that?

When she arrived back in the basement, she peeked in to see if anybody was in the studio. Dingo was in the control booth alone with headphones on; he looked up and gave her a friendly wave.

She wandered down to the rehearsal room that had become the little love nest she shared with Peter and found Peter sitting on a chair playing guitar. "Sumner got caned," he sang, "it damaged his brain . . ." He looked up at her. "Hey! So I was thinking about why I was a history major, and it was because of this thing we learned junior year in high school about how Charles Sumner was caned on the floor of the Senate by some pro-slavery thug of a senator, so I thought, what the hell, maybe there's a song there."

He was cute. Sarah kissed him. "How's it going?" she asked.

"Not so good. Well, you heard. I don't think I can use the caned / brain rhyme. It sounds too comical. I wanted it to be a song about a hero, not some Punch-and-Judy show thing."

"Mmmm." Sarah was only half paying attention; the Fibonacci song was trying to write itself in her brain.

"Hey, do you think you could help me out with this?" Peter asked. Sarah looked at him and wondered, just briefly, if Pamela had been right. No. He had helped her with plenty of songs.

"Um, yeah. Well, I've got a song in my brain I have to get down right now, so maybe when I'm done we can play for each other and help each other out."

Peter looked disappointed. "Oh. Okay. Sure." Then, as suddenly as it had fallen, his face animated again. "So, you're gonna play for me?" he said. "I get to watch you play?"

Sarah smiled. "Would you like to watch me play?"

"Yeah. I think I'd like that a lot."

"Okay, okay, don't make me horny, I have to get this song down before it goes away."

Peter smiled. "Okay."

Sarah grabbed her guitar and looked down the hall. "Anybody else here?"

"No. Julie and Levon went off to have a *talk,*" Peter said.

"Okay," Sarah said, not wanting to get into a conversation about that. She found an empty practice room that didn't reek of sex and cast all her doubts about Peter out of her mind by filling it only with thoughts of Fibonacci.

She had needed the bathroom since returning from lunch, but the demands of the muse had kept her out until it was too urgent to ignore.

She went to the bathroom, and, before flushing, she examined the contents of the bowl. It appeared she still had some work to do.

14.

LEVON

LEVON CHECKED HIS watch, looked at the door of Julie's building, and decided to circle the block again. He had put her off this morning by promising to have The Talk this afternoon, and by now she was supposed to be done tidying her apartment or walking her dog or whatever it was that she was doing.

And so it was time for The Talk. But Levon had no idea what to say. Why did they have to have The Talk at all? Well, maybe it was a good idea. If they had eleven more months of working closely together, they kind of had to figure out what last night meant. If anything.

Levon saw three options. Option one: Fuck it and forget it. Since he certainly was still attracted to her, and he figured she was still attracted to him, and there would probably be more occasions when they would be drunk and/or high and alone together, with or without Peter and Sarah's pornographic soundtrack, the idea that this was one-and-done seemed kind of unrealistic.

Okay. Option two: Occasional and casual. They could still fuck whenever the mood struck, but it wouldn't be a *relationship*. It would just be them working together and occasionally burning off some tension and energy together. This was probably the best option, but Levon wasn't too sure it would work. He knew himself enough to know that he'd start to get jealous, and that when, at the end of the year, she went off to Greenwich to marry some white guy with three names and a country-club membership, he'd feel used and sad. He couldn't say this, of course, because it sounded way too girlie, but he'd had enough of that treatment in college. He liked sex as much as the next guy, but being the guy who was okay for a tussle in the dorm room but had to hide on parents' weekend just made him feel ashamed of himself.

But then there was option three: Have an actual relationship. In some ways, this was the most appealing. He did like Julie, and whatever their differences, they had music in common. Music had always been the part of his life that was simple, the part of his life that worked, and Julie was the first woman he'd ever been able to share that with. It got to the point where Julie knew what piano parts he imagined in his songs, and he could lay down a bass line for Julie's songs before she even finished playing them through once.

Calvin had believed firmly that women belonged in the audience and backstage but not in the band. And now Levon understood why. Get them in the band, and then things get complicated. The one thing in his life that had been uncomplicated, where he hadn't had to think about being black, about Dad, about anything but being funky, where he could just relax—all of the problems from every other part of his life had suddenly come flooding into the music. If only he'd gone on tour with Calvin and the Supersonic Funketeers, he'd have a series of one-and-dones in a series of little towns and nothing at all to think about.

Because even in the unlikely event that Julie was willing to horrify her parents by getting serious with a black man, Levon knew that getting serious with Julie would pretty much make him an orphan.

Already there was the confrontation brewing with Dad when Levon revealed what he'd really been doing, and that he'd stopped looking for an engineering job, but he knew that at least Mom would be in his corner, that Mom would support him no matter what.

Well, no matter what with an asterisk. Mom had tried to pretend she didn't care who Levon dated throughout high school, but he could see the disapproval lurking behind the friendly "nice to meet you" she dished out whenever Levon brought a white girl home. Since she'd never made it explicit, Levon had never had to ask her why the hell she'd moved him to Ridgewood, New Jersey, if she'd wanted him to date black girls, since, as near as he could tell, there weren't any within three towns of him.

Levon was back at Julie's place, but he was no closer to figuring out who he was or what the hell he was doing. He felt like the person he wanted to be right now was a musician with a white girlfriend whose parents could love and be proud of him. But that person couldn't exist. So which part would he give up? The only solution was Julie. Okay then. One and done. Move on. We got carried away and that was that. One and done.

He pushed the button next to Julie's name, and the door buzzed to let him in.

He walked up the stairs and knocked timidly on the door on the second-floor landing that was slightly ajar. "Hello?" he said, peeking his head in the door.

He saw Julie coming toward him and, in front of her, a big, slobbering, barking dog charging in his direction.

"Whoa!" Levon yelled, pulling his head outside the door and closing it.

"Sorry," he heard Julie say from behind the door. "Simone! Easy! Simone! SIT!" The barking stopped, and the door opened. Julie was holding the big brown-and-white dog by its collar, and it immediately started barking at him again.

"Sorry, she's really friendly. This is just her way of saying hi. Can you just hold your hand out for her to sniff?"

"You want me to put my hand by his mouth?"

"Her mouth. No, but just her nose, yeah. Please."

Well, he was already working a whole lot harder than he wanted to for this. This could have been a five-minute conversation at ATN, but now it had to be a big event, with him coming to her place and facing her killer dog and probably not getting out of here for an hour. God, women were frustrating.

Tentatively, he held out his hand, closing his eyes because he couldn't bear to watch the dog's killer jaws close down on his hand and end his music career. In an instant, he felt the dog licking his hand, which was certainly better than biting it, but still pretty disgusting.

"There you go! She likes you!"

"Hey, that's great," Levon said. Julie released her grip on the dog, who looked at Julie and then trotted away and lay down under the kitchen table.

"I'm sorry," she said. "You know, single woman in New York. I felt like I needed a dog."

"Okay!" Levon said.

"So, uh, listen, do you want a cup of tea or anything?"

"No, no thanks, I'm good."

Julie paused briefly, as though she were considering making a joke about that remark, then said, "Okay. So, I, uh, I guess we need to talk."

"Yeah," Levon said, even though he really wanted to run out of the apartment and go pick up his bass and maybe get high with Peter and not ever have this conversation.

"So, listen, Levon, I really like you and I really like working with you . . ." Levon could hear the approaching *but* from the beginning of the sentence, and he wanted very badly to just cut to the end of this and say, *Okay, one and done, my thoughts exactly, thanks, see you back at the office.* But no, she was still talking, about how she'd never dated a co-worker before, and she wasn't really sure if it was a good idea given their rather unusual work situation, blah blah. She wasn't saying anything about him being black, but Levon somehow knew that if she'd ended up sleeping with Peter, this conversation would not be going this way.

See, Levon thought, this is why I wanted to cut to the end. Because he didn't really care about her reasons, but, more than that, he couldn't stand for her to be thinking that he was a poor Negro here on his knees hoping she would deign to accept him, which was obviously the way she was looking at it. *See, you being who you are isn't a problem for me even though it should be! Ain't I liberal?* The hell with it.

"Yeah, I agree, I mean, it definitely complicates an area of my life that has always been simple. You know what I mean? Music has always been the place I go to get *away* from my problems."

"Oh." Julie clearly didn't like being characterized as a problem. Good. "Well. Okay then. I guess . . . I mean, I just hope we can keep working together without it being—I mean, you're a great musician and a great songwriter and I really like working with you. And I feel like . . . my songs are better when you play on them, and my playing is better when you're writing the songs, and I would feel terrible if it got ruined because I couldn't control myself."

Levon felt his annoyance melt away.

"Well, I wasn't actually in control either. And I feel the same way about your—you are incredibly talented, and it's a lot of fun to work with you."

She smiled. "Thank you. Well, okay. I guess as long as Peter and Sarah can remember to shut the door, we'll be fine."

"Yeah," Levon said, smiling. "They sure were loud."

"Yeah," Julie said, a faraway look in her eyes. Then she turned her eyes to him. "So were we."

Levon looked at her, and, as his conscience screamed *No! Don't do it! No!*, pulled the emergency brake lever until it broke off in its hand, and finally slumped down in disgust as it was ignored, he grabbed Julie, and kissed her.

TWO HOURS LATER, he was back at ATN. Dingo was gone, and Peter and Sarah were working on songs together. He popped in and sat, listening to Peter's song about somebody getting beaten. He didn't really understand why that was an important event that a third-grade cartoon watcher would need to know. Then he listened to Sarah's song about how we'd all be doing base-eight math if we had four fingers on each hand, which was comprehensible to Levon, who understood the mathematical principles very clearly, but not exactly riveting grade school material. He couldn't imagine what a third-grader would make of that.

Still, he smiled and told them both that their songs were good, which wasn't exactly a lie, since they were both catchy, even if the lyrics were not exactly there.

Finally, Levon was too jealous of Peter and Sarah to stay in the room. They had found each other, and their relationship seemed easy and uncomplicated. They were getting a little out there in terms of their lyrics, but they believed completely in what they were doing and took very seriously Pamela's instruction to think about their passions. Sarah even seemed to be taking Pamela's dietary nonsense seriously.

"You know, Pamela told me some interesting things about bowel movements today," she said, and Levon looked intently at her to see if she was messing with him. She wasn't. His eyes flashed to Peter, who was biting his lip trying not to laugh and who gave Levon a quick shake of the head to indicate that no, this wasn't a joke, and he shouldn't laugh about poop right now.

"You know what, I think I feel a song coming on, so I'm gonna have to ask you to hold that"—his choice of words made him snort, and he was afraid he'd crack up—"thought."

He ran from the room and into his own, closing the door to soundproof his laughter. Once he was done laughing, though, he started to feel sad. He envied Sarah's certainty. She was sure of everything, and Levon was sure of nothing.

He didn't want to sit in here thinking—in fact, he didn't want to think at all. Fortunately, he had been made custodian of the toilet bong and Captain Sunshine's fine scotch. He filled and fired up the toilet bong and thought about what kind of obscure thing he could write a song about. A few bong hits, and it came to him.

"Position and momentum, you can't measure both / even with a perfect microscope," he began to sing. He cracked himself up, so he kept at it until he'd actually completed a song about the obscure, incomprehensible-to-third-graders subject that suited his mood best. He called it "Heisenberg's Uncertainty Principle."

15

DINGO

INGO WAS PISSED. He sat in the tunnel, not moving, trying not to think about the tons of water on top of him, and spoke to the imaginary Cass riding in the passenger seat.

"I mean, Christ, what do I have to do? You're pissed 'cause we don't have a yard, I get you a yard. You're pissed that I'm never home, now I'm home and you're pissed anyway! What the hell do I have to do?"

He felt helpless, and not just because he was trapped under the river unable to move, entrusting his life to engineers and construction workers from decades ago. Why the hell was Cass so mad at him all the time?

"Move! Goddammit!" Dingo yelled, pounding on the steering wheel. It wasn't like anybody was going to care if he got to work on time. Actually, he had no idea what on time was. He just hated sitting in traffic.

And he was starting to hate his job. The reason he'd been a musician his whole adult life was that he didn't want to have to go do some pain-in-the-ass nine-to-five straight job.

He hated touring, hated being away from the kids, and

thought he hated the monotony of hotel rooms, but he had no idea what monotony was until he had to go to the exact same place every single day. It was like touring without the excitement.

Well, that wasn't true. The first week had been really exciting— coming in every day and not knowing what kind of cool songs the kids would have come up with, working on arrangements, getting to know the old equipment in the studio. Some of it was horrible crap, but some of the stuff had a richness to the sound that he didn't think you could duplicate on modern equipment.

He had even bought into the idea that they were doing something important, especially after sitting with Davey one Saturday morning and feeling like he needed a shower as half hour after half hour of shitty programming washed over them.

But then Pamela came back, and the vibe changed, as it always did when she entered a situation. She'd returned on a Monday, and it was now Friday. Today they'd record another song or two for Pamela's new album, and then Pamela and the kids would get high and sit around and write increasingly weird songs that were completely unsuited to the project, and Dingo would sit around twiddling his thumbs.

Well, no, he'd go over the stuff they'd recorded, he'd take a long lunch by himself, and then he'd work on an arrangement for one of Pamela's songs and maybe one of the songs by the kids that would never be recorded.

He was a competent drummer and, if he did say so, a hell of a producer, and here he was spinning his wheels. Nobody cared who played drums on a cartoon, and Pamela would probably find a way to steal the producing credit from him on whatever they recorded.

Which might not matter so much if things were better at home. Maybe he and Cass just needed to adjust to being together all the time. They'd never really had to get adjusted to each other's annoying habits the way most couples had. Or maybe, Dingo thought as the traffic finally broke free and he sped into Manhattan, it was just that he was extra cranky and resentful because he spent two hours a day in the car by himself and was stuck in a dark basement all day so he could keep Cass in the house she wanted and Davey in the school district they wanted.

Maybe he was a little impatient these days, but that didn't excuse what happened last night. Davey was being a real snot and refusing to get in the bathtub, and after sitting there for ten minutes listening to Cass talk to Davey about his *feelings* and still not getting him into the tub, Dingo had had enough. He stomped into Davey's room, grabbed him by the shoulders, and boomed, "Your mother told you to get undressed ten minutes ago! Get your butt into that tub *now*!"

Davey had simpered and cried, but he'd gotten undressed and gotten his butt into the tub. He thought Cass would thank him for getting the job done. Instead she'd said, "You didn't have to *yell*. You really upset him."

"Well, I guess I did have to yell, because not yelling wasn't getting him into the bath!" he'd said.

"I have been giving him baths for years without your help," she'd said, and she didn't have to say any more, because he could read the whole thing clearly on her face. You haven't been here, you don't know what you're doing, just let me handle this, will you, just bring the money home and shut up.

Well, maybe she wasn't thinking that, but that was how he felt. Which made him even grumpier. Which made Cass grumpier. Which meant no sex, which made Dingo grumpier still.

He showed his parking pass in the ATN garage like he was some kind of secretary, took the elevator up to the lobby and then down to the basement.

Pamela was standing outside the elevator.

"David!" she said. "I am so glad you're here! We're all ready to record 'Demiurge,' and I was hoping to do 'Droplets' as well. So we were just hoping you'd get here."

Dingo looked at the clock on the wall. It was ten after nine. This was the first time he'd ever seen Pamela in here before ten. "I was in traffic," he said.

"Ah yes," Pamela said. "The only drawback of life in New Jersey." She laughed.

Dingo walked toward the studio in order to avoid saying something to Pamela that he might live to regret.

In the control booth, Dingo called out for everybody to check their mikes, then double-checked the controls before exiting the booth and taking his place behind the drum kit. Pamela's happy little army were all there in place, ready to bring her songs to life.

"Hi, Dingo!" they all said, and Dingo just nodded. Their cheerfulness annoyed him. Why the hell shouldn't they be cheerful? They had no responsibilities, they got all the sex they could handle, and they had somebody coming in and telling them how great they were all the time.

Well, maybe that wasn't fair. They *were* great. Or at least they used to be, before Pamela started telling them how great they were. So far she'd only had her little meetings with Sarah and Julie, but Dingo could see the quality of their work decline almost immediately following the meeting. He suspected Pamela had puffed them up by telling them what little geniuses they were, because instead of being tentative and eager to please, they started acting like they were incapable of writing a bad song and disproving it by writing really obscure crap.

Dingo sat behind the drum kit for five minutes not taking part in whatever banal chatter the kids were engaged in. Jesus, she acted like it was so important that I was ten minutes late, and now she's making us all sit here with our thumbs up our asses.

Finally Pamela walked into the studio. "Ah," she said, "the en-

ergy in here is perfect for creativity." Lady, Dingo thought, my
energy is perfect for kicking your ass. He went back into the
booth, hit the button, shouted "Rolling!" and went back to his
drum kit.

He took his annoyance out on his drums, and they got through
"Demiurge," probably the closest thing to a rock-and-roll song
Pamela had ever written (at least it was once Dingo had gotten
through arranging it for her), in only seven takes, a record for
Pamela. Twelve (!) takes of "Droplets" later, Pamela pronounced
the work for the day done and commanded Levon to fire up the
toilet bong.

This annoyed Dingo. Everybody was clearheaded when they
did Pamela's work, which was not, by the way, something any of
them were being paid to do, and then they'd all stagger in later
high as a kite with some song about logarithms or something and
hope to be able to do something with it.

"I'm gonna go take a walk," Dingo said. "Maybe grab some
lunch."

"Groovy," somebody said in an indifferent tone. Dingo got in
the elevator planning to go up to the lobby and go for a walk, but
when he got in and saw the bank of buttons, he decided to go a
little farther.

Heart pounding, he pushed the button for Clark Payson's office.

DINGO WALKED INTO Clark Payson's outer office and caught a
phony smile from the secretary, a pretty girl with dark hair and
cruel eyes. She looked Dingo up and down and said, "Mainte-
nance?"

"Uh, no," Dingo said, suddenly feeling awkward and stupid.
He shouldn't have just walked up here. He shouldn't be here at

all. These kinds of meetings, where you sold out everything you thought you were, should be held in parking garages late at night, not in broad daylight, and Kara Newhouse, as her nameplate identified her, had just reminded him that guys who looked like him had no business in places like this unless they were fixing something.

It occurred to him to turn around, get in the elevator, and really go to lunch, but that would be handing Kara Newhouse a victory. *If I want a woman to treat me with contempt and boss me around, I'll go home,* Dingo thought, and smiled to himself. That wasn't fair, but it gave him some of his bluster back.

"David Donovan to see Clark Payson," he said, because that's exactly what people said in situations like this on TV.

Kara Newhouse smiled even more broadly. Dingo recognized the bared teeth as a threat display that any animal would be proud of. "Do you have an appointment . . . *Mister* Donovan?"

Had she just been nicer to him in the first place, Dingo would have been out of here already. He realized he was doing the wrong thing here, selling out his co-workers, but there was no way he was going to let this painted security guard make him feel inferior to her. He had to get into Clark Payson's office now. And, he reflected, his Borscht Belt joke about going home might have had some truth to it. He always knuckled under to Cass, because that's how you stay married, but he didn't have a relationship with Kara Newhouse to maintain. He decided to go for arrogant.

"I don't, but Clark told me I should stop by anytime."

There was a pause as Kara Newhouse looked at him as though he'd just explained that he'd ridden Mr. Ed up the stairwell. "Ah. I see. Well"—she looked down at a book on her desk—"Mr. Payson has a full schedule today, and I'm afraid there's no way he's going to be able to squeeze you in."

"Well, can you check with him?"

Kara Newhouse smiled even more broadly. "I'm afraid I can't possibly. Mr. Payson gave me explicit instructions not to disturb him."

She smiled again, confident that she had Dingo on the ropes. If he tried to call, he'd reach her again, and anytime he tried to show up in person, she'd be guarding the gates.

But he couldn't go away; he could beat Kara Newhouse, and he would. He had her at a disadvantage: He didn't care about following company protocol, and she had to be the model of company protocol, especially if she hoped to keep this job when Clark Payson took over ATN. So Dingo strolled over to the inner office door and knocked.

He glanced at his adversary; he had to hand it to her, she was really good. She didn't waste any time with feeble protests about how he couldn't do that—she'd probably taken stock of the situation and realized he had ten inches and at least a hundred pounds on her, so she merely got on the phone and called security.

"Kara?" Clark Payson's muffled voice behind the door said.

"No, Mr. Payson, it's me, Da—uh, Dingo."

One second later the door opened, and a smiling Clark Payson stood there. "Dingo! I'm so glad you stopped by!"

Dingo glanced at Kara Newhouse. "Shall I cancel the call to security, Mr. Payson?" she said, smiling.

"Please do, Kara," Clark said. "And thank you."

Dingo smiled at Kara Newhouse, who smiled back, and then entered the office as Clark Payson shut the heavy wooden door behind him.

CLARK PAYSON INDICATED a fancy chrome chair with leather straps for Dingo to sit in. Dingo eyed it, wondering if the leather would hold his bulk, then eased himself into it carefully. The leather gave a little creak of protest, which didn't help Dingo to feel any more comfortable.

Clark went behind his desk and eased into his own chair. "I hope Kara didn't give you too much trouble," he said.

Dingo smiled. "She's pretty fierce."

"She's a Doberman in panty hose," Clark said, drawing a smile from Dingo. "Which is exactly what I want in a secretary."

Dingo just looked at him, unsure what to say. Clark Payson finally broke the silence. "Uh, so, what can I help you with?"

"Well," Dingo said, "I . . . I mean, I hate to say this, but there seems to be a problem."

"Okay," Clark said. The expression on his face was still calm and pleasant, and it unnerved Dingo. "Tell me about it," he continued.

"It's just . . ." Dingo paused, suddenly unsure how much to reveal to Clark, suddenly horribly uncomfortable in the narc role, in his own skin. "It's getting a little claustrophobic down there, and I . . . I'm . . . well, you know how Pamela is, right?"

Clark rolled his eyes. "Only too well."

"So she's kind of got the kids thinking that they need to take a journey to the center of their minds, and everybody's kind of walking around with their heads up their ass and not doing anything relating to kids. I mean, I'm the only one down there who has kids, and I can tell you that kids who watch Saturday-morning cartoons are not going to get a song about the Heisenberg uncertainty principle."

"What's that?"

"Hell if I know. But we've got a song about it."

Dingo waited nervously as Clark Payson thought.

"Okay," Clark said. "I'm going to come down—no, no. I'm going to call everybody up here on Monday for a meeting about what kind of progress is being made. And then I'm going to put on a show that would make my father proud."

"Uh, okay," Dingo said. "I was thinking if you just leaned on Pamela a little bit . . ."

"I don't think Pamela is really susceptible to being leaned on. I do think I can scare the kids, though. At least I hope so. Listen, do you have . . . do you have anything recorded?"

Here was the moment he'd been expecting. It was a relief to be able to say, "Yeah. I got a whole bunch of stuff the first week. I do think we've got some stuff we can use."

"Great. Do you think you could get that to me so I can listen to it over the weekend?"

"Yeah. I'll dupe the tapes this afternoon and send them up to you."

"All right," Clark said, rising from his chair. Dingo, with some difficulty, extricated himself from the leather-and-chrome trap of his chair. "Thank you," Clark said, shaking Dingo's hand. "I really appreciate it."

"Okay," Dingo said, probably sounding as uncomfortable as he felt. He really hoped he'd done the right thing. It felt bad, but so did sitting by and watching Pamela lead the project that was paying his mortgage down the toilet.

He went home early, and, as soon as he walked in the door, Cass started in on him about some goddamn thing she'd wanted him to do that he hadn't done.

He stared at her quizzically; her words couldn't quite penetrate his ears. "You know," he said, "I just betrayed everything I thought I was for you. That ought to count for something."

Cass stopped talking and looked at him. "Honey, what are you talking about?" she said, and her face was soft where it had been hard just a moment ago.

"I can't . . . I have a . . . I'm ashamed of myself."

"Why, baby?"

"Because. Because I just . . . I didn't think I became a musician so I could rat my co-workers out to guys in suits."

"Sweetie, you know I have no idea what the hell you're talking about, right? Can you tell me the story?"

He looked at her. "I guess. Just promise not to hate me."

"Did you cheat on me?"

"Of course not."

"Kill anybody?"

"No."

"Then I don't hate you. Now talk to me."

16

PETER

PETER LAY AWAKE in the dark listening to Sarah breathe.
When his music career had been foundering and he'd
been unable to make rent on his rat-infested apartment, Peter
had spent hours staring into early-morning darkness and worrying, but he hadn't done that since he'd moved into the ATN
basement.

Until today. Things with Sarah felt a little weird, and while he
could ignore this or explain it away when he was fully awake, it
occupied all of his thoughts here in the early morning. (Or what
passed for early around here, he thought. It was probably after
eight. His semiconscious panic used to arrive at five AM. He supposed he should be grateful.)

She wouldn't eat with him anymore. Or, anyway, he wouldn't
eat what she was eating—usually some combination of an unsalted boiled grain and an unsalted steamed vegetable—and she
explained that she felt the impurities in what he was eating were
affecting her cleansing process. So if he wanted to eat real food,
he needed to do it away from her.

And then there was the songwriting. She told him that she really needed to work alone to explore her own passions, so they'd stopped the creative give-and-take that had been one of Peter's favorite parts of their relationship.

So without eating and songwriting, they were essentially just sex partners now, and while that continued to be fun, Peter worried that it was only a matter of time before he became one more toxin she wouldn't want to put into her body. And Peter was afraid that the quality would start to decline. Because they shared this intimacy outside of bed, sex with Sarah felt more intimate, more meaningful than it ever had before. There were times when he felt like putting their bodies together had actually allowed their souls to touch. Would that ever happen again?

And did the fact that he was even thinking this way make him female? Probably. He couldn't imagine telling Levon or any other man that he was worried about endangering the spiritual connection he felt in his nightly sex.

Well, maybe this was the instant karma John Lennon was talking about. Way back at Antioch, he'd adopted the sensitive singer-songwriter persona as a way to get laid, and now he was getting too sensitive about getting laid.

He looked at Sarah, wondering what she was dreaming, wondering if she was worrying about anything. More instant karma: She'd initially been the one who wanted to have the Big Conversation, and he'd wanted to avoid it. Now he was dying to ask her, *Where are we headed? What's going on with us? Have I done something wrong?*—but they rarely had any time alone anymore except at night, and he continued to choose sex over a Big Conversation, because at least you know you're going to feel good after sex.

Sarah continued to breathe, to sleep the undisturbed sleep of the undisturbed. Peter got up and started to get dressed, hoping he could be loud enough to wake her up and quiet enough to plausibly deny that he'd been trying to wake her up. Fortunately, Dingo took care of that.

"Rise and shine, everybody!" Dingo's voice bellowed down the hallway. Peter stuck his head into the hallway and saw Levon peeking out of his room. Julie, dressed and obviously showered, walked down the hall with Dingo. Peter supposed that meant she hadn't slept here last night. What the hell was going on with her and Levon anyway? If Sarah knew anything from Julie, she wasn't sharing, and all Peter ever got out of Levon was "I don't know, man. It's complicated."

"Just got a call from the boss," Dingo said, "and we've got some important stuff to do today."

Suddenly Sarah appeared behind Peter's shoulder. "Great!" she said. "When is she going to get here?" As she said this, she slid her hand into the back of his jeans and gave his butt a squeeze. That seemed like a good sign.

"No no no," Dingo said, "not Pamela. The *boss*. The man in the suit who signs your paychecks."

"I haven't seen any paychecks," Levon said. "Is everybody getting paid but the black guy?"

"No. It takes a week to get your information into the payroll system, and then the checks come biweekly. We're supposed to get paid on Friday, but Clark Payson agreed to move things along, since so many of us are in really dire need of that check. So we're all supposed to go up to Clark Payson's office and collect our checks and tell him what progress we're making," Dingo said.

His words hung in the air, and though nobody said, *Oh shit*, Peter could hear everybody thinking it. Including him. He left the basement so rarely that he had kind of forgotten that he actually had a job. It wasn't like he'd had a paycheck to remind him, either. The way he ate—stealing food from the employee cafeteria or the

buffet on the morning news set or whatever was left over in dressing rooms and green rooms all over the building—made him feel
more like a basement-dwelling rat than an employee.

And Pamela certainly hadn't been encouraging them to be
productive. Once they recorded a song or two for her, they just
kind of sat around smoking, and occasionally they wrote songs.
Peter knew that most of the stuff that he'd been writing wasn't
going to make the final cut, but Pamela had told them all that
they had to be fearless about writing bad songs, that opening the
channels to the creativity of the universe would eventually lead
them to the best work of their lives, but they might have to go
through some bad work too.

Peter didn't buy into the whole energy thing, but it had been
a great relief to just write songs without worrying about how
they'd sound in performance. He was proud of a lot of what he'd
written, and he saw the wisdom in what Pamela was having them
do. If he was ever going to find his voice as a songwriter and have
it sound like his own voice rather than a pale echo of Dylan's
voice with a little John Lennon thrown in, then he'd have to just
write song after song after song until he had his own identity
rather than a reflection of someone else's.

And it was fun to think about history, about causes and effects,
about patterns, about all the things he'd liked about history but
had given short shrift in college while he focused on sex and pot.

There was still a lot of both here, but he had hours and hours
to pore over the box of history books he'd moved into the corner
of his practice room and just to think.

That is, when he wasn't thinking about why Sarah was drifting away from him and whether he was frightened or relieved
about it.

All of this artistic and personal exploration had been fantastic,
but now the ride was over, and there was a guy with money in his
hand who expected to actually see some work done for the

money he was spending. Which was, Peter supposed, the way it actually worked in the real world. But was this the real world?

Well, it was now.

"SO WHAT Mr. Payson told me," Dingo said, "was that he'd love to hear what we've been working on. So I would like to suggest that you all get your best work ready to play for him this afternoon."

Peter looked around. He could see Julie intently going through her mental catalog of songs and picking out the best one. Levon was rubbing his eyes and trying to wake up. Sarah said, "Where's Pamela? I'd really like to talk to her about my selection."

"Well," Dingo said, "it's only eight thirty, and I'd be real surprised if we see Pamela before ten. So you can go back to bed if you want, or get up and work, or whatever, but we are due in Clark Payson's office in four and a half hours."

One o'clock! Shit! Peter always hit the employee cafeteria at ten minutes till two, when they were getting ready to throw stuff out and you could get really big portions for free. Now he'd be sitting in Clark Payson's office with his stomach growling. Then again, if he walked out of the office with a paycheck in hand, he'd actually be able to buy some food. Like a regular person.

"Oh, one more thing," Dingo said. "You probably understand this anyway, but just to get it completely out there, none of us are getting paid to record Pamela Sanchez songs that have nothing to do with making educational cartoons for kids. So you should probably not mention that while we're in Clark Payson's office. Okay. I got doughnuts in the lounge if anybody wants some."

Peter headed straight for the doughnuts.

Sarah looked like she wanted to tell him about the evils of eating sugar and fat for breakfast, but she held back. Instead, she just said, "I think I'm going to try to get some more sleep. I can't—I mean, there's no point in me picking a song until Pamela gets here."

As he walked to the lounge, guitar in hand, Peter thought that if this had happened a week ago, Sarah would have at least asked him for his opinion on which song she should play for the boss.

He grabbed a chocolate-glazed and sat down on the couch opposite Julie, who was sitting in a chair. "So what are you gonna play?" he asked her.

"I don't know," she said. "I'm thinking about 'Tell Me How.' You know, the adverb song?"

"That's a great one," Peter said. "I was thinking about 'Bicameral, by Gum.' "

"That's good," Julie said, "but I think 'Emancipation Proclamation' is more of a showstopper."

Peter popped the last bit of doughnut into his mouth and started to pick out "Emancipation Proclamation."

"In eighteen hundred and sixty-three / Abe Lincoln ended slavery / keeping slaves is really wrong / he knew it went on far too long . . ."

He looked over at Julie, who was looking distressed.

"What? Is it bad?"

"Oh, no, I'm sorry, Peter, it's not your song, it's just that . . . we've got to go up to Clark Payson's office, and I didn't see a piano up there, and so once again my song isn't going to sound the way I want it to. I know it's dumb, I'm being a baby, but I'm the only one who plays an instrument that isn't portable, and I just get a little sick of it sometimes."

"I'm sorry," Peter said. "You know, we all know that song. We can make it sound really good, especially with the harmonies with you and Sarah."

"Yeah," Julie said in a flat voice. "Thank you. I don't mean to be a brat. I do really appreciate what you guys have brought to my songs."

"Thanks!" Peter said. "And, uh, you know, you too."

That was nice, and more of a conversation than he'd had with Sarah about work for days. But now he felt guilty about continuing to play in front of Julie, so he decided to go get showered.

He showered and dressed and went to the empty practice room and played through all of his songs. At ten fifteen, he decided he'd check to see if Pamela had arrived. Sure enough, she was in the lounge, surrounded by Sarah, Julie, and Levon.

"Oh, Peter," she said, smiling brightly. "I'm so glad you're here. We've been talking about song selection for our little show this afternoon."

"Great," Peter said. "What do you think abut 'Emancipation Proclamation'?"

Pamela was silent for a moment, and Peter winced. Okay, he could play something else.

"It's just that," Pamela said, "I really want to . . . I want Clark to really get a sense of the creative journey we're on, so I don't think playing things we wrote in the first week will really give him a sense of what we're doing here. You know? We've come so far in such a short time, and you're all doing such a wonderful job of exploring the corners of your subject where your passion for it began, and I think it's important for Clark to see that, to see that we're engaged in something more than just writing catchy commercials for learning"—Peter's eyes darted to Julie, whose smile faltered just enough that Peter could tell she was seething—"that what we're doing here is trying to ignite a passion for learning in the youth of America, to really make them learners instead of just memorizers."

THREE NERVOUS HOURS passed, with everyone locked up in their own practice rooms trying to hone their songs while Pamela recorded a solo acoustic number with Dingo.

Finally, it was time to go. Peter packed his guitar in his hard case and walked over to the elevator. He had that called-to-the-principal's-office feeling, and, looking around, he could see that everyone but Pamela seemed to be going through it too. Pamela had this blissed-out grin on her face, and seeing that helped Peter feel better about this whole thing. Whatever was happening, Pamela wasn't concerned, so it couldn't be that bad. Right?

Nobody spoke in the elevator. Pamela hummed something unrecognizable under her breath. When they arrived at Clark Payson's office, his very attractive secretary said, "Good afternoon! Mr. Payson realized that he doesn't have a piano in his office, so he asked me to tell you to meet him in studio 8-J. Do you know where that is?"

"Eighth floor?" Dingo said.

"That's right. It's the home of the Misty Lee show." Peter looked to Sarah to see if the mention of Misty Lee would set off a spark of jealousy. If it did, she kept a very tight lid on it—she didn't even look back at him or seem to notice that he'd looked at her. Well, she was probably nervous about the meeting.

Another silent elevator ride, and then they all wandered around the eighth floor in a pack, finding studio 8-F and studio 8-R. "What the hell happened to the rest of the alphabet?" Julie said. "I mean, this is my area of expertise, and I'm pretty sure they're missing some letters." She looked around, smiling, but nobody even acknowledged her. Peter guessed she'd been encouraged by the news that she'd have a piano to play.

Finally they found 8-J and walked in. "Whoa," Peter said as he looked around the small studio. "It looks much bigger on TV."

"So do Misty Lee's tits," Julie stage-whispered, glancing at Sarah, who gave her a polite smile.

Clark Payson was sitting on the stage, next to Dr. Andrews, the education expert who'd created the binders everyone had ignored for such a long time that they had finally disappeared from the basement entirely, probably because Pamela had thrown them out. "Hi folks!" Clark Payson said. He didn't seem pissed off.

Dr. Andrews, who was busy scribbling something on a piece of paper, looked up at everyone, waved, and went back to scribbling.

"So," Clark Payson said, "most important things first. Your paychecks!" They all filed up to the stage, and Clark looked each one of them in the eye, shook their hand, and handed them a check.

"I feel like I'm graduating," Peter joked as Clark handed him his check. He felt a stab of fear as he wondered if it had been a good idea to make that joke, but Clark Payson smiled.

"Okay!" Clark Payson said when they had all tucked their checks into their pockets. "I'm just so excited about what you're doing that I couldn't wait to hear something, and I know Dr. Andrews shares my excitement. Now, we know you're probably still in the works-in-progress phase, but I'm just dying to hear some of what you've got. So who'd like to go first?"

"Well," Pamela said. She got up on the stage with Clark Payson and gave essentially the same speech about the fantastic creative journey they were on that she'd given them in the lounge before. Clark nodded politely, and Dr. Andrews didn't even pretend he was paying attention. Pamela cast a dirty look in Dr. Andrews's direction, and then she said, "Okay, Peter, would you go first, please?"

Peter was relieved that he wouldn't have to sit here worrying about how his song stacked up to the others. As he took out his guitar, it occurred to him that playing the song Pamela had recommended—"Smoot-Hawley Boogie"—might not be the best choice, that it was far safer to go with "Emancipation Proclamation," especially with the educational theorist now looking straight at him, pen poised above the piece of paper.

He looked at Clark Payson. He looked at Pamela Sanchez. Well, he thought, if he pissed off Clark Payson, he'd hopefully have Pamela and Dingo to take some of the heat for him, and if he pissed off Pamela, life in the basement was going to get very difficult for him.

"People said, 'We don't really think it's fair if / you hit all our goods with these tariffs,' / but President Hoover said, / 'It's the Smoot-Hawley boogie for me . . .' " When he finished, everybody applauded. He couldn't read Clark Payson's face, but Pamela was beaming. Dr. Andrews scribbled furiously and shook his head.

Sarah followed this with "Fibonacci's Tree," Levon played "Non-Euclidean Space," and Julie, in direct contradiction of Pamela's instructions, strode to the piano and played "Tell Me How."

Peter looked nervously at Pamela, who was obviously unhappy. He looked back to Julie and wondered why she'd done it. Was she jealous of Pamela? Or did she, the only one of them who'd ever held a real job outside of comic-book retailing, have a better sense of whose ass to kiss than anybody else?

When she finished, Peter started the applause. Pamela notably did not put her hands together. Dr. Andrews notably did, for the first time today.

Clark Payson leaned in to talk to Dr. Andrews. The two of them conferred in whispers for what seemed like an hour while everyone else stared at them. It occurred to Peter to scream an obscenity just to break the unbearable tension, but he managed not to.

Finally, Clark Payson nodded at Dr. Andrews and turned to address everyone else. "Folks," he said, "I have to say I'm a little disappointed. And I really hate to say that, but there it is. I was—I didn't expect finished products, but I guess I just feel like you guys are going in a direction here that runs away from what this project is supposed to be. The average viewer of our Saturday-morning cartoons is"—he looked in his notebook, flipping pages until he found the number—"a nine-year-old boy with one sibling and a dog.

"Now, I don't know about you, but I can't imagine being a nine-year-old boy and understanding anything about non-Euclidean space, or the Smoot-Hawley Tariffs, or Fibonacci numbers. I haven't been a nine-year-old boy for twenty-nine years, and I graduated from Princeton, and I have no idea what Fibonacci numbers are. Dr. Andrews?"

"Thank you, Clark," Dr. Andrews said. "I feel—I can't help feeling partly responsible for the debacle that's taken place here today. It's clear to me that you all need some grounding in educational theory. In particular Vygotsky's concept of the zone of proximal development, which I mentioned to you a few weeks ago, but which I clearly need to explain in depth. I'm going straight to my office to prepare a translation—from the French, of course—that you can read, and please, *please* understand that I'm here as a resource to you, and if you have questions about the appropriateness of what you're writing, which, frankly, you should, come and talk to me."

"Thanks, Dr. Andrews," Clark Payson said. "I don't know if you guys know my father, but believe me when I tell you he will literally physically kill me if I walk into his office and explain that I've spent tens of thousands of dollars of his money and gotten a song about the Smoot-Hawley Tariffs.

"Now, I know you don't know me well, but I hope you don't want to be responsible for my death. I don't know if the rest of you have anything like the adverb song Julie played, but if you do, that's really the direction I want you going in. We can't be so obscure, guys. I will of course expect you to read the material that Dr. Andrews prepares for you, but, for now, I can just tell you to remember your audience. We're talking about kids here. Stuff that's obscure even to college students is just not going to

fly with our nine-year-old boys. Now, I'd like to meet again in another week, and I really hope you'll have something more suit-
able for me."

They all sat silently. Peter felt the weight of Clark Payson's
words pressing him into the floor. When he was nine, he'd liked
superheroes and the Cisco Kid. He wouldn't have given a shit
about the Smoot-Hawley Tariffs.

Pamela got up and said, "Clark, I'd love to explain. You see,
we're on a creative odyssey here, and just like Odysseus had to
meander in order to find his way home—"

Clark Payson got up from his seat and walked toward the studio door. "I'm sorry, Pamela, but I've got another meeting that
started five minutes ago."

They all went back to the basement in silence. When they got
off the elevator, Julie headed down the hall, and Pamela called
after her, "Julie! We need to talk in here!"

"I'm sorry," Julie said, "but I really need to get to work. I feel
like I'm really . . . I have some songs to write." She disappeared
into the practice room, and Pamela looked after her, absolutely
fuming.

"She undermined all of us there," Pamela said. "I hope you all
noticed that. I couldn't possibly convince Clark of the importance of the journey we're on when she played her song from the
first week!"

Nobody spoke. Peter wasn't sure what he thought, but he was
leaning toward Julie's point of view. He was embarrassed that he'd
actually played "Smoot-Hawley Boogie" out loud when it was
obvious to him now that it was a complete piece of shit, and he felt
like he really wanted to go write some songs he could be proud of,
songs that his nine-year-old self might have sung along to.

"Now, I just want you all to know something," Pamela said.
"What happened today is never going to happen again. If Clark
wants progress, I'll take him some recordings, but I will never

allow you to be put through that humiliation again, to be paraded before some self-styled expert who can't even write comprensibly for adults . . . It's my job to deal with the commercial demands of this project, not yours, and I'm sorry. I should have insulated you from that. And I don't want you to despair. The fact that where you are now is not where the network wants you to be should not discourage you from continuing the journey. Rrrgh, I'm really angry right now. I *told* him we were on a journey of artistic growth and exploration! Of course we haven't arrived yet! Ah—the money people never understand art."

They all stood there looking at each other, not knowing exactly what to do next. Peter looked at Levon, who shrugged, and Sarah, who was looking intently at Pamela. Pamela had closed her eyes and was breathing deeply. Peter shot Dingo an inquisitive glance. Dingo made a face, then said, "Well, anybody got anything they want to record today?"

Pamela opened her eyes and gave Dingo a withering glance that did not actually make him wither. "No, David. We are not recording today. We've all just been dealt a serious blow, and we're going to recover in our own ways. I'd like to suggest . . . well, Peter, I was going to meet with you to talk about your journey today, and I think it's still a good idea to do that, if you don't mind."

"Uh, yeah, that's fine," Peter said. Might as well. It didn't seem like much else was going to happen this afternoon. He looked over at Sarah, who gave him a little nod.

"Okay then," Dingo said. "Well, if we're not recording, I guess I'm gonna head back home then. I'll see everybody tomorrow." He walked out, and Pamela looked angry but said nothing.

"All right, Peter," she said. "Shall we go?"

"Sure," Peter said. He wasn't sure where they were going—maybe a museum, or the park? He thought that might actually be good. Clearly he needed to get the hell out of this basement and into the real world again. Maybe looking at some paintings or trees or something would help him to get a better sense of what he should be doing. Right now he felt totally lost—should he continue to write crap in the hope of arriving at something wonderful, or should he just go back to what he was writing before, knowing it was good enough, even if it wasn't the best he was capable of?

Outside the ATN building, Pamela hailed a cab, and Peter felt disappointed when she gave the cabbie her address. Sarah got to walk around outside, and I get to go sit in another dim red space. Well, maybe he'd walk back to ATN or something, remind himself that there were other people in the world living lives that had nothing to do with *Pop Goes the Classroom.*

In the cab, Pamela said, "Well, I really like your tariff song."

"Really?" Peter asked.

"Yes really. Where Clark is . . . see, this is why I'm so frustrated by this whole thing. Clark is right, of course, that a nine-year-old isn't going to care about the Smoot-Hawley Tariffs, but that's not the point of what we're doing now. What I hear in that song that's important is a Peter Terpin song about the Smoot-Hawley Tariffs. I don't mean to disparage your early efforts, which I also like—you're certainly the most talented songwriter we have—" Peter couldn't help but be thrilled to hear that—it was easy for him to hear how talented Julie and Sarah and Levon were, but he was never as sure of his own work. And here Pamela had told him he was even better than them! He wasn't sure about that, but at this point it was nice even to feel like he was as good as any of them. "—but what I hear in your Smoot-Hawley song, in both the lyrics and the music, is *Peter* writing a song about some obscure part of American history rather than Peter trying to imagine what a John Lennon song about American history would sound like. Do you know what I mean?"

"Yeah!" Peter said. "I do! I was thinking the same thing!"

Pamela smiled at him. They arrived at Pamela's place, and she paid the cabbie and led Peter inside.

"So," she said when they'd gotten inside, "after that *meeting*, I need a little natural decompression." She reached into a box by her bedside and pulled out a Baggie of pot and some rolling papers. She rolled the joint quickly and efficiently, lit up, took a drag, and passed it to Peter, who inhaled deeply.

He felt almost instantly like he was a hollow shell filled with smoke. And the smell of the pot mixed with whatever smells of incense and/or perfume smells permeated this place anyway reminded him of sweating with Pamela amid the same smells years ago at Antioch. Did she remember? He couldn't help wondering. He'd long ago gotten over the illusion that his one night with Pamela had been as important to her as it had been to him, and in the end it didn't matter, because having Pamela Sanchez tell him she liked his songs and then sleep with him gave him the confidence in both the musical and sexual arenas that had made the rest of college so much fun.

Still, he was curious about whether she even remembered.

"Mmmm," she said as she inhaled again. "For some reason I was just remembering being in an apartment in Yellow Springs, Ohio, several years ago. Do you remember that?"

Peter's throat was suddenly dry and his penis was suddenly erect. "Yeah. I remember."

"Well, of course I could never forget. You were fantastic." She passed him the joint, and he took it, grateful that his hand was a smoke-filled balloon and not trembling.

Peter inhaled and didn't say anything, because he didn't know what to say. He knew on some level that she was lying—he'd certainly been eager and appreciative, but not exactly skilled, and he'd been much more of a sprinter than a marathoner back then. So why even say that? It wasn't like she needed to give him a review at this point. His mind felt cloudy and his stomach, the only part of him not replaced with lighter-than-air smoke, was churning a mix of arousal and guilt, excitement and fear. He inhaled again.

"Sarah's very lucky to have you," Pamela said. "I hope she appreciates how lucky she is."

The mention of Sarah's name dropped Peter back into reality. If Pamela had actually mentioned Sarah's name, then she couldn't be just an idea in his mind that he could ignore. She must be an actual person, a person he cared about, a person who would be hurt if he betrayed her. *Or would she?* his penis whispered to him. *She's pulling away, setting you up for the big breakup, and you're going to regret it if you act all noble and faithful and end up getting dumped anyway.*

When Peter didn't immediately jump in telling Pamela that of course Sarah appreciated him, Pamela pounced with, "I mean, is everything going okay with you two?"

"I dunno," Peter said. "She seems to be getting a little distant or something. Maybe it's just that we spent too much time together at first and she needs a little personal space."

"Well, Sarah's going to take a while to find herself," Pamela said. "What you have to remember is that not only is she younger than you chronologically, she's also a younger soul. So while you have a pretty clear sense of who you are and what you are doing, Sarah is going to need to spend some more time on a quest to figure herself out. She's going to be going through some changes. It will be a beautiful rebirth for her. But birth is always painful."

Peter didn't know what to say to that, other than, "Mmm."

"Peter," Pamela said. "I'm having a hard time getting past my memory."

Peter's brain, full of smoke and the smell of Pamela and the memory of her body against his and resentment of Sarah, spun around and around and didn't help him. "Uh . . . um . . . I see," he said.

"Yes," Pamela said, rising from the couch and sitting astride him, "I think you do." She leaned in and kissed him, and though part of Peter wanted to push her away, that part didn't seem to be in control of his body at the moment. He grabbed Pamela's back and pulled her closer, pushing his tongue into her mouth. She held his head in her hands, then slid one hand down, between their legs. She gave him a squeeze.

Decision time.

He flashed back to a similar scene in Yellow Springs. It had certainly been fun but, taking away the thrill of Pamela's celebrity, nothing special. Nothing like what he had with Sarah, which he was jeopardizing right now, which would be seriously compromised if Pamela ever freed him from his zipper.

His mind raced. If he didn't sleep with Pamela, things might improve with Sarah, and if he did sleep with Pamela, then he was making the decision to cut off the best thing he'd ever had. It was a gamble, but he'd rather kick himself for not sleeping with Pamela than for ruining the best thing he'd ever had. He reached down and grabbed Pamela's hand and gently pushed her away.

"I'm sorry," he said, "I've got to go." He squirmed out from under her.

"Peter," she said, "we need to—"

"Sorry," he said again. "Sorry. Gotta go."

He ran from Pamela's apartment into the sunshine and headed uptown. He was ten blocks away before he stopped running.

17

SARAH

SARAH WAS AT loose ends after Pamela and Peter left. Julie was holed up in her practice room, Levon had taken his paycheck out to cash it, so Sarah was alone with Julie.

Sarah picked up her guitar and strummed chords that didn't go together. Nothing worked. She felt awful. She closed her eyes, breathed deeply, and tried to look inside herself and figure out why she felt so horrible, why her creativity was not flowing. Pamela said when you found this happening, you had to search yourself, really search yourself to find what it was in you that was blocking the path of the universe's creative energy.

Sarah breathed and listened to herself breathing. She realized that it was a wonderful thing to be breathing, to be alive, to be drawing air in and pushing it out. She felt the tension drain from her shoulders as she continued to breathe. She pictured the air flowing into her lungs as a golden light filling the shell of her body until she glowed. She exhaled, pushing out all of the negativity, all of the fear, all of the tension. Golden light flowed into her; gray, polluted smoke poured out.

If she could keep this up, she would be bathed in the universe's luminous energy, she would be—she opened her eyes and felt her lungs and arms and stomach and legs fill with the tense pollution she had been trying to rid them of. It was so difficult. She wanted so badly to be like Pamela—comfortable in her own skin, confident, and at peace, not tormented with self-doubt, with her mother's voice in her ear telling her she was making a terrible mistake.

So she tried all the stuff Pamela told her—the breathing, the meditation, the cleansing. And yet, apart from the fact that her colon was working like a Swiss watch, she still felt like ugly little Sarah Stein, not the being of light that Pamela assured her she was inside.

She closed her eyes again and forced herself to examine the gray smoke that filled her body. She saw shame—Sarah, after all, had never so much as been called to the principal's office, had gone through sixteen years of school being the quiet, good little girl in the middle of the class who did well but didn't draw attention to herself.

She knew there were girls—her next-door neighbor Robin Cornwall, for example—who were always getting in trouble at school and who didn't care, who laughed on their way out of the principal's office. Sarah had always wondered how they did it.

Right now she was feeling chastened and ashamed. Clark Payson, who had manipulated them so well by handing them their checks—reminding them that the money came from him—had hated her song. Had actually mocked it. It felt bad. Sarah didn't know enough about Clark Payson to know whether she should value his opinion or not, though she suspected that Pamela was right, that he obviously didn't understand anything about the creative process—but she wanted him to like her work anyway. She wanted him to like her work the way he'd liked Julie's.

Sarah continued to breathe, and she found, floating in the gray smoke, a large hunk of resentment about Julie's kissing up to Clark

Payson by playing her little adverb song. Julie had pretended she was one of them, had seemed to believe that they were doing the right thing, but when it came down to it she wasn't really an artist. She was an advertising jingle writer, and she was used to crafting little songs for pleasing people with money, and when given the choice between her friends and her paycheck, Julie had stabbed them all in the back. It made Sarah angry, but, more than that, it hurt. Where was that confused girl who'd come barging into the bathroom to tell her about having sex with Levon? Wasn't that something you did with a friend? How could Julie just pretend to be a friend and then turn around and make Sarah look like an idiot?

Sarah thought back to all the hours they'd spent playing music together, getting high together, growing into the kind of creative community that could produce some really remarkable art. And apparently the whole thing had been a lie to Julie.

Sarah continued to breathe, exhaling her anger and hurt and breathing in golden light. After a few minutes, she began to feel lighter, but she realized there was one more thing. Peter was alone with Pamela, and Sarah was jealous.

But that was silly. Pamela would never betray Sarah that way. But Peter might fall in love with her. What man wouldn't want Pamela instead of Sarah? Even if Sarah continued along and had a music career rather than a teaching career, she'd never be on her album cover spilling out of her blouse (for one thing, boobs as small as hers just didn't spill out of anything) with teenage girls wanting to be her and teenage boys wanting to sleep with her.

Sarah opened her eyes. Her creativity was blocked. Pamela told her that when she felt blocked, she had to identify and remove the obstacles in her way. She got up and walked down the hall toward Julie's practice room. Julie opened the door just as Sarah was preparing to knock on it.

"Hey!" Julie said. "I just wrote two songs! Do you wanna go take these paychecks and treat ourselves to a nice dinner?"

"Uh," Sarah sputtered. She'd been gearing up for a big speech about how Julie had really hurt her, and Julie's bright, friendly disposition had taken the wind out of her sails. "Well, I'm really not eating restaurant food right now—you know, I'm still trying to cleanse my system, and Seeds is the only place that really serves the kind of thing I need to be eating, and they're closed on Mondays."

Julie looked disappointed. "Well, that's too bad. I guess I'll see you tomorrow, then."

"Yeah," Sarah said, as flatly as she could.

Julie walked a few steps away, then turned around. "Is something bothering you?" she asked.

"Well . . ." Sarah started, then hesitated. Her nerve was failing in the face of Julie's self-assurance. "I guess . . ." The authoritative denunciation of Julie's betrayal she'd been preparing melted away. "I guess I'm just wondering why you played that song today."

Julie looked at Sarah closely. "I just felt like, you know, my experience with the Clark Paysons of the world is that they don't want to hear about your artistic growth. They just want a product for their money. And I didn't think that my song about synecdoche would have gone over too well."

Sarah's anger suddenly flashed out, and it felt good. Powerful. "But if you'd played it, then maybe he would have understood what we were doing. You made Pamela look stupid. You made us all look stupid."

Julie's face contorted into a mask that looked just like Julie's imitation of her mother in frosty politeness mode. "I don't think Pamela needs my help looking stupid," Julie said, then turned to walk away.

"I can't believe you! I can't believe you said that! You've been—none of us would be—you really do just care about the money, don't you? Pamela was right about people who write songs on the clock."

Sarah had backed off calling Julie a whore at the last minute, but she'd invoked Pamela calling Julie a whore, which might have even been better.

Julie whipped around, face red. "You know what?" she yelled—then, as if she'd heard herself yelling and been surprised, she closed her eyes, breathed deeply, and smiled a cold, hard smile at Sarah. "You know what, Sarah? I forgive you. If my boyfriend were alone with Pamela Sanchez, I'd be very worried too. I don't blame you for taking it out on me, because of course neither of them are here for you to take it out on. But don't worry. I'm sure nothing will happen between them."

Julie spun around, leaving Sarah alone and defeated in the hallway. Fuming, Sarah retreated to her practice room and kicked at the spongy soundproofing, punctuating each kick with a nasty word about that traitorous bitch. "Fucking! Uptight! Hypocritical! Bourgeois! Whore!" she yelled. The wall didn't respond, and Sarah felt stupid and out of control. She knew she should breathe, she should exhale all this negativity, but it was no longer gray smoke—it was white-hot lava that couldn't simply be breathed away.

She felt like everything she'd accomplished under Pamela's guidance had evaporated. Pamela had told her that she was transforming, leaving the caterpillar shell of her former self behind. "If you want to work with children because it's what you love and excel at," Pamela had said, "then it's a wonderful, noble calling. But if you are working with children in order to hide from adults, then you'll never fully be an adult."

That had stung, but it was the same way iodine stings in a cut—necessary, and healing.

And so she'd been trying to emerge from her cocoon, and she had certainly felt like it was working, that she'd changed an incredible amount in a relatively short time. With Peter, for the first time ever, she hadn't been shy about telling him what she wanted. Maybe he wasn't actually all that much better than anyone else she'd ever had—maybe it was just that she was better at speaking up for her pleasure, at being an active lover instead of a passive receptacle. And her songs had gotten so much better—she knew in her heart that she was growing and maturing as a songwriter, that working with Pamela was helping her become more fully herself and less a shadow of Pamela.

But here, now, in an afternoon, it had all come undone. She couldn't write a song, and the artist she was trying to become had just been rejected, and Julie, with her cruel beauty, had reminded Sarah of her own ugliness, of the fact that she was timid for a reason—because when you are unattractive and not talented, you can't make yourself vulnerable, because people will hurt you. As Julie had hurt her. And as Peter would hurt her when he came back and seemed distant and pulled away from her and pined after Pamela.

Sarah's scalp felt tingly, her palms were sweaty, and her heart was pounding. She was out of control, and she needed Peter to tell her she was beautiful again, she needed Pamela to tell her she could still write songs, she needed someone to pull her from the avalanche of doubt and self-loathing that was covering her, crushing her butterfly wings.

She wished she could call Peter or Pamela, but she didn't even know where they were! Well, she could try Pamela's house. She left the room and ran down the hall to the lounge to use the phone.

There, in the lounge, she saw Levon. "Hey, Sarah!" he said.

She just glared at him—of course he liked Julie, with her height, her blond hair, her little button nose always held high in the air. She picked up the phone and dialed Pamela's number. After ten rings, she gave up and slammed the receiver down. "Dammit!" she said aloud.

Levon, who was sitting on a couch picking a guitar and staring at her, said, "Uh, are you okay?"

Sarah spun around. "Do I look okay to you?"

Levon kept picking and did not miss a beat. "Nope. That's why I asked. I suppose I really should have said something like, *What's wrong*, but I was trying to be polite, you know. Sorry about that."

Sarah looked at Levon and felt bad. He hadn't done anything. Except sleep with Julie, and even Sarah didn't know what a two-faced backstabbing bitch Julie was until today. She wondered how people like that slept at night.

"I'm sorry," Sarah said. "I'm just—I'm really mad at *your girl-friend*, but that's not your fault."

Levon raised an eyebrow and put the guitar down. "I've got a girlfriend all the sudden?"

Sarah paced back and forth, eyeing the phone, eyeing the ele-vator doors, and occasionally glancing at Levon. "Don't be cute. You know what I mean."

"Hey, sister, I can't exactly help being cute. You'll have to take that up with the people who passed the genes on to me," Levon said, smiling.

"Funny," she said flatly.

"You smiled," Levon said. "Whatever Julie is to me, which, not that it's your business or anybody's, but whatever she is to me, it's not a girlfriend."

"But you . . . ," Sarah said, stopping.

"Sarah, did you go to college?" Levon said.

"Well, yeah, of course, you know that."

"So in your experience . . ." He paused. "Among girls you know, did you find that sleeping with somebody automatically made them his girlfriend?"

That sentence yanked open the file drawer of Sarah's memory and pulled out three or four painful memories from freshman year, before Sarah had figured the whole top-tier/bottom-tier thing out. "Not according to the guys, anyway. I was on the wrong end of that misunderstanding more than once." Sarah felt the pain and shame burning in her chest as though the wounds were fresh. After the third time, she'd gotten the message—I'm okay to fuck when you're drunk, but not okay to be seen with in the daytime—and what she hated more than anything was that knowing this hadn't prevented her from hoping the fourth time would be different.

"Well," Levon said, "there's no misunderstanding here. She's not my girlfriend. I'm not her boyfriend. End of story. And I am damn sure not going to be responsible for her pissing you off."

Sarah stopped pacing and looked at Levon. "I'm sorry. I really didn't—I'm just beside myself. She said awful things, and it really got to me. And I really thought she cared about what we were doing here, and she betrayed us all."

"Well, yes she did," Levon said, calmly, "but she spent the last three years making a living by pleasing the boss. People don't overcome their pasts in just a couple of weeks. Right? I mean, look at you."

"What do you mean?" Sarah said, ready to fight.

"I mean, when I met you and you said you were going to be a grade school teacher, you reminded me of Miss Keener from the fourth grade, who was this meek little white lady who cried when we were bad, so we started being bad just to see if we could make her cry."

"Thanks a lot!" Sarah said, and began to stomp away.

"Would you let me finish?" Levon yelled.

Sarah spun around, feeling like a cornered bear, and said, "What," in a tone that made it clear that she meant she would rip him to shreds if he dared to piss her off.

"What I was *trying* to say is that my first impression of you was wrong. You're not some mousy teacher—you're a sexy, talented artist, but here you are at the first setback getting all mousy again."

Sarah felt a big portion of rage drain out of her. Tears came to her eyes. "Oh," she said. "That's just so . . . that's the nicest thing anybody's ever said to me." She laughed. "I mean, not the part about me getting mousy again, which wasn't all that nice, even if it was true, but the other part. Thank you."

"It ain't nothing, which Julie would probably tell me is a double negative, but you know what I mean," Levon said, smiling.

Before Sarah could savor the warm feeling of being the recipient of kindness, the elevator doors opened, Peter walked in, and Sarah was filled with cold fear again.

He walked toward her. "Hey, beautiful," he said. He kissed her, but she didn't kiss him back. He pulled away and handed her a bouquet of daffodils. "I know you like yellow," he said.

Without saying anything, Sarah walked away. "Uh . . . hello?" she heard Peter calling after her.

She walked into the practice room and closed the door. Peter came running after her, still holding the daffodils. "Um, what's going on?"

"I should ask you the same question," Sarah said as coldly as she could.

Peter looked shocked. "What are you talking about?" he said.

"Peter, you've never bought me flowers before. Why are you buying me flowers?"

"Because I love you! Jesus! I never bought you anything before, because I've never gotten paid before! Did you notice me stealing food for the last three weeks?"

"You smell like Pamela. I smelled her when you kissed me. Why do you smell like Pamela? Did something happen?"

Peter hesitated for less than a second, probably only a quarter of a second, not very much time, not really, but it was a tiny bit of time that Sarah knew was the time his guilty, racing brain took to compose a lie. "No! Nothing happened! We went to her apartment, we talked about songwriting, she made me tea, we smoked

a joint! She doesn't exactly have a light touch with the perfume—
I mean, come on, baby, you've been to her apartment. You know
everybody walks out of there smelling like pot smoke and her
perfume."

"Don't call me baby. Do not call me baby. I am not an infant. I
am not some cranky infant to be soothed and placated with your
lies. I am a woman. You do not call me baby. Not now. Not ever
again." Sarah spat these words out, turned on her heel, and
walked out, leaving Peter stewing in his guilt. Baby. He was lucky
she hadn't killed him for that.

"You didn't mind me calling you that last night!" Peter yelled
out.

"That was before I knew you," Sarah said. She ignored Levon's
staring, pushed the button, and got into the elevator.

OUTSIDE, MIDTOWN WAS beginning to empty out as people
headed for bridges and tunnels and subway stations. Sarah
joined a throng heading underground and got on the first downtown train that came by. She didn't know what she was going to
say when she got to Pamela's place. She couldn't believe that
Pamela and Peter would both betray her, and yet why was
Pamela getting Peter high? And why was Peter lying? God, he
was such a bad liar. He really should take lessons from Julie.

Sarah stood wedged between two tall men in gray suits. She
looked around the car and saw a really skinny unshaven white
guy darting his weaselly eyes around. When they landed on her,
Sarah looked right through him. You junkie bastard, she thought.
You try to rob me, I'm gonna give you a fix like you won't believe.
I'll give you a straight shot of pure rage, imported straight from
my guts. I am not afraid of you.

The junkie looked away. A black guy with a huge Afro stood
four people away from her and looked over the car with a heavy-

lidded, predatory gaze. Sarah stared at him until he looked away. Not tonight, she thought. I'm not your victim tonight. I am woman, hear me roar, feel me kick.

Someone, she thought, is going to get hurt tonight. She wondered who it was going to be. The only thing she knew was that it wasn't going to be her.

She shoved her way out of the car when it reached the stop near Pamela's place. What was she going to say? She had to know what happened, because everything hinged on that. If Peter and Pamela had slept together, she was done with Peter, and after she murdered Pamela, she would have to quit the project, and there she would be with no job and no apartment, no music career, no teaching career, no friends, nothing, nothing at all. She'd have to run home to her parents like a little kid, like the little lost girl she was.

As she walked down the street, Sarah wondered how she had let it come to this in such a short time. Just a few weeks ago, she had a future and a life all planned out, and if she was letting her dreams die, at least she could look forward to having a normal life where she had a job and some nice co-workers and an apartment and maybe a boyfriend she saw only on weekends. Now her career, her social life, even the roof over her head depended on a man keeping it in his pants. She asked herself Levon's sarcastic question: Did you go to college?

She reached Pamela's door and rang the bell. No one answered. She rang again. This time, a sleepy voice said, "Hello? Who is it?"

"It's Sarah."

"Come on up," Pamela's voice said. The door buzzed, and Sarah ran up the stairs. At the top of the stairs, she saw a slightly disheveled Pamela, attired only in a silk robe, standing in the door.

"Sarah," Pamela said. "What brings you here?"

What makes you need a nap at this hour, Sarah wanted to ask. Did he wear you out? Instead, she just said, "I need to know what happened."

Pamela looked puzzled. "I'm sorry, honey, I really don't know what you mean."

"With Peter. Did something happen? He was . . . just tell me what happened."

Pamela sighed and looked sad. "Dear, please come in and have a cup of tea."

Sarah wanted to just let Pamela take charge of the situation, because lurking behind the angry woman scorned was a sad, tired, scared little girl who was hurting and just wanted some-body to make it better. But she couldn't give in. Not yet. "I . . . I'm really sorry, Pamela, but I can't . . . I can't even come in to the apartment until I know what happened."

Pamela sighed again. "Okay. We . . . we took a taxi down here, and we were talking about songwriting. I was feeling out of bal-ance, as you can imagine, after our encounter with Clark this af-ternoon, and especially Julie's betrayal of the whole project and process . . ." Just tell me if you slept with him, Sarah thought, I don't care about anything else.

"And," Pamela continued, "so I rolled a joint, and of course I had to share, and before I knew it, Peter was talking about what happened back at Antioch—"

"What happened? What happened at Antioch? What are you talking about?" Sarah was yelling, and though she'd asked the question three times, she already knew the answer. She knew what happened at Antioch. Dammit! She'd been so stupid! How could she ever think she was going to be an elementary school teacher when she didn't have as much common sense as a six-year-old?

"Oh. Oh dear. I'm so sorry, dear, I just assumed he would have told you. When I played at Antioch a few years ago, Peter was a student there, and we . . . were together."

"Oh God" was all Sarah could say before her stomach clenched. She hunched over and vomited, mostly a yellowish, watery mess, since she hadn't eaten since breakfast. She knelt before Pamela, vomit pouring from her mouth, stomach acid burning as strings of vomit dripped from her nostrils.

"Oh God," Sarah finally said, "you slept with him. How could you do that to me? How could you?"

"Darling, Peter and I were together years ago. Long before either of us knew you."

"But . . . ," Sarah said, but that was the only thing she could say before she started to cry. She wiped the vomit from her mouth with her sleeve and cried. "But . . . ," she choked out, "you said . . ."

"Sweetheart. Please come in and let me make you tea."

"No! Tell me the end of the goddamn story!"

"Okay, honey. You know I would never have told you this . . . I never wanted to hurt you."

"What? Tell me what?"

"He mentioned . . . the time we were together, and I told him that that was a long time ago, and he . . . he kissed me. And I asked him to leave. And he did. And that is the end of the story."

Sarah looked up at Pamela, and Pamela held out a hand to her. "Stand up, sweetie. It's okay."

Sarah got to her feet with Pamela's help and collapsed against her, crying. "It's not okay," she said, "it's not. I thought he . . . I . . . oh God, I'm such an idiot! How could I not see? How could I not know who he really was? Oh God, I thought I loved him!" Pamela enfolded her in a hug, and Sarah rested her head on Pamela's shoulder and cried and cried.

18

LEVON

EVON SAT ON the couch with an acoustic guitar, picking out notes from Booker T. & the MG's' "Green Onions." He thought wistfully that it was really more of a keyboard-driven song, and it would sound much better if Julie were here to add a keyboard part. He sighed.

He'd watched Sarah pace around the basement and counted himself lucky that he hadn't been five minutes later sneaking into the basement in his interview suit, because then he probably would have had to endure some of her rage as well. She had come completely unhinged.

And now Peter was pacing. "I mean, what the hell! We just . . . everything we've been through, and she just completely lost her mind!"

"Pete," Levon said, "what have you been through, really? A few weeks together."

"Yeah," Peter said, "but they were really intense weeks, and I thought we had a connection! You know? I mean, I thought it was more than . . . aaah, well, forget it. Obviously it wasn't."

He paced. Levon plucked, and smiled as he realized that Peter was walking in time to his rendition of "Green Onions." It was none of his business, but he was curious, and he did think Peter would tell him. "So did you?"

Peter stopped and looked at him. "Did I what?"

"Did you do Pamela?"

"No! Jesus! No! That's what kills me! I mean, I could have, you know—well, you know, obviously. I mean, I could have, and Sarah would have been like this, and that would have been only fair. But I didn't!"

"That's a shame," Levon said.

"Well, maybe. I don't know. I mean, I did sleep with Pamela, but it was years ago, when I was in college, and she was touring."

Levon stopped plucking. "No shit. How was it?"

"Well, it was my first time, so . . ." Peter started blushing.

"Little Speedy Alka-Seltzer," Levon said, laughing.

This drew a smile from Peter, who responded, "Nestlé Quik. But that was years ago. I didn't feel like I had anything to prove, and what I have, or, I suppose I should have with Sarah was really . . . I don't know, special, I guess . . . hey, do we have any liquor down here?"

"Did you drink all the gin we got from Walker Wallace's dressing room?"

"No. Where is it?"

"I think it's in the fridge. Behind a big bowl of brown rice."

Peter rummaged in the fridge. "Fucking brown rice," he said. He pulled out the bottle of gin, grabbed a plastic cup from the cabinet, and poured. "You want some?"

"No thank you," Levon said. "My folks are coming into the city to take me out to dinner."

Peter froze. "Whoa. That's nice. I mean, that's really nice. I kinda wish . . . well, I'm just really far away from my folks." He took a big drink from the tumbler of gin.

"Shit," Peter said, taking another big swig of gin. "This whole thing is completely messed up."

"On that we agree, my friend," Levon said. He glanced at his watch. "Whoa. Shit, I gotta get changed and go meet my folks. You take it easy on the gin there. You'll be okay." He debated saying that Peter was better off without a crazy bitch like that, but then if they got back together, it would be awkward.

Though it was certainly possible that he wouldn't be around for very long anyway. He got changed and took a taxi to the steak restaurant. His parents were waiting outside. They hugged him, and Mom said, "I am so proud of you for not giving up. You are a strong man, just like your father."

Levon couldn't help looking around to see if anybody else heard. What was it about being with his parents that made him seventeen again? The maître d' led them back into the restaurant. It was dark, with oak paneling on the walls. Each round table had its own dim light. The tables were covered with white tablecloths, and there were cloth napkins folded into water glasses. They were seated, and Levon and his mom spent the first minute at the table convincing Dad that they hadn't gotten a shitty table because they were black, they'd gotten a shitty table because they'd called at the last minute. "We're lucky to get a table at all," Mom said.

"Don't you teach my son that attitude," Dad said.

"Oh goodness, James, all I meant was that we were lucky to get a table because we called so late."

"I know," Dad said, grinning. "I was making a joke! Don't you know a joke when you hear one?"

"Now, since when have you ever made a joke about something like that?" Mom asked.

"Since my son had a great interview with a big engineering company!" Dad said, just a little too loud. Levon looked around the restaurant guiltily before realizing that there was no way that anybody connected with *Pop Goes the Classroom*, with the possible exception of Clark Payson, would be eating here.

People at a couple of other tables did look over and smile. "Better get used to eating steak," Dad said. "That's all they eat in Texas."

Levon rolled his eyes. "Okay, Dad."

The waiter brought rolls, and Dad ordered a bottle of wine that cost fifteen dollars. He really was splurging, and it made Levon nervous. "You know, Dad, I don't have the job yet."

"You'll get the job, don't worry," Dad said.

The wine came, and the waiter poured a little bit for Dad to taste. "Are you gonna present the cork?" Dad said.

"Oh, I'm sorry, sir," the waiter said. "It completely slipped my mind."

"It slipped your mind?" Dad said. "You just present the cork. It's an essential part of serving the wine. That's like forgetting to pour it."

The waiter looked flustered, and Levon tipped his head down and covered his eyes with his hands. "James," Mom was saying.

"I'm very sorry, sir," the waiter said.

Dad looked like he was about to unleash another lecture about serving wine, but instead he just sipped, swished it around in his mouth, and swallowed. They all waited while Dad very theatrically examined and sniffed the cork. "It's good," Dad said.

"Very good, sir," the waiter said, and he poured for all of them. It occurred to Levon that he should have told his dad no, he didn't want to go out, he really missed Mom's cooking, but Dad was so proud, so insistent, that he couldn't say no to him. And now he was enduring Dad being embarrassing, which was a pretty high price for a free steak dinner. Still, Levon thought it was worth it just to see his dad's face so full of pride, his whole body looking like he was about to explode with joy.

"So tell me about the interview," Mom said.

"Well," Levon said, "they've been around making components for years, but they're just moving into making stuff for the consumer market. They're putting out a calculator—it's like a little electronic adding machine, but it also subtracts and divides and multiplies—and they're already at work on the next one, which is going to have a lot more functions. It's really amazing stuff. I mean, when I think about the stuff I did with a slide rule, and probably in twenty years every college student will carry one of these things around and won't even recognize a slide rule."

Mom beamed at him, and they ate steak that nearly melted in their mouths, and at the end of the evening Levon felt better than he had in weeks. This wasn't just because he'd been fed properly; it was because he'd been dreading a confrontation that now never had to happen.

He hugged his parents good-bye and returned to ATN. Peter was passed out on the couch in the lounge, so Levon went back to the practice room. He picked up his bass and started playing Supersonic Funketeer songs and thought. He probably would have left anyway, even if he was having a wonderful time, but the fact was, he'd been feeling like this whole thing was a mistake. Who the hell was the boss, anyway? And he knew that Clark Payson had been right about how the songs weren't working for the project, but he'd gone along with it anyway, just because everybody else was, and now he was wishing he'd had the guts to play one of his good songs like Julie did.

But it was a lot easier to piss off the boss—or whoever the hell Pamela was, since it looked like Clark was the boss—when you were not the only black person on the staff.

More important than this, though, more important even than

displeasing his parents, there was the fact that he just wasn't having any fun with the music. Music had always been his escape from all the stress and problems of the rest of his life, a wonderful sonic space he could escape into, and now all of his problems—Pamela's insistent come-ons, what to do about Julie, how to make his parents proud of him, everything—it was all wrapped up in the music. Which just made it less fun. All the songs he'd written in the last week contained all of his uncertainty and fear, so playing them didn't release him from it.

He'd rather work in an office all day helping to make little calculators and play once a month in a half-assed funk band than continue to suck the joy out of his favorite thing by doing it for a living.

LEVON FELL ASLEEP and awoke to the sound of yodeling. Sleepy-eyed, he staggered down the hall to Peter's practice room.

"What the fuck is that?" he said.

Peter turned around. "It's 'Long Gone Lonesome Blues.' It's Hank Williams."

"You're yodeling. What are you, the fucking Swiss Miss?"

Peter laughed. "Yes. I am the fucking Swiss Miss. No, I just have to play country music when I'm sad."

Levon pried his eyelids open and looked at Peter. "So why do you have to wake me up with it? Yodeling. Shit." He turned and walked away, and heard Peter's apology coming down the hall. Well, he wasn't thinking clearly.

Levon showered and dressed and returned to the lounge. The phone rang, and, heart pounding, he picked it up. "Hello?"

It was his mom. "Baby, they called! They called! Call them back right now!"

"Okay, Mom, okay, I will. I'll call you in a few minutes." He went back to the practice room and pulled out the roll of dimes he'd gotten when he cashed his check. He ran out to the street and found a phone booth.

Once inside, he called Thomas Long, from Dallas Technology. "Mr. Hayes!" Thomas Long said. "Great to hear from you! So to make a long story short, we'd like to offer you the job!"

"Fantastic! I'll take it!"

"Wonderful. We're doing some really exciting things, and I'm sure you'll be a great addition to our team. We'll pay for your move to Dallas, of course, and we've got an apartment you can stay in until you find a place of your own. Do you think you can get your stuff together to be down here in two weeks? We're on a deadline with the new project, and we need all the help we can get."

Levon thought about his stuff, piled in a corner of the practice room in the basement at ATN. Yeah, he thought, I can probably manage to get it all together in a week. "Yes. Shouldn't be a problem."

"Wonderful. I'll send you some plane tickets, and you can be in touch with Shirley, my secretary, she'll be arranging the move."

"Thank you. Thank you so much!"

"Thank you. You're going to make us a better company."

Damn right I am, Levon thought. They said good-bye, and Levon gave his parents' address for the moving truck to come to next week. Then he called his mom back and heard how wonderful he was again. Mom insisted he call Dad at work, so he did, and Dad actually started to cry while he was on the phone. "I'm so proud of you," Dad said, "I'm so proud that you're my son." Well, that was a hell of a lot better than the *I'm going to be a musician* conversation ever would have turned out. He glided back to ATN.

When he got into the basement, Levon looked around the

lounge. Peter had disappeared, and the lounge was empty and bathed in dim red light. It was going to be such a relief to get into an office with bright fluorescent lights and not feel like such a mole man down here.

He opened the fridge. Brown rice and booze. The fact that there was actually some booze left was a good sign—it suggested that Peter had taken his advice and was doing more yodeling and less boozing. As long as the door was closed, the yodeling was pretty harmless.

Levon wandered down the hallway to Julie's practice room and knocked on the door. It opened a crack, and then Julie smiled and opened it all the way. "Hey," she said, smiling. "Come on in."

"Hey there, Benedict Arnold," Levon said to Julie.

"You know what?" Julie barked. "If you came in here just to give me shit, you can just—"

"Whoa whoa whoa," Levon said, "I was joking!"

"Well, it's not funny," Julie said, and then she collapsed against him, crying. "I just didn't know what to do! I mean, I couldn't go in and play some piece-of-crap song for the guy who hired me! I mean, there—she acts like she's some kind of big pure artist, but why the hell is she here? Do you think for one minute she gives a shit about the youth of America? She's here to make money!"

"Hey now," Levon said. "That's not fair. She's also here to record her new album for free." Julie looked up at him and laughed, wiping her tears away. "Anyway, I'm gonna join you on the wrong side of the fence. Actually, I think pretty much everybody but Sarah is on the wrong side of the fence these days anyway."

"What do you mean?"

"Well, you could see how pissed she was at Dingo, and Sarah let Peter have it right after she let you have it—"

"But what about you?"

Levon debated whether to tell her. It wasn't that he didn't trust her, it was just that getting the job felt like it belonged to another world, another life, a life that wasn't going to include anyone from here, and he wanted to keep it for himself. Not because he cared if anybody knew, but because he liked having this information belong to him alone, and to share it with anybody from this fucked-up environment might contaminate it.

But then again, if there was anybody here he was close to, it was Julie. Even though they'd established many times that they weren't boyfriend and girlfriend, the sex kept happening, and Levon felt himself getting attached. Another good reason to run away to Texas.

"I . . . well, I . . . it's kind of a secret."

"What is it?"

"I'm leaving. I got a job . . . I mean, a real job, you know, one I can actually tell my dad about. So I'm starting in two weeks."

Julie pulled away and turned her back to him. "Great," she said. "Fantastic. So you're leaving."

"Yes," Levon said.

"To get a *real* job." Uh-oh. He'd heard that tone from enough girls to know he'd just stepped in something, just said something innocuous that had pissed her off to the core. He'd been stupid to try to include her in anything from his other life, his real life. He took a deep breath and worked very hard trying not to roll his eyes. This was the kind of thing that made having a girlfriend a pain in the ass. You had to spend hours groveling and trying to convince them that whatever weird interpretation they'd just put on your words actually had nothing to do with what you meant, and if you managed to get them to calm down and stop crying, they'd be too upset to have sex anyway. The hell with that.

"So you've basically just said that the way I've chosen to spend my life, the career I've chosen, isn't *real*. You find yourself singing my commercials all day long, but my work isn't *real*. No, not like the square root of negative one. Now, *that's* real."

Levon knew the boyfriend drill at this point was to say, No, baby, I didn't mean that at all, I think your work is important, blah blah blah. But he wasn't her boyfriend. Which meant he didn't even have to have the fight at all. He said nothing and turned and walked out while Julie was still talking.

Levon wondered what he should do. He'd written a few good songs, but he guessed he should probably write a couple more, just so he wouldn't feel too guilty about leaving with the work undone. He wasn't feeling particularly inspired right now, at least musically. He already had one foot in Dallas Technology. He went back to the lounge and thought about making small calculators. He sat next to a lamp draped in a red scarf. He looked at it for a long minute, and then he tore the scarf off the lamp and went over and stuffed it deep into the kitchen trash. "I've had enough of red and dim," he said aloud to nobody. "How about some light on the subject?"

The one lamp casting yellowish white light looked out of place in a lounge with three other red lamps, so Levon went and trashed another scarf. The other two lamps had red bulbs, so nothing could be done about those yet, but he might even go out and buy some nice white bulbs so they wouldn't have to sit in this room that looked like a whorehouse anymore.

He started thinking about how electric lights made it possible to work in a windowless basement, made skyscrapers possible, made Dallas Technology possible . . . it all came back to Edison. There had to be a song in there somewhere.

Half an hour of picking and frantic scribbling later, he was nearly done with "Some Light on the Subject" when Peter came shambling into the lounge. He looked like complete shit, but Levon decided not to inform him of that. Instead he just watched as Peter headed to the fridge, opened it, said, "Goddamn brown rice," and closed it.

"What are you doing?" Peter said.

"Writing a song about Edison," Levon said. "What about you?"

"Writing a song about the Louisiana Purchase," Peter said.

"You done yodeling for the day?"

"Yeah, I played pretty much every Hank Williams song I know, and I ended up playing 'Jambalaya,' which isn't really my favorite, because it's a little too upbeat, but anyway, that got me thinking that you couldn't really have big fun on the bye-yo and stay in the United States if it weren't for good old Thomas Jefferson . . ."

"Slave owner."

Peter stopped. "Well, yeah, but . . ."

"Who raped his slaves."

"I thought it was just the one, but okay. How about immoral old Thomas Jefferson and the Lousiana Purchase."

Levon smiled. "Cool."

"Hey," Peter said. "Let's go see if Dingo wants to record these."

"You think yours is ready? Because mine sure isn't. And anyway, I don't think Julie's speaking to me, so no piano, and Pamela and Sarah aren't here."

"Hey man, guitar, bass, and drums is all you need!" Peter said.

"Well, what the hell," Levon said. "Not like we have a lot of other stuff to do. But what if Pamela comes back?"

"Fuck Pamela!" Peter said.

They looked at each other for a minute, and then they both started laughing. "I'm considering it," Levon said.

In the studio, Dingo nearly hugged them when they suggested recording something.

"Thank you," Dingo said. "I am so bored I'm starting to hallucinate."

The next time Levon looked at the clock, it felt like five minutes later, but two hours had passed, and they had completed what Levon thought were pretty decent takes of "Some Light on the Subject" and "I'll Take One of Those," and while they were playing, Levon felt that familiar feeling—he was just here, having fun, not worrying about anything, just lost in the thrill of making music. It was like the three of them had just stepped outside of time somewhere, made music, and been transported back.

Dingo was grinning like a maniac, and Levon, for the first time, felt a big stone of sadness in his stomach. He was giving this up. He would have money, and respect, and probably a feeling of accomplishment at Dallas Technology, but what he wouldn't get was this feeling. It would be a great job, but it would never be magical.

"All right!" Dingo said. "First actual work we've gotten done here in over a week! Who wants a beer?"

"Me," Levon and Peter said together.

"Great," Dingo said. "Pete, you get the hell out of your pajamas and meet us in the lounge. I'll take you guys out of this hole in the ground."

Half an hour later the three of them were seated at the bar in a dingy, smoke-filled hole-in-the-wall.

The first pitcher was dedicated to Sarah, as Peter went on in boring detail about his heartbreak. Levon, his tongue appropriately loose from the beer, said, "Pete, man, you need to forget that crazy bitch. What are you, twenty-four? There's plenty more girls out there."

Peter looked at Levon, and Levon was afraid that Peter might take his anger out on him, but instead he just looked sad. "I know! But I can't forget her just because she's a crazy bitch! I mean, shit, they're all crazy! Might as well find a crazy one you can connect with."

Dingo snorted beer out of his nose laughing, and Peter turned to him and said, "What? Am I wrong, O wise family man?"

The smile disappeared from Dingo's face with what looked like pretty significant effort on his part. "I . . . I really don't think I can get into this, guys."

"Come on, Dingo!" Levon said. "How long you been married?"

"Fifteen years," Dingo said, and drained his glass of beer. "Hey, how about another pitcher over here?" he called out to the bartender, an ancient white man with a red vest on over a dingy white shirt.

"So what's the verdict, then? Is this worth saving, or should he just find another one?"

Levon and Peter both looked at Dingo, who smiled. "Well, I don't know enough about the particulars of this situation," he said, "but I think you're both right. I mean, on the one hand, it's worth fighting for something special, and yes, they are all crazy, but there's crazy and then there's *crazy*. I mean, there's crazy like the way they'll see that sock you left on the floor as proof that you don't appreciate them, and then there's burn-your-house-down crazy. You can't avoid the first kind, but you need to get the hell away from the second kind as fast as you can."

This response left Levon convinced that he was right, but he could tell by looking at Peter's face that it left Peter thinking he was right. Dingo smiled and sipped his beer.

"Okay then," Peter said, "should Levon sleep with Pamela?"

Dingo looked at him in surprise. "You mean you haven't yet?"

Levon shook his head. Dingo looked to Peter. "You?"

"Well, five years ago, but not this year."

Dingo shook his head slowly. "She's really slipping. How the hell should I know if he should sleep with her? I mean, obviously nobody should go into that situation expecting to be her boyfriend or even her musical protégé or anything. As long as you go into the situation with your eyes open, I guess there's no harm in it."

"Well, I got Peter's review," Levon said, "but what about you?"

Dingo looked puzzled. "My review? Of what?"

Levon took another sip of beer. "Of Pamela."

Dingo looked at Levon and said, "I can't speak about that from personal experience. I've been married for fifteen years."

Levon looked at Peter, and they both looked at Dingo. "Fifteen years on the road, and you never . . ."

Dingo shook his head. "I made a promise."

"But, I mean, you must have had girls just throwing themselves at you," Peter said.

"I didn't say I never wanted to," Dingo said, "I just said I never did."

"But *why not?*" Peter said, like the idea was unbelievable to him. Actually, when Levon thought about the kinds of propositions he got whenever he played with the Supersonic Funketeers, the idea of turning that down every night for fifteen years, especially if you were drunk or high, did seem pretty incredible.

"Because when you find the right one, you don't do that to them. I mean, I was young when I got married, but not too young to know I got really, really lucky. I see the way single guys my age live. It's pathetic. There is no pussy on earth worth throwing a good life away for. And besides, Cass is—besides everything else, she's my friend. And you don't treat your friends like that. You make a promise, you're supposed to keep it. And yeah, you're only human, and shit happens, but that's all an excuse. It never just happens. You make a decision to shit on somebody you care about just so you can get somebody else to do for you what you can do for yourself."

There was a pause as Dingo's serious words settled into their brains, but Levon was too buzzed to stop himself from saying, "Damn, Dingo, you can suck your own dick?"

Peter and Dingo laughed, and then Peter got up. "I gotta go. I gotta talk to her," he said. "Thanks, Dingo. Thanks for everything. I'll see you tomorrow."

Peter left, Dingo and Levon drank their beers, and Levon said, "Now, that guy is seriously pussy-whipped."

"Yep," Dingo said. "And if you're lucky, you will be too, one day."

"Damn, Dingo, you are the fountain of wisdom today," Levon said.

"Every day, my friend, every day. It's just that people so rarely choose to drink."

"Okay then," Levon said. "Let me ask you this. Do you ever— do you feel like doing this for a living has ruined it for you? I mean, I . . ." For just a second, Levon considered spilling the beans: I'm trading a life of coolness for about the squarest environment you can imagine, I'm about to kill my chances of being a professional musician, and all I want to know is if I'm making the right choice. Instead he just went with, "I had fun whenever I played with Calvin. I mean, there was work, you know, but it was always fun. But the last few days, with all this bullshit going on, it hasn't been that fun for me. It just feels like another job."

Dingo took a long drink and finally said, "Every once in a while, I get together with the guys I first started playing with in high school. Howard and the Hot Rods." Levon snorted, trying to hold back laughter, and Dingo said, "Yeah. Well, that was one reason that band never made it big. Anyway, we get together once in a while and play 'Hard Headed Woman' and 'Ooby Dooby' and 'Flying Saucer Rock and Roll,' and those are the only times I love playing music. Every other time, it's a fun job, but it's still a job. It beats the hell out of what most of the other guys are doing—Howard is a roofer, and his knees are shot to shit, he's broke every winter and sunburned every summer—so it's better than any other job, as far as I'm concerned. Although Ed, our bassist, is a plumber, and he makes shitloads of money—more than the rest of us combined. But it's still a job."

Levon thought that over. It seemed kind of tragic. Like if you did something you really loved for money, that would make you stop loving it. Well, the fountain of wisdom came through again. He was making the right choice. Now he just had to figure out who to tell and when to tell them. Well, maybe he'd go straight to the top and give Clark Payson his two weeks' notice. Because at the end of the day, whatever anybody else pretended, this was just a job. He wasn't part of some elite squad of world-saving jingle writers or anything. He was a guy who needed food money before his engineering job came through. And so he owed the boss a real resignation, because that was professional. But as for everybody else—well, just like he didn't have to try to talk Julie out of a tantrum for some unintentional slight if she wasn't his girlfriend, he didn't have to listen to two weeks of *How can you betray us, how can you abandon the most important cartoons ever made* if he wasn't really saving the world.

He thought about how naïve he'd been just a few weeks ago, how he really had believed that they were engaged in something important, something that was going to change both his life and the world. It was kind of sad to give that up, but, more than that, it was a huge relief.

19

JULIE

JULIE WAS ALONE in the basement. She knew that Dingo and Peter and Levon had been recording, and she was jealous. She really wanted to record too.

She clearly had a lot of work to do before she could ever hope to approach Elizabeth's level of proficiency. She'd cut Sarah off at the knees by being calm and merciless, and Elizabeth certainly would have been proud of that, but then she'd gone home and not slept at all, feeling horrible about hurting Sarah, who was confused and hurt already and whom Julie had really considered a friend. The remorse was not Elizabeth at all. Or else maybe killing the memory of being awful to someone was one reason Elizabeth drank so much.

Nah. She really didn't think Elizabeth ever felt remorse, and Julie did, which is why she'd never win a fight with her mom and she'd never be as good at this stuff as she aspired to be.

She was already sleep-deprived and fragile when Levon announced that he was leaving because he needed to get a real job. And then he'd walked out before she could fully explain to him what an asshole he was.

So she'd attacked the piano with a vengeance. She had now written songs for every part of speech, and if "Darren's Gerunds" and "The Principle of Participles" were maybe a little on the obscure side, she felt satisfied that she'd covered pretty much every kind of word there was. And she really wanted to get some more of them recorded.

But the studio was empty, and anyway, she didn't want to record anything with Levon right now. Especially because he was right. This wasn't a real job. That's why everybody hated her. At a real job, you do your work and you get paid and you try to please the boss so you can keep getting paid, and that was all she'd done.

But at this job, apparently, you were supposed to get high all the time, and find your passion, and blur the lines between your work and the rest of your life, and also have sex with your co-workers right there in your workplace. No, this wasn't a real job by any stretch of the imagination.

Maybe she should apologize to Levon. But he'd walked out on her! He was the one who should apologize.

Why did he have to leave? She didn't want him to leave! How could he leave her? Just because they'd both said that this was just casual, nothing serious, could never be serious? Well, maybe he'd actually meant it. Julie thought she had too, but if she had, why would she be feeling so betrayed that he was leaving?

She opened the door and walked out into the hallway. She peeked into the studio and saw no one. She tapped on the door of Peter's practice room and heard nothing in response. She walked past Levon's door three times, then finally knocked swiftly and hard. He didn't answer. Pamela was not holding court in the lounge, and she suspected that she was keeping Sarah on a short leash, so Sarah wouldn't be around anyway. Not that she deserved an apology.

It was three thirty. Realizing she wasn't going to get any more songs written today, Julie decided to go home.

Simone bent into a circle when Julie got home, and Julie bent down and rubbed Simone's head. "Yes. You still love me, don't you, baby? Yes. Simone still loves me." They went out to the park, and while it was relaxing to just be walking around green space with Simone, Julie felt wistful. Back when she'd worked at McMahon & Tate, she'd walked Simone on a rigid schedule, and she'd seen the same people day after day. She didn't know any of their phone numbers or last names, but she had gotten used to seeing them every day, and she missed them. Here she was at four—a full hour and a half before she ever used to come out. Well, tomorrow morning she'd make sure to come out at seven thirty, just like she used to, and maybe she'd see Karen and Ben and Amy and Ruth and Leroy again, and Simone would see Buster and Wilson and Apollo and Seamus, and things would start getting back to normal.

Well, Simone's life would get a little more normal, anyway. Julie would still be stuck in some bizarre music commune in the basement at ATN. She had money saved, but not enough that she felt comfortable chucking the whole thing and being unemployed. Besides, she'd placed a pretty big career bet on Clark Payson, and if she abandoned him before the project was complete, she would probably be burning the television bridge, and she might have a hard time explaining to an ad agency why she'd quit McMahon & Tate and couldn't get a reference from ATN.

She was trapped. She felt awfully young to be trapped. Leaving the park, a little light-skinned black boy wearing a Superman T-shirt approached her and Simone tentatively, while a tall, dark-skinned woman pushing a baby carriage looked on. "He bites?" the kid asked.

"No," Julie said. "She doesn't bite. She's actually very nice. Would you like to pet her?"

"It's a she?"

"Yeah. Here, just hold your hand out like this—" Julie held her hand in front of Simone's mouth, and the little kid did the same. Simone gave the kid's hand a sniff and then received some very light, very tentative pats. Julie looked at the mom and figured she was about her age. She looked at the dark-skinned mom and the light-skinned kid and wondered if this mom was some road-not-taken version of herself. See, you did it, she thought, you didn't let the obstacles stand in your way, you started a family, you let love conquer all.

Not me, Julie thought. Not me. Of course, she wasn't actually in love with Levon, and he certainly wasn't in love with her, and they probably never would have been. But they'd never given themselves a chance to find out. They'd looked at the first hurdle, declared it too high, and not even tried to jump. Cowards.

"She's nice," the kid said.

"Yeah," Julie said. "She really is. She's a good girl."

"Okay, Albert, let's go," the mom said, then smiled at Julie and said, "Thanks!"

"Oh, you're welcome. Simone always likes making new friends."

Julie walked home. She looked around her apartment where nothing smelled like pot, there were no red scarves on lightbulbs, and natural light flooded through the windows. It felt huge, which was partly because of the light, but also because the air wasn't stuffy with anger and jealousy and hurt, and she felt like she could actually breathe.

The only problem was that it also felt quiet and empty and boring. Julie grabbed today's unread *Times* off the kitchen table and saw that a new Catherine Deneuve movie was playing downtown. Perfect. Maybe Catherine Deneuve—blond and impossibly beautiful but, even in that prostitute movie, always classy and elegant—maybe she could give Julie a little encouragement. And maybe there would be interesting people there.

There were plenty of interesting people there, and they were all couples—mostly young, college-student-looking couples, but also a few older, better-dressed couples out getting a little dose of European culture.

Unfortunately, the movie was weird—some guy treated Deneuve like a dog, down to leashing and collaring her, and Deneuve on her hands and knees wearing a leash wasn't exactly the classy role model Julie was looking for tonight.

The movie left her cold, but it quite obviously heated up some of the couples coming out of the movie theater, and this made Julie's cab ride back uptown feel especially long and lonely. When she got home, Julie had a hard time quieting the voices of Sarah and Levon in her mind. She really didn't want to keep replaying those scenes all night. She made herself a gin and tonic, hoping it would help her sleep.

It did. She woke up with a really dry mouth at quarter to eight. Simone jumped up when Julie got out of bed, and Julie realized she'd missed getting Simone back on her normal walk schedule. Dammit. She really couldn't do anything right.

After walking Simone and seeing nobody, Julie returned to ATN, and, feet feeling like lead, she stepped off the elevator into the basement.

Nobody was in the lounge, so she wandered down to the studio. Peter and Levon were sitting there with Dingo.

Well, Julie thought, if we're not boyfriend and girlfriend, then there's no reason for this to be the least bit awkward, so I'm just going to pretend it's not.

"Hey, everybody," she said brightly. "What's up?"

"We're going to try to record some stuff," Peter said.

"Great!" Julie said. "Can I play?"

"Of course," Dingo said. "I promised Levon we'd do one of his first. You got anything ready to go?"

"Tons of stuff," Julie said. "I've kind of been on a tear lately."

"Great," Dingo said as he adjusted a microphone stand. "Give me about five minutes here. Maybe Levon can teach you the new song, and we'll see if there's a piano part in there somewhere."

Dingo bustled off to turn some knobs in the booth, leaving Julie alone with Peter and Levon. "Well," Peter said, putting his guitar down, "I'm, uh . . ." He looked at both Julie and Levon and started backing away " . . . bathroom. Seeya."

And so they were alone. Julie supposed that if this were a love affair, if it were anything more than two people grabbing each other in the dark, this would be where she begged him not to go, or something. She said nothing for a minute, then said, "Sorry."

Levon looked up. "Me too. Ready to learn a song?"

"Okay," Julie said. She sat at the piano and listened as Levon played, following him on the piano. Julie smiled. She guessed this was their "we'll always have Paris" moment, but it was more like, "we'll always have catchy little songs about grade school curricula." Not quite as poetic, but as they went through the song a second time, Julie felt good. Whatever else was or was not happening here, the act of making music felt uncomplicated and good. Peter came back, looked from Julie to Levon, sat down, and started to play.

They heard Dingo's voice from the booth. "That sounds great, guys. Let's do it with me and put it on tape."

Dingo emerged, sat behind the kit, and propelled them through a perfect take of Levon's "Gravity Got Me Down." He disappeared into the booth again, and before he could give them the verdict on the playback, Pamela and Sarah walked in.

Well, it was actually more like gliding. Pamela always glided and swept into rooms, but Sarah had always been a walker until today. Now she was gliding.

Pamela looked around and smiled. Julie looked at Sarah, who was carefully avoiding looking back at her.

"David?" Pamela called out.

"Yeah?" Dingo said through the speaker.

"I'm so glad you're set up to record. Sarah and I have been working on some wonderful songs, and I believe they are ready to put on tape."

"Okay," Dingo said. "Let me just put some more mikes up."

"All right," Pamela said. "Now, I'd like to work on three or four today, but Sarah will begin by playing the first one."

"Okay," Sarah said, "this is one Pamela and I wrote together. It's called 'Modifiers'" Modifiers? That wasn't a math term. Julie's brain spun as she realized Sarah had paid Julie back by taking over her turf. She seethed, feeling like she could spit acid, and wishing she could, but at the same time, she couldn't help realizing she'd been outmaneuvered, and she was impressed at Sarah's cunning.

Modifiers,

Sarah sang,

> *Modifiers tell you what kind or how*
> *Nouns, verbs, and adjectives need modifiers now.*

It continued in this vein. The melody burrowed into Julie's brain and would probably prove very difficult to dislodge. It was perfect, musically, but lyrically it was a mess. You can't teach categories before you teach the specifics, Julie thought. You can't teach a kid about modifiers and then explain what modifiers are by saying they sometimes modify other modifiers. Julie had never had an education class in her life, but she knew that much. This was muddying the issue. Sarah had studied to be a grade school teacher, and this was what she came up with? Julie ground her teeth and played a perfunctory piano part.

They spent hours in the studio, working more and harder than they had since this whole thing started. Once they finished "Modifiers," they went on to two new math songs that Sarah had written, neither one of which had a melody as good as "Modifiers," but both of which, though Julie hated to admit it, had lyrics that managed to be both clever and simple.

The process of recording, though, was not simple at all. They had to do take after take as Pamela decided she hadn't liked something, and the awkwardness in the room wasn't smoothed over by the music. It made everything feel stiff and strange. Julie knew that Pamela and Sarah were both mad at her, and while she could still play and sing, she just wasn't feeling the music the way she had earlier today. She also knew that Sarah was mad at Peter, and he looked uncomfortable too. There were no jokes between takes, there was no sense of camaraderie. It was just a long, boring day of drudgery.

Finally Pamela pronounced herself satisfied with the day's output. Everybody began to file out of the studio, and Pamela said, "Oh, Julie, dear, can I talk to you for a moment?"

Everybody froze. Julie steeled herself and prepared for the onslaught. Remember, she told herself, this is like a lapdog nipping at your heels. Annoying, but nothing to be afraid of, and nothing you can't dismiss quickly and easily. Pamela shot a meaningful look at everyone else, and they all fled the studio. Julie knew if the door weren't soundproofed, they'd all be outside trying to listen in.

Julie raced through several tactics in her mind, and eventually decided on disingenuous.

"So I'm sure you're wondering about the modifier song," Pamela said.

"No," Julie said, planting a puzzled expression on her face. "What about it?"

"Well," Pamela said, "it's the first time anyone's written a song outside their own subject area."

Julie smiled and looked at Pamela, forcing her to fill the silence.

"And I just felt it was important for our creative journeys for us to try a different perspective."

She's waiting for me to fight back, Julie thought. She's not going to yell at me without getting me to yell first. Well, she has no idea who she's dealing with.

"Okay!" Julie chirped. She turned to leave the studio.

"And," Pamela said, "after the events of the other day, I'm just not sure I can trust your creative vision anymore."

"I don't know what you mean," Julie said, aiming for puzzled and slightly hurt.

"Well, your choice of songs just revealed that . . . well, forgive me, but knowing your background, I feel that you're approaching this project from a sensibility that may be too commercial, that you might not be dedicated to really getting to the creative heart of what's possible here."

"Gee," Julie said, still acting perky enough to wake the dead, "I guess I don't understand. I mean, Mr. Payson seemed to like my song."

Pamela sighed. "Yes, dear, but Clark is not an artist. Clark is a pencil pusher. He has a feel for commerce, but not art. He hired me to make the artistic choices knowing that his artistic senses weren't as finely honed as my own."

"Gosh," Julie said. "Well, how does Mr. Payson like *your* new songs?"

Pamela paused, and for a moment Julie almost felt sorry for her. Pamela didn't even realize she'd dealt every one of them a trump card. "Uh, well, uh, given Clark's . . . that is, while my songwriting is part of the creative milieu here, part of the atmosphere of mutually nuturing artistic growth we're trying to develop, my songs aren't . . . I mean, obviously they're not bound for Saturday-morning cartoons—"

"But gee," Julie said, going for the full-on Eddie Haskell, "Mr. Payson seemed kind of upset about the progress we were making. Don't you think he might be happy to know we'd spent so much time putting together the album you're making for him?"

Pamela started sputtering. "Well, I . . . as I said, these songs are more of a background, a foundation for your work. I thought if you all saw a professional at work, it would help fuel your own process. Yes. I'm glad we had this chance to talk," Pamela said before sweeping out of the room.

"Me too," Julie said, smiling.

She walked calmly to the bathroom and took several deep breaths and waited for her hands to stop sending her the message that they really needed to form fists. She suddenly realized it was four o'clock and she hadn't eaten anything since breakfast, so she made a beeline for the fridge in the lounge.

She rummaged through the fridge but found only brown rice and steamed vegetables. "Dammit!" she said aloud. "First thing tomorrow I'm buying some real food to put in this fridge. If I never see another grain of brown rice, it'll be too soon!"

Julie heard applause, and she turned around and saw Dingo, Peter, and Levon clapping. She was puzzled. She suspected everybody hated Pamela's food, but she didn't think she'd said anything worth applauding.

"Fan-fucking-tastic!" Peter said.

"Uh, yeah, well, I just got tired of the—hey, what are you doing?" she asked, as she saw Dingo threading tape into a reel-to-reel player.

Dingo looked up and smiled. "You knew you were having that discussion right in front of open mikes, right? I kind of accidentally left the tape rolling. We all just went into the booth for playback."

"No way were we missing that," Peter said.

"You weren't kidding about that WASPy fighting style," Levon said, grinning, then broke into a bad accent and tried to move his mouth out of sync as though his words were dubbed. "Your

word-fu is pretty good. But I come from Westport. WASP style!
Hiiiiiiya!"

Julie laughed.

"Play it!" Peter said, and Dingo obliged.

It was somewhat surreal to hear the whole argument played
back. She'd been replaying the arguments with Sarah and Levon
all night in her brain, and now her latest one was actually committed to tape. She heard Pamela say this was the first time
someone had written outside their subject area.

Dingo looked at his watch, then paused the tape when Pamela
began to speak again. "Five seconds!" he said. "Five seconds of
silence that you made her fill up! I have to say, girl, I have been
working with Pamela for four years, and I have never seen anyone get the better of her."

"Teach us, O wise one!" Peter yelled.

"Yes," Levon said, still in his martial-arts movie voice, "we will
become your students, O master of word-fu. I must avenge my
father's death."

Julie looked at him for a second and decided, what the hell,
she might as well play along and celebrate her triumph. "You
must put your anger aside, young one," she said. "To find true
success in verbal combat, you must keep your anger in check.
Your anger is the fire on the burner, but you must be the cast-
iron pan atop the fire. Cold, hard, and slow to heat up."

Peter and Levon both placed their hands together and bowed
their heads.

"Aright aright," Dingo said, "I wanna hear my favorite part."
He pressed PLAY and started laughing hysterically when Julie
said, "Gosh."

"Gosh, and then Gee," Dingo said, fighting his laughter for
breath. "That's great! Gee, Pamela, what about your recordings?
Oh, shit, that's great stuff."

They listened to it again, and Dingo was cuing it up for a third play, and Levon had fetched some of the purloined Walker Wallace gin, and Julie was thinking Thank God I don't have a real job.

Just as Dingo was pushing PLAY again, the phone rang. Everybody looked at it somewhat guiltily. Though she knew it was crazy, Julie half expected it to be Pamela on the other end, screaming at all of them for laughing at her.

Levon shushed everybody and picked up the phone. "Hello?" he said. "Oh. Yes, he's still here. Just a moment."

He held out the phone to Dingo. Dingo looked at it suspiciously, then said, "Hello?" There was a long pause. "Yeah, Clark. Sure. Okay. I'll see if I can find her. Okay. We'll see you in a few minutes." He hung up and looked at Julie. "You and me. Principal's office."

"Ummmmmmm . . . ," Peter and Levon said.

Julie rolled her eyes. "Geez, I still haven't eaten anything. I'm starving. And I have gin breath."

"Tell you what," Peter said. "Here's a stick of gum. While you guys are getting in trouble, Levon and I will get us some food, maybe a couple of beers or a bottle of wine or something."

"And I'll make sure Peter's cheap ass actually buys some food this time. I can't eat that employee cafeteria shit anymore," Levon said.

"Sounds good," Julie said, smiling. And she wondered what Levon's friendliness was supposed to mean. Did this mean they were going to make the most of the two weeks they had left and just be content with the fact that it was over at that point? Or was he being friendly because they were just friends? Well, she supposed a few beers would answer that question one way or the other.

Julie and Dingo headed into the elevator, and as it crept skyward, Julie said, "Can I ask you something?"

"Sure," Dingo said.

"Is it . . . I mean, you know I worked in advertising, right, so this is really my first experience working in any part of the music industry that isn't about selling soap."

"Yeah?"

"And I just . . . I don't want to go back to advertising, but if this is what it's like to work outside of advertising, I don't think I can do it. I mean, is this what it's like?"

"You mean the backstabbing and the jealousy and all that stuff?"

"Yeah. I mean, is this normal?"

"Well, you'd probably know better than I would, since music is the only job I've ever had. I mean, I guess in most jobs you are rarely drunk or high at work, and the, uh . . . well, there's usually more, uh, *privacy*, but I think people being assholes and betraying each other is pretty much the way it goes all over the place. I mean, isn't it?"

Julie thought about McMahon & Tate, about the rivalries among the jingle writers to land accounts, about the sales reps hanging each other out to dry in front of clients. "Yeah. It is."

"Only sometimes," Dingo continued, "in this job, you get to make something beautiful."

Julie looked up at Dingo and wanted to say something about how wise and cool he was, how much she appreciated and looked up to him, how glad she was that he was there. But that kind of gushy crap just wasn't her, and now, having seen Pamela gush on numerous occasions, Julie doubted that showy displays of emotion could ever be genuine. Instead she just said, "You know I wouldn't tell Clark about Pamela's album without checking with you first. I mean, I know you're the real grown-up here, and I wouldn't tell him if you thought it would get you in trouble or something."

Dingo looked down at her. "Thanks," he said, and the elevator doors opened.

20

DINGO

INGO SMILED AT Kara Newhouse, his former adversary. "David Donovan and Julie Waterston to see Clark," he said. "We're expected."

"Yes," Kara Newhouse said, smiling. "Mr. Payson will be with you shortly."

Dingo knew that this was Kara trying to make up for her defeat last time. She hadn't called back to tell Clark they were here; she was just going to make them cool their heels for a few minutes to punish Dingo for going around her last time. Well, that was fine.

He and Julie sat. Dingo considered having a loud conversation with Julie to antagonize Kara Newhouse, but he thought it would probably be wiser to just allow her this little victory. Then, hopefully, she'd have nothing to prove in the future and they could have a normal working relationship.

Because, if things went as he expected, he'd be working for Clark Payson for quite a while, and not as a nursemaid. That wasn't quite fair. Dingo really liked the kids, even poor lost Sarah, who had completely fallen under Pamela's spell. And he did like, for once, having his age be a bonus—he liked feeling older and wiser. But at the same time, he was tired of wiping their noses. It was, after all, just a job, just a girlfriend, just a boyfriend, whatever. Maybe that was what happened when you didn't have kids. Their whole selves were wrapped up in where they were working and who they were fucking because they had no idea what it meant to do something really important. They didn't have the first idea what a life-or-death experience or problem was, they'd never sat in the NICU twenty-four hours a day for three weeks while their baby fought for life, so they thought who wrote the grammar song and who fucked who was something that mattered.

Well, breaking promises mattered, but Dingo had seen enough of people's antics on the road to know that who you fucked meant exactly as much or as little as you wanted it to.

He felt Julie looking at him and turned to face her. "Didn't he send for us?" she whispered.

"Yeah," Dingo said. "I pissed off the secretary last time I was up here, so now she's punishing us both. Sorry."

There was a long pause, and then Julie turned to him again and said, "When were you up here?" Oops. Dingo had unintentionally revealed himself to be a corporate stooge. Well, if anybody could understand that, it was Julie, who had stood alone in picking Clark over Pamela.

"Uh," Dingo said, "when I told Clark that you guys were writing dumb songs and he needed to step in." He saw shock on Julie's face, and a little wave of anger as she undoubtedly realized that he'd caused the crisis that forced her to make an unpopular decision and piss off Pamela.

"Oh. Does he know about the album?" Julie said.

Dingo shot a panicky glance over to Kara Newhouse, who was typing with some sort of headset on. "Not yet," he said. But he will, Dingo thought.

He'd been thinking about it for several days, ever since he finally got sick of shutting up and going along as Cass got grumpier and grumpier with him.

"You really don't want me here at all, do you?" he'd yelled. "I can't do anything right except make you angry. I'm doing a fucking great job of that. Otherwise, you'd just rather have me on the road, wouldn't you?"

Cass had screamed at him that he was the one who was always getting mad, that he obviously missed being on the road with all his *mistresses,* that maybe he should go back on tour so he could go be with all of the other women he wanted more than her.

He'd been so angry he was beyond speech for a long time, and as he sat there silently trying to tamp down his anger and choose his words carefully, he saw Cass get a slightly afraid, *maybe I've said too much* expression on her face.

Finally, Dingo had said, very quietly, "Fifteen years, Cass, I've never touched another woman. Every single night for the last fifteen years, I did the right thing. I guess I thought I'd earned some kind of trust or respect. Just one more thing around here that I'm wrong about."

He'd walked out of the house, wandered around the deserted suburban streets, and when he got back, the house was dark.

He'd debated whether to just sack out on the couch, but then thought, No, the hell with it. She was wrong, not him. If anybody was going to sleep somewhere uncomfortable, it damn sure wasn't going to be him.

He undressed in the dark and slid into bed next to Cass's unmoving body.

He lay there for ten minutes with his eyes open, knowing he wasn't going to get to sleep, but unwilling to leave the bed. Finally, he heard Cass say, in a completely normal, wide-awake tone of voice, "I'm sorry."

Well, that was unexpected. Their fights always ended with him deciding that keeping the peace was more important than being right, and sucking it back and coughing up the apology rather than continuing the fight forever. Because Cass was always right. Except this time.

Dingo was stunned into silence, and Cass said, "Are you awake? Did you hear me?"

"Uh, yeah. Thank you," Dingo said.

"I've been . . . I haven't been . . . I know I've been impatient lately."

"Yeah. Well, I . . ." Dingo was going to offer up an olive branch, but Cass wouldn't take it.

"No, wait, just listen. It's been really, really hard not having you around, and I've just been—I'm afraid to let you help, I'm afraid—it's so nice to have you here, sleeping next to me every night, and I'm just . . . I don't want to get used to it, because I know you're going to be out on the road again, and if I get used to having you around, I'm going to have to relearn how to do it all myself again."

"I'm sorry," Dingo said. "I mean, I knew it must have been hard for you." It took a tremendous effort not to point out that the constant touring had paid for the house she wanted in the place she wanted, that it was hard for him too, that he would have liked to say no to a number of those tours, but there were bills to pay.

"Well, I knew I was marrying a musician. I mean, I kind of signed up for it. It's not like you lied to me, and I wouldn't . . . I mean, it would have been worse to have you unhappy all the time working over at the Nabisco plant or something."

Dingo had said nothing, trying to imagine that life.

"But yeah," Cass had said. "It hasn't been easy. And now I just . . . I want you back. I want you here all the time. I don't want phone calls from St. Louis anymore. I want you here where you belong."

Dingo had leaned over to kiss her, and the resulting sex was the best they'd had in years.

And she was right. He was tired of it all too. He didn't want to tour anymore. He just wanted to be home. And he thought he knew how he was going to arrange that. He wished that Julie didn't have to be here to see the depths to which he was willing to sink to get what he wanted, but they would all know soon anyway.

Actually, maybe he'd take her place on the hot seat and she'd be grateful. Well, he couldn't worry about Julie. His loyalty was to Cass and Davey and Jenny.

Finally, Kara Newhouse reached over and hit the intercom button. "Mr. Payson? Mr. Donovan and Ms. Waterston to see you."

"Great. Send them in," Clark's voice said through the speaker.

Dingo looked at Julie, who looked even more nervous than Dingo felt. Well, she was afraid she was going to get yelled at, whereas Dingo knew he was about to sell out completely.

They stood and walked into Clark's office, and Clark stood, smiled, and shook their hands. Julie sat in the chrome chair with the leather straps Dingo had sat in last time, and Dingo sat in this big square chair that forced him to lean back a little. It was uncomfortable. It struck Dingo that Clark had filled the office with good-looking impractical furniture and never really expected to have anybody sit in here.

"So," Clark said. "I'll get right to it. My father is . . . shall we say *very* anxious for this project to reach completion. As is typical for him, he's demanded results in half the time he originally asked for. He has a meeting at the FCC in two weeks, and he is . . . very eager to have something to show the commissioners. My father, as you may know, is a friend of the president, and he has given enough money to enough senators that there's no danger of anything actually happening, but he does not enjoy being raked over the coals."

"Uh, okay," Dingo said. "So what's this mean in terms of a deadline? Or, I mean, we don't know exactly how many . . ."

"Right, right, right. I've been a pretty negligent boss in any number of ways, but I think you guys can save my butt. I have the twelve songs you've given me—those are actually with the animators in Cincinnati right now. And I need twelve more. As soon as possible. I mean, if you've got anything in the can, I need it today, and if you don't, I need it tomorrow."

Dingo looked at Julie. She was obviously doing the same thing he was doing—counting the number of usable songs they'd put on tape since Julie had defied Pamela.

"Well," Dingo said, "I think we've got four we can use."

Clark smiled. "Fantastic. And how many can you get me in the next couple of days?"

Dingo looked helplessly at Julie.

"Well," she said, "I have two more ready to go, and I'll have to check with Peter and Levon, but . . ."

Clark waved his hand. "Okay, Julie, this is the reason I matched your salary from McMahon and Tate. I know that you know how to work quickly under pressure. So I don't care how many songs Peter has, or Levon has, or anything. If you have to write every single one yourself, that's fine. Dingo, you're obviously in charge of the recording and producing, and Julie, you are the artistic director. You're deciding which songs are getting put on tape. I know the others have written some good songs, but you're the only one of the songwriters I really trust to understand the project. So what you say goes, and anyone who has a problem with that can come to me." Dingo looked at Julie. So this kid that he'd felt so protective of was actually out-earning him and had just, by virtue of defying Pamela, gotten a big promotion. Well, good for her. She didn't have a family, but she was looking out for herself too, and that, Dingo thought, was what you did in a business. So much for the Age of Aquarius.

Julie looked scared. "What about Pamela?"

Clark rolled his eyes. "Remember when I said I was a bad boss? It's become clear to me that hiring Pamela was a huge rookie mistake. I mean, it was a good decision only in that it brought us Dingo."

Dingo tried his best to look cool, like he got these kind of compliments all the time, but he caught himself grinning.

"So," Clark said, "I'm going to have to relieve Pamela of her duties, and probably have a gigantic messy contract dispute."

Dingo thought for a second. This was his opportunity. "Well," he said, "I think I have a better idea. Do you—is Pamela on the same kind of work-for-hire contract that I signed?"

"Well, of course that's confidential information," Clark said, nodding in the affirmative.

"Because if she is, you probably don't want to terminate the contract," Dingo said. Julie looked at him, slack-jawed, for a moment, and then her look of surprise turned to a smile.

"Explain," Clark said, leaning forward, elbows on his desk, chin atop folded hands.

"Well, if Pamela was on a work-for-hire contract, you might want to just hold her to it, because she's got an album in the can." He looked nervously at Clark, who looked surprised. This was the point at which Clark might be so pissed that they'd recorded the new Pamela Sanchez album behind his back that he'd blackball Dingo forever, in which case his grand plan to get off the road forever would blow up in his face. Well, nothing to do but keep going. "So, if she's on a work-for-hire contract, then the album belongs to ATN. It was recorded in the basement at ATN using musicians under work-for-hire contracts, and, I mean, I haven't really looked carefully at the terms of the contract, but ATN certainly owns the recordings. I guess your lawyers could argue about who owns the copyright and publishing for every song on the album."

Clark leaned back in his chair and folded his hands in front of his face, saying nothing. Dingo's heart hammered in his chest. He couldn't bear to look at Julie, because as much as she was on the outs with Pamela, he imagined that any songwriter would feel like he was helping Clark Payson steal Pamela's new album.

Finally, Clark said, "Is the album any good?"

Julie piped up with, "It's the best thing she's ever done."

"Really?" Clark asked.

"Yeah," Dingo said. "It's fantastic."

"So if I own it, what do you think I should do with it?"

Here goes. Phase one was a success, but this part was the really tough sell, and Dingo had never been all that good at this stuff. "Well. I mean, this depends on your . . . whether you want . . . well, you've already got the album, so what I would do if I owned this album would be to start a new division of this company that's a record label. Sign a distribution deal, and you've got the album in stores for the price of pressing and printing. Pamela will be touring like crazy—she doesn't have enough money not to—so she'll be promoting the hell out of it at no cost to you. The record company will be profitable right away, and you can use the profits to build a whole roster of artists. And, I, uh . . . you know, record labels need A and R guys, and, I mean, I've been in this business long enough, I mean, I've seen a lot of bands, and I, uh, I mean . . ."

Clark smiled and said nothing for a long minute. Dingo searched his face, but it was impossible to read. "Okay," Clark said. "Well, like everything else around here, it depends on the approval of my father, but I think he'll like the whole profitability part, and the fact that we own an album by somebody with two number one singles under her belt. So, assuming my father

says yes, we'll get started with ATN records as soon as this project is complete. And you can be the A and R department."

Dingo smiled. Success! Probably. Assuming Briggs Payson
said yes, but it was practically a risk-free proposition. All the
money had already been spent on the *Pop Goes the Classroom*
project. Pamela's album was just a bonus. And if he was working
for the record label, he'd make damn sure he got the production
credit this time.

"But for now," Clark said, "I need you guys to put this into
high gear, work late, work all night if you have to, I'll have food
delivered. I know my father will be much more receptive to the
idea of becoming a music mogul if I have the children's programming to give him before the FCC meeting. So send up what
you have, and I guess we need eight more songs. I'd love it if we
had ten."

Clark stood up, and Dingo and Julie followed his lead. He
shook their hands, and they walked out, past Kara Newhouse,
and Dingo pushed the elevator button. He didn't look at Julie.
There was a part of him that was ashamed of what he'd just done.
After all, if Pamela hadn't brought him in on this project, he
would probably be out on tour right now, or hustling around trying to find work in commercials, maybe even considering up-
rooting his family and heading for LA, where there was a lot
more session work. Pamela was responsible for his being home
and seeing his kids and his wife and having some reliable in-
come, not worrying about money for the first time in a long time,
and he had just repaid her with a knife in the back.

They stood there, and the elevator just would not come. Even
without looking at her, Dingo could feel Julie's condemnation,
and finally he couldn't stand it anymore. "Listen," he said. "I
know I'm a piece of shit. Maybe when you have a family you'll
understand. It's not like I'm proud of that."

"Why not?" Julie said, and Dingo finally looked over at her. She was smiling, and she didn't seem to think he was as horrible as his conscience kept whispering that he was. "That was just . . . Jesus, that was masterful. I mean, I've never seen anybody just completely take control of a situation and turn it completely around like that. Elizabeth would be proud."

"Who's Elizabeth?" Dingo said, as the elevator finally arrived, and they stepped in.

"Elizabeth's my mom," Julie said. "The master manipulator. Well, she was until today. I think maybe you just usurped the throne."

Dingo felt his face get hot. "I know, it's just that I've been touring for so long, and my kids . . ."

"You don't owe anybody here anything," Julie said. "Do you think Pamela would cut your heart out if she thought it would help her?"

Dingo chewed on that for a second. "Yeah. And eat it."

"Exactly. So she got beaten at her own game for once. I think it's great. So you wanna hire me to work at your record company?"

Dingo smiled. "Maybe. But you can't keep making more money than me." Julie laughed. Dingo got off in the lobby and said, "I've gotta call home," and left Julie to go do whatever it was artistic directors did.

He ran out of the ATN building, fed some coins into a pay phone, and called home.

"Hello?" Cass answered.

"Hey!" Dingo said. "It worked! It worked!"

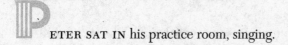

21

PETER

PETER SAT IN his practice room, singing.

> *Three-fifths of a person*
> *I'm only three-fifths of a person*
> *That's what the Constitution said*
> *In the land of liberty*
> *Where a person can be free*
> *There's only sixty percent of me*
> *And I'm trapped in slavery . . .*

He looked up and noticed Julie had opened the door and was staring at him. "Great song," she said. "But you know it's not going to work. They'll never put that on the air."

"Yeah," Peter said. "I know. The story of America is about how we overcame all of our problems, not about the hypocrisy at our very core."

"*Our very core*? Have you been drinking?"

"Strangely, no. I'm just drunk on spite and despair."

Julie looked at him for a long moment. "Well, listen, I'm sorry about that. But I have something to ask you."

"Yeah?"

"How many usable songs do you think you have? I mean, songs that might actually make the air, but that we haven't recorded yet."

Peter thought about it. "Red Genocide" was probably out, as was "Man Oh Manzanar" and almost everything else he'd done in the last few days. This left him with "Nothing Civil About War" and "A New Deal."

"I guess I have two. Probably 'Tuskegee Syphilis Experiment Got Me Down' isn't going to work, huh?"

Julie smiled. "No. Okay, listen, things have . . . well, uh, Clark's put me in charge."

Peter said nothing. Despite everything that had happened, the idea that somebody other than Pamela could be in charge of this project had never even occurred to him. It felt exciting and a little scary, like finding out your fifth-grade teacher was gone and the girl who sat two desks behind you was the new teacher.

"Uh . . . well, congratulations? I guess?"

"Yeah, I'm actually very excited about it. So listen, here's what we have to do. Clark needs ten more songs two days from now. So I see us recording tonight, writing tomorrow, and recording again tomorrow night."

"Uh, when do you see us sleeping?"

"Not sure that's going to be an option. Well, maybe an hour here or there, but we're pretty much going to be working flat-out for the next few days."

"And then what?"

"What do you mean?"

"I mean, we work flat-out for two days, and then we've got our ten songs done, are we done?"

"I guess . . . I don't really know, Clark didn't make that clear . . ."

"Because, I mean, I can do this, you know, but I was counting on getting paid for a long time. If this project is done in three days, what does that mean for my paychecks?"

Julie looked flustered. "I can't answer that, Peter. You're just going to have to check your contract." Peter looked over at the pile of his crap in the corner of the room and hoped his contract was in there somewhere. "Listen, I have to go home to walk the dog. I'm going to be back in two hours, and we're going to record. So please get ready." She spun on her heel and started to walk out.

Peter knew it was a terrible time to ask this, but he couldn't help it. "Hey, can I ask you something before you go?"

"Quickly," Julie said, standing with one foot in the hallway.

This fear had been eating him alive, had been consuming his guts so much that it actually hurt, so much that he had to ask about it, but now, when it came time to actually ask, he felt stupid. "Well, uh . . . I mean . . . I know Dingo said that she . . . um . . ."

"Peter, I really need to get home to my dog. Can this wait?"

No, he thought. Not another two hours of this question running around his mind. "Did Pamela ever make a pass at you?"

"What? Jesus Christ, Peter, why the hell . . . oh." And Julie's hard face softened. "No, Peter, she didn't."

Peter felt no relief. In fact, having spoken his fear aloud just made it harder to shoo away.

Julie turned to go, then stopped and said, "You know, whatever's going on, I think Sarah's lost to us. I think she's down the rabbit hole—sorry, bad choice of words—I think she's gone into Wonderland, and I don't know if she's ever coming back. I know it's difficult, but for the next couple of days, I really need you to focus on your work. I think it'll help."

"Yeah," Peter said. "Thanks." Julie smiled and closed the door quietly behind her.

Peter stared at the closed door for a minute. He wondered if Pamela knew she was fired. He wondered if Sarah was with her right now, and what they were doing. He wondered why he couldn't just write Sarah off the way Julie had. They'd only been together for a couple of weeks. Why couldn't he just let it go?

Because it hadn't run its natural course. Because Pamela had come in and broken it up. And he couldn't accept the idea that he'd been so wrong and so stupid. If he'd felt, well, love—he supposed he could admit it to himself, if nobody else—for the first time, then how could he just pretend it wasn't important that it was over? He knew he'd get laid again—as long as he had the guitar, that wouldn't be a problem—but would he find love again? Everything Dingo said about finding a good friend, and the way you treat somebody special and all that stuff—he'd been married for four years when he was Peter's age.

He just didn't know how many shots you got at finding the right one, and he couldn't let Pamela take her away. And he had to know how much Pamela had taken. Was she sleeping with her? For being so shy, Sarah had been surprisingly open-minded . . . Peter's guts boiled with fear, rage, and humiliation and his brain burned with some very deep, very ugly kind of arousal.

He barely felt human. Maybe Julie was right. He'd been trying to work, after all—that's why he had so many songs. But why should he bust his ass and go without sleep for two days if all it was going to get him was unemployed? His head was swimming. Too many changes in too short a time.

He picked up the guitar, then went to the corner. He dug through his clothes and found some fragments of love songs he'd been writing for Sarah that were painful and humiliating to even look at now, but which he still couldn't bring himself to crumple up and throw away. He found a flyer for a sale at a shoe store that some guy had given him. A two-day old *New York Times* with the story about the Tuskeegee Syphilis Experiments on the front page. And down at the bottom, rumpled and reeking of pot, his contract.

Peter scanned down and found the relevant clause: *The term of employment shall be one year; employment may be terminated by ATN if employee fails to follow the provisions of the contract or in the event of extraordinary unforeseen circumstances.*

Well, that clarified nothing. He had no idea why they were suddenly on a tight schedule, but since it had arisen kind of suddenly, he supposed it might well qualify as an extraordinary unforeseen circumstance. Jesus, had he even read this thing before he signed it?

He had to talk to Levon. Still holding his contract, he walked down to Levon's practice room, but he wasn't there. He was in the lounge, picking out a song.

"Hey," Levon said. "New boss lady, huh?"

"Yeah," Peter said.

"It's going to be really fun to watch when Pamela finds out."

"You mean she doesn't know?"

"Nope. I asked. I guess she's going to find out whenever she decides to show up next."

Peter imagined the scene. Levon was right. It was going to be entertaining, if also awful. Good. He knew Julie would cut Pamela to ribbons, and he'd be there cheering the whole time. Probably.

"Hey, can I ask you something?"

"Go ahead."

"So I'm just looking at the contract here, and it looks like we could bust our butts for the next two days and then be out of a job."

Levon looked strangely unconcerned. "Huh. You don't say."

"Yeah, I do say! Don't you care? I mean, doesn't that make you a little bit nervous?"

"Not at all." Levon smiled and picked some notes on the guitar.

"Why not? Are you high? And if you are, can you share, because I'm jumping out of my skin here."

Levon said nothing. "I'm not high, but that's probably a good idea. I think I still have enough in the bong to get us nicely toasted for a nice night's work. Might help get the creative juices flowing."

"Great, but what about money? I mean, I don't get why you don't care if you're going to have a job in three days or not!"

Levon smiled. "Because, my friend, I am going to have a new job in a week and a half. So whether my employment here ends in three days or ten doesn't really make a whole lot of difference to me."

"Jesus! What the hell? I mean, everything's completely going to shit around here! I can't believe . . . I mean, how can you . . . I mean, what am I . . . shit!"

"You know what?" Levon said, "I'm just gonna go grab the bong. You sit right there."

Peter couldn't sit down. He paced the room instead. How could Levon leave? What the hell was he . . . that would leave him here all alone, with Sarah and Pamela making him miserable, and Julie trying to be hard-assed boss lady, and Dingo always going home to his family, and Peter alone with his guitar. Shit.

Levon returned with the bong, lit it up, took a hit, and passed it over. Peter took a hit and immediately felt some of the tension and insanity seep out of him as the smoke seeped in.

"There," Levon said. "Now, as I was saying, I will be starting a job with a company in Texas called Dallas Technology, and actually be putting my engineering training to use."

"That sucks," Peter said. "I mean, congratulations and everything, but that's going to leave me in a pretty crappy situation here."

"Sorry," Levon said.

"So," Peter said, "I actually don't have another job lined up, and the contract looks a lot like I'm not going to get paid if I finish up in three days. So I'm thinking about refusing, at least until I get some assurances that I'm actually not screwing myself out of a job by doing all this round-the-clock work."

"Yeah," Levon said. "I'm with you. I mean, like I said, I don't care at all, so I might as well make it easier for you."

"Thanks," Peter said. "But, I mean, won't that make things difficult with you and Julie?"

"Who says there's *things* with me and Julie? There aren't any *things* to make difficult."

Peter didn't really believe that, but since this point of view was working to his advantage, he decided not to press the point.

They sat on the couch talking and laughing and arguing about music for about ten minutes, but then suddenly the elevator opened and Julie was standing there, so it must have been closer to two hours.

She looked uptight. "Okay, guys, let's get to it," she said.

"Uh-uh," Levon said. "We're on a sit-down strike."

For some reason this struck Peter as very funny, and he started to giggle.

Julie's face turned red. "Okay, funny, but now we really need to get to work, so can you guys get yourselves together?"

"Not until I know I'm gonna keep getting paid," Peter said.

"Peter, I told you to look at your contract!" Julie snapped. "I can't answer your question!"

"Well," Peter said, "see, I did look at the contract, and it says my employment can be terminated in the event of unforeseen circumstances, which could mean just about anything, including finishing this project."

Julie took a deep breath. "Okay," she said. "I can ask Clark about this tomorrow. I promise. But right now we have to get to work."

"See, the thing is, no we don't," Peter said. "And until I know for sure that I'm not playing myself out of a job, I'm not playing."

"Me neither," Levon said.

Julie took another deep breath, then turned and walked out. She came back a minute later with Dingo in tow. "Listen, guys, you are not irreplaceable. Dingo, can you get me a guitarist and a bassist in here?"

Dingo looked at Peter and Levon, then back to Julie. He looked profoundly uncomfortable. "Yeah," he said, kind of sadly. "I can have musicians here in an hour. I don't know about song-writers, though. I mean, I know a lot of guys who play, but I don't really know anybody who can write for shit, except guys who are out, you know, fronting their own bands and stuff. Nobody I could get here on short notice."

Julie's face was crimson. "Guess you better call Clark," Levon said, smiling.

Julie stormed off down the hall. Dingo looked sad. "I'm sorry," he whispered. "I wish I could support you guys more. You're doing the right thing, you know. Nobody else is gonna look out for you if you don't look out for yourselves."

Peter smiled and nodded. It was sure a long way from the Kumbaya campfire feeling they had at the beginning, but that had all been bullshit anyway. Dingo was right. You have to take care of yourself, and expecting anybody else to care about you is just naïve. But Levon is looking out for me, he thought. He's got nothing to gain and Julie to lose, and he's doing it anyway. He looked over at Levon and was about to tell him how great he was, how much he appreciated his show of solidarity, when Julie came back in the room.

"Well," she said through clenched teeth, "I can't reach Clark."

"That's too bad."

"Listen, guys, please. We're friends, right? I mean, can you just help me out here? I promise I will go to bat for you with

Clark, hell I'll ask him for bonuses, but please. He's counting on me to deliver something here, and I need you."

Peter softened, suddenly feeling sorry for Julie. She was about his age, and she'd been put in charge of a fairly big-deal project. Peter never wanted to be in charge of anything like that, and Julie had always been a good friend. Maybe he should do it after all. Maybe he was being a jerk. He was about to agree when Levon spoke up.

"And Pete needs to get paid. And what if you go to bat for him and strike out? Who's gonna look out for him? Are you personally going to cover his salary because he did you a favor as a friend?"

Julie was silent.

"That's what I thought. So it's all great to be friends and everything, but this is business, Julie. It's not a friendship thing. It's about the money."

Julie stared at Levon for a long time and then said, flatly, "It's about the money. It's—" She looked like she was about to cry, but then she pushed her tears back. "It's just business. It never was anything else, was it. We're all just cordial co-workers here. Or I suppose we were until I became the enemy. Well, that's fine. You guys are making a business decision, and I don't take it personally. But you understand that I've got to act in a business-like way. So, since the day's work is obviously done, I'll be expecting all ATN employees to go home now. I'll have security down here in fifteen minutes to remove anybody who's in this workplace not working."

Wow. Well, Peter figured he really shouldn't be surprised. It had only been a day ago they'd been bowing down to Julie for getting the best of Pamela. There really wasn't any reason to expect she wouldn't get the best of them too.

"Our workday begins at eight AM. I'll expect everyone here and ready to get some work done at that time. Tardiness will be

a breach of your contractual obligations. I will see you gentlemen in the morning. Good night."

She turned and walked away. Dingo, looking sheepish, said,
"Listen, guys, if you need a place to crash, I mean, I can call
Cass, we've got a couch and everything, I mean . . ." Peter imagined the awkwardness of trying to sleep while Dingo's wife radi-
ated waves of hate, and getting up in the morning with Dingo's
kids running around, asking who the hell he was and why he was
sleeping on the couch. He'd rather stay up all night and roam the
streets getting shitfaced.

"Thanks, Dingo, but I'll pass. I'll be fine."

"You sure?"

"Yeah, Dingo."

"Levon?"

"I am fine, Dingo. But I do appreciate it."

"All right then, guys, I'll see you in the morning," Dingo said.
His relief was obvious and kind of depressing. He walked over
and pressed the elevator button.

"Well, I'm not even wearing shoes," Peter said to Levon, "so
I'm just gonna go get some."

"You do that," Levon said. Peter went back to the practice
room and put some shoes on and grabbed the tape and note-
books with all of his songs. Just in case he was fired tomorrow, he
wanted to make sure that they wouldn't get their hands on any of
his work without paying him.

When he emerged from the practice room, Levon was not in
the lounge. Peter went back and knocked on the door of Levon's
practice room. Nobody answered, and when he opened the door,
the room was empty. Peter gave a little humorless laugh. For
somebody who didn't have any *things* with Julie, Levon had certainly run off fast enough to try to patch things up. Leaving Peter
alone with nothing to do for the next ten hours. Great. Well, he
couldn't really blame Levon. He was looking out for Peter

money-wise, and Peter was an adult and could certainly find a way to spend a night in New York City without help.

He wondered if he should just go get a hotel room and collapse, but if he was out of a job, he certainly didn't want to blow money he'd need for eating next week on one good night's sleep tonight. Hell, he was going to go out and have a great time tonight and not even think about this place. It was actually going to be a relief to get out of this dungeon. He'd have to remember to thank Julie in the morning for forcing him into the real world where nobody gave the tiniest shit about what was going on in the basement at ATN.

Peter got out of the elevator in the lobby just as one of the security guards was standing there pressing the DOWN button. So Julie had been serious. Not that he'd really doubted it, but it was kind of weird to see a security guard heading down into the sacred womb of creativity. He hoped somebody had remembered to hide the pot.

Peter pushed the glass door open and stepped out onto a sidewalk filled with people who didn't care about any of this, which was adjacent to a street filled with taxis filled with people who didn't care about it, on their way to apartments or restaurants filled with people who also didn't care. He breathed in a lungful of car exhaust, and it came from a car full of people who didn't know or care about any of the problems consuming him right now, and it was ambrosial. "New York City," he said, smiling, "just like I pitchered it."

He looked both ways on the sidewalk and decided, all things considered, if he had to be dining and drinking into the wee hours of the night, he'd rather be downtown than uptown. He started walking downtown, and he just felt free for the first time in a long time. He wasn't carrying anything but money enough to get full of good food and top-shelf booze, and that wasn't a feeling he'd had in a while. Okay, okay. Ever. If you looked at the big picture, he was screwed: The love of his life hated his guts, he might or might not have a job, and he certainly had no place to live. He had no way to fix any of these problems. But tonight, he was putting his history major training aside and not looking at the big picture. Because, after all, if you looked at the big picture, everybody all the time was screwed. So tonight was a small-picture evening. He had a wallet full of money, he was young and healthy, and he had to spend a whole night out in New York City. Many, many people around the world would envy him tonight. Oops—there he was thinking about the big picture again.

He walked for a good long time, soaking in the sights and sounds and smells of New York, and when he was good and hungry, he stopped into a tiny little bistro that he used to pass on his way home from the comic-book store. He'd always walked by and gotten the tantalizing smells of hot onions and garlic, and this had always made going home to spaghetti with butter or peanut butter and, when he was flush, jelly sandwiches that much more painful.

He spent an hour and a half drinking wine and eating from the five-course prix fixe menu and flirting with his delightfully cute waitress. By the end of the meal, he was feeling that disgusting, too-full feeling he hadn't felt since his last Thanksgiving in Ohio. It was unpleasant but, then again, not as unpleasant as the gnawing emptiness in his guts when he hadn't had enough to eat. Yeah, he'd definitely take too full over not full enough any day.

He tipped extravagantly, and only when he stood up to walk out the door did he realize how incredibly drunk he was. It was kind of a shame, really, because that was probably the most expensive bottle of wine he'd ever have, and after the second glass, he might as well have been drinking a jug of Gallo Hearty Burgundy, which had always been the jug wine of choice in the folk music scene he'd belonged to what felt like a hundred years ago.

He could feel his mind beginning to walk through the time

that had passed between the last time he'd smelled the food cooking at that bistro and the time when he'd just tasted the food. He tried to force his mind onto a different track, but there was Sarah in his mind, there was that beautiful, tentative first kiss, there was her face when she was coming, there were the jokes, the lines that had flown back and forth between them while they were writing songs together.

He missed her body, he missed her smile, he missed laughing with her.

Suddenly his insides were a volcano of grief, and there, on the street, they began to erupt as big sobs forced themselves up from his stomach and out of his mouth. He could live without Sarah. He'd done it before. He just didn't want to have to.

He imagined the rest of his life stretching out in front of him with no Sarah in it. There were other girls, sure, but right now he didn't want other girls. He just wanted Sarah. Which is why he'd turned Pamela away.

Wiping the tears from his face, Peter made a decision. He was going to Pamela's, and when he got there, he was going to get Sarah back. He wasn't going to take this lying down. He'd always had girls drifting in and out of his life, and the idea of fighting for one never really made sense to him—he'd see movies where people vowed to fight for their true love and just think they were idiots. But now he was the idiot. And he was going to get her back.

He rehearsed everything he was going to say as he walked to Pamela's house. Not petulant and whiny—not begging pathetically, why did you leave me, please take me back. No—stronger, more manly. Dammit, you have to give me another chance, because what we have is too special to let it die over a misunderstanding, it's too precious to let it be sabotaged by Pamela Freaking Sanchez, who writes good songs but clearly doesn't know shit from shinola when it comes to life.

He felt his anger at Pamela bubbling up, and he nursed it. He would be on her turf, and she'd probably be lying, and he had to be strong, he had to withstand the force of her personality and make Sarah see the truth, see that one of them had betrayed her and one of them hadn't. (Unless, a little worried voice in his mind whispered, you count a kiss as a betrayal. Which Peter probably would have if Sarah had kissed anyone else.)

He reached Pamela's building, and felt less nervous than he'd imagined he would. He was on a mission, he was in the right, and he was going to get this done. He punched the bell angrily, re-hearsing his tone of voice in his mind. *It's Peter,* he would say. *I need to talk to Sarah.* Or maybe just *I need to talk to Sarah.* Or possibly, *Give me back my girlfriend now, goddammit.*

THE BOX NEXT to the door did not squawk at him. He punched the bell again. Nothing happened. Thirty seconds passed. He leaned on the bell. One minute. Clearly there was nobody home. Or else there was just nobody answering the bell. Because they were in bed.

The hot fury that had filled his body turned to cold fear. He knew it was crazy, but he knew that Pamela wouldn't be satisfied with just wrecking their relationship, she would punish Peter for rejecting her by visiting the ultimate humiliation on him—she'd take Sarah's body as well as her mind.

He knew, he just knew, that right now they were upstairs in that gigantic bed, their bodies entwined, Sarah making that face for Pamela, that face that belonged to him, that face that was for him alone.

There had to be some way in. He had to know. He had to know right now. He wouldn't wait anymore. He ran to the side of the building and found only sheer walls. Around the back, though, there was a fire escape. The bottom level had to be twelve feet up. There was no way he could jump high enough to even reach the ladder. But there must be a way.

The Dumpster was too far from the fire escape to be of any use. Unless there were some way to move it. Moving closer, Peter saw that it was on wheels. "Thank you!" he whispered.

He walked around the Dumpster and kicked aside a pile of garbage bags. Three rats went skittering away, and Peter nearly screamed. He put both hands on the metal and pushed. And the Dumpster wouldn't budge. He leaned against the Dumpster and shoved with all his weight. Still nothing. Not even close to moving. Well, he thought, maybe if he took all the trash out, it would be easier to move. Somewhere inside, he knew that emptying out a huge Dumpster in an alley in the hope of moving it so he could jump onto a fire escape so he could catch his ex-girlfriend in bed with a folksinger was insane. But he shut that part of his brain up. Because if there was a way—any way at all—for him to know for sure, to just end the torment of wondering and worrying, then he had to do it now. What else could he do? Wander the streets in a drunken fugue, eaten alive by jealousy and fear and anger? No, goddammit. He had come here to do something, and he was going to do it. He opened the Dumpster and was assaulted by the smell. He pulled out one bag, which dripped a grayish liquid. He tossed it onto the ground, then quickly did a little dance step away from the rivulets of foul-smelling gray goo that ran from the holes in the side. He looked to see if his shoe was wet, and, as he did, he noticed that the wheels on the bottom of the Dumpster had little locks on them.

He quickly ran around and unlocked the wheels and tried to push it again. It was heavy, but it rolled about as easily as his friend Mark's VW Microbus that they used to have to kick-start all the time.

When he'd gotten it under the fire escape, Peter climbed onto the top of the Dumpster, balancing precariously over its yawning, trash-filled maw. Even with his arms outstretched, he was still several inches below the fire escape. A picture of him sprawled in the alley with a broken leg, screaming to an uncaring city for help, flashed across his mind, but he managed to push it away. He squatted down and sprang up as high as he could. His fingers closed around the bottom of the fire escape.

Now he was hanging from a fire escape over a Dumpster. For the first time, he wished he'd done more pull-ups in his life. Arms straining, he pulled himself up, grabbing at the fire escape for a better hold until he could pull his scrambling lower body up. Not exactly the graceful, Batman-like swing onto the fire escape he'd pictured in his mind when he'd first conceived of this plan, but it would have to do.

He climbed up to the landing outside Pamela's loft. He crouched down and felt at the windows. One was open a crack, and it took a little fumbling, but he was able to pull the edge slowly toward him, making the window swing open. He was only able to get it open about eight inches, though. He pulled harder, but he still couldn't make it open.

There was certainly enough room to stick an arm through the window, but he thought it was probably too narrow to even get his head through. So all this for nothing. No . . . not for nothing, because he could hear something . . . it was a woman, and she moaned.

Peter was filled with a caustic mixture of emotions, aroused and hurt and humiliated and enraged, and he looked around the fire escape for something to break the window with, because goddammit he would go in there right now and pull Sarah out of that bed, he would kill Pamela with his bare hands. He saw nothing on the fire escape, and frantically, he stuck his hand into the window and flailed around. What was he hoping to find? Something, anything he could use to break glass. His hand felt a hard, flat surface—some kind of desk or countertop. Stapler, he thought, there's got to be a stapler, a big heavy Swingline I can chuck at the window and stop this horror, stop it right now.

The noise inside turned to a hiccup that Peter remembered as a distinctly Pamela noise of pleasure. Oh, God, he couldn't even think about it. And he wanted to see it so badly. He contorted his body, turning his head sideways to try to squeeze it into the opening. He got his forehead in and got stuck when his ears caught on the window and the frame. He was debating whether to give a big shove that might bloody his ears and get him completely stuck in the window when he heard another sound. It was a distinctly male grunt.

Peter paused and slowly, carefully, withdrew his head. He heard Pamela's voice echoing through the loft. "Oh, yes . . . my sweet black angel . . ." Wasn't that a song on the new Stones album?

And suddenly the man spoke. He sounded annoyed. "You know, they make 'em in black."

"What?" Pamela said.

"Dildos," the voice Peter recognized as Levon's replied. So apparently he wasn't lying, and there were no things with Julie and he was making no effort to patch any of them up.

"I . . . I don't understand . . . ," Pamela said.

"It's just that that's like the eighth time you've said black this or black that, and I just thought you should know that you could get something black inside you without the trouble of having an actual human being attached to it."

Ouch! "What . . . I don't . . . I mean, baby, I never meant . . ."

"I know you didn't. You . . . I guess I deserve it. I mean, I came over here for one reason, and so I guess it's pretty fucking stupid for me to get upset because you don't care about me."

"Oh, baby, you don't . . . I do care, I care about you, I just . . ."

"I thought this would make me feel better, and I just feel worse," Levon said. Was he crying? It sounded kind of like it.

Suddenly Peter was embarrassed to be listening to this. Weird, he thought, that he felt no embarrassment or shame about listening to his friend having sex, but he really couldn't listen to him cry.

As quietly as he could, Peter snuck down the fire escape. Hanging down, he looked down at the Dumpster. Why the hell hadn't he closed the lid? Oh, right—insane with liquor and jealousy. Steeling himself, he dropped down into the trash. He landed with a wet thump and felt something seeping into the back of his pants. Gagging, he began to scramble out of the Dumpster when he noticed something spilling out of the ripped bag in front of him. Well, he noticed a few things. Several bags that had contained brown rice. From India. Some burnt-to-the-nub sticks of incense. An old phone bill. And a postcard from Sacred Heart High School in Cherry Hill, New Jersey. "Hope to see you at the fifteenth reunion next year!" it said. It was signed Barbara Palmintieri (née Demarco) and Janet Pallazolla (née Cattanaro). It was addressed to Pammy Sanchez (née Finocharrio).

He pocketed the postcard and pondered his next move. Well, he was going to have a pretty hard time going out for a night on the town reeking of garbage. And, having burned through his adrenaline, he was suddenly exhausted. He decided to close his eyes for just a few moments while he tried to plan out what was happening next. Twenty seconds later, he was asleep.

22

SARAH

SARAH BREEZED PAST the security desk in the ATN lobby and headed for the elevator. "Miss?" one of the guards called out. "Miss?"

"Yes?" Sarah looked at him.

"I'm sorry, but can you tell me your destination in the building?"

"Uh, yeah, I'm going to the basement? I'm working on the music project dow—"

"Yeah, I'm sorry, miss, but it's after hours, and the project manager told me not to let anybody down there."

The project manager? Who the hell was that? Did Pamela lock her out of the basement after kicking her out of her apartment? Or was Clark just finally tired of people crashing down there? This was very, very strange. She needed to call Pamela.

"Uh, can I use your phone?" she asked the guard.

"I'm sorry, miss. Pay phones are next to the restrooms."

"Thanks," Sarah said sarcastically. She rummaged through her pockets and found a dime. She dropped it in the pay phone and called Pamela's number. No answer. She had a moment of panic.

It was nine o'clock at night and she had nowhere to stay! What was she going to do? She felt sure that Pamela could help her out—would know someone she could crash with, some place she could go. But Pamela wouldn't answer the phone, and anyway she'd been kind of mean about kicking Sarah out.

She'd gotten some mysterious phone call, and then she'd said, "Well, dear, I'm afraid you're not going to be able to stay here tonight."

Sarah had been shocked. "But why . . . I mean . . . okay, I guess I'll just . . ."

"Sweetie, I really need you to leave right away."

"What . . . okay. Did I do something?" Sarah had asked, feeling suddenly on the verge of tears.

"It's just that . . . well, I've been putting a lot of energy into your personal growth, and your artistic growth, and it's been a real drain on me and I need you out of my space so that I can re-connect with my own creativity, so that I can continue my own journey without distractions."

Sarah felt like she'd been smacked. It was true that she had been getting a lot from being with Pamela—but Pamela made it sound like she was just a leech. She'd stayed here at Pamela's in-sistence, and it wasn't like she had put any demands on her or anything. She'd felt suddenly embarrassed and ashamed. She'd thought they were friends, but it was clear that Pamela just saw her as an annoyance, a puppy dog to be stroked now and kicked later.

She left the loft and got a taxi uptown, racking her brains the entire time trying to figure out what she'd done wrong. By the time she reached ATN she still hadn't figured it out.

But it must have been pretty bad, because Pamela had locked her out of ATN too. She wondered if everybody else had suf-fered the same fate.

Sarah stared down the empty lobby and wondered what she

was going to do. She fought back the urge to cry, because she suddenly felt more lost and alone than she had in a very long time. Peter was a lying traitor, and she'd somehow offended Pamela, and she had alienated Julie, and she supposed Levon was the only one who still liked her, but she had no idea where he was. She couldn't even go and sing the bleak despair out of her body, because her guitar was locked up downstairs. It was dark, and she was friendless and alone.

She dug through her pockets and found some change, but probably not enough. So she called collect.

Mom accepted the charges. "Are you okay, sweetie?" she said. "Is everything all right?"

And now the tears that Sarah had been fighting back came rushing out, and she knew the security guard could probably hear her crying, but she didn't care. "I . . . I'm fine, Mommy, I'm just . . . I'm not hurt . . . my body's not hurt . . . I just . . . I'm sorry, you don't have to worry. I'm just feeling terrible, I've messed everything up and everybody hates me and I'm all alone."

"Well," Mom said, "I doubt that everybody hates you, sweetie. "

"They do," Sarah said through tears, her nose starting to run. She wiped the snot on her sleeve. "They hate me!"

"Sarah. Sweetie. Have you ever seen me and your father have a fight?"

Sarah laughed at the absurdity of the question. "Only like every five minutes."

Mom actually laughed. "Well, but we still love each other. The fact that we've had a fight doesn't mean we don't love each other. You know that, honey, right?"

"Yeah," Sarah said, feeling very small. "I just—I don't know what to do, Mommy, I messed everything up."

Mom sighed. "I doubt it's as bad as that, but I know how you feel, honey. It's very hard what you're doing. And I'm not going to lie to you—we'd still like you to be a teacher, but we also know how hard it is to try to make a living as a musician. And we're proud of you for having such a talent that people are going to pay you money to write songs. And we're proud of you because you're a kind and compassionate woman."

"I . . . I . . . thanks."

"All right. Are you going to be okay?"

"Yeah, Mom, I am." She didn't dare tell Mom that she didn't have a place to sleep tonight, because she didn't want her to worry about her physical safety. "Thank you. I love you."

"I love you too, honey. You're going to be fine."

"Okay," Sarah said. They said good-bye and hung up. She still had no idea what to do, but at least there was one person in the world who still loved her, and the problem of where she was going to sleep tonight felt easier to tackle knowing that. She'd even said they were proud that she was making a living as a musician! That was certainly news to her.

Then she realized she'd been a total idiot. She was making a living as a musician. They had gotten paid, and she had money in her purse. And it was hard to walk two blocks in Manhattan without hitting a hotel. She had enough money—money she had earned with her songs!—that she wouldn't have to crash in some scary shooting gallery, she could treat herself to a nice night's sleep in a big hotel bed. She smiled just thinking about it. She was going to go get in a big, soft, comfortable bed, and, what's more, she was going to order something fried from room service. And she was going to eat ice cream and watch Johnny Carson.

She paid for her single room in cash, took the elevator up, unlocked the door, and immediately dropped her clothes and ran a bath. It felt wonderful to actually soak in a bath. She looked down at her legs, and it occurred to her that she could stand to shave. She wasn't sure if that would be caving in to male opression or not, but she just didn't like the way her legs looked like this. In fact, looking at her body, she was starting to look a little bony. Maybe subsisting on brown rice and vegetables wasn't so great after all. She was starting to get angles where she used to have curves, and she didn't like it.

She soaked in the warm water and just thought about how good it felt. But, of course, after a while, thoughts about Peter and Pamela and Julie started creeping back into her mind. To stop herself thinking, she climbed out of the tub and into a thick white bathrobe. She called room service and got a big dish of ice cream sent up, and she sat on her bed in her bathrobe holding the bowl of ice cream in her hands. She tried not to hear Pamela's voice talking about how revolting it was to eat cow pus, how humans were the only adult animals to drink milk.

She dipped the spoon into the ice cream and put a sweet, creamy, chocolatey spoonful in her mouth. She gasped as she experienced what felt like a taste bud orgasm.

The rich, decadent flavor of the ice cream was a beautiful shock to her system made that much more pleasurable by the sense that she was doing something wrong.

She watched television, and she quickly found herself drowning in the sweet mindless narcotic that was ATN's prime-time lineup. She woke up at some point with the empty ice cream bowl in her lap and the test pattern with the Indian head in the middle on the screen. She turned off the TV and crawled back into bed.

She woke up at seven, feeling better rested than she had in weeks. She bid a sad farewell to the bed and vowed that she was going to find an apartment today whatever happened, and she was going to get a big, beautiful mattress, and she was never going to sleep on anything that rolled or folded up again.

She walked out of her room, took the elevator down to the lobby, went into the restaurant, and feasted on pancakes and coffee. She could feel the white flour turning to glue in her stomach, and she could feel the coffee pumping up her blood pressure. She felt jittery and tired at the same time, and she had to admit that maybe a whole-grain cereal and some fruit was a better way to start the day, but, at the same time, she really liked pancakes.

She ate slowly, and it was nearly eight o'clock by the time she finished. She debated whether she should head in to ATN and get there before anybody else, or wait until later. Well, she was dreading seeing everybody but Levon and Dingo, and she really had nothing else to do, so it looked like her choices were getting it over with and going in to ATN or else wandering the streets and fretting for a few hours.

She walked over to ATN and tried to sort out what she was going to say to everyone. It wouldn't be impossible to keep working there, but it would certainly be impossible to keep living there. She needed her own space: Then even if everybody hated her, she could at least go somewhere else at the end of the day. But what would she say to everybody? Pamela had hurt her, but so had Peter, with his betrayal, and Julie, with hers. But for all that, she was tired of being upset, she was tired of the intensity of the whole experience. She just wanted to write some songs about math. She felt kind of bad being in conflict with everyone, but she just didn't feel up to fixing it. She just wanted to be by herself for a while, to figure out who the hell she was.

It was comfortable being Sarah Stein, boring elementary school teacher with a secret music jones, and once she'd given that up, who was she? Peter's girlfriend? Hell, Peter's life mate? They hadn't spent more than a couple of hours apart until Pamela came between them. Pamela's protégée? That was comfortable too, because there was no thinking to do. It was kind of embarrassing now in the light of day on the street in Midtown Manhattan, but there had been something wonderful about giving up all of her authority. Here's what you eat, here's who you sleep with, here's what you write songs about. When you didn't make your own decisions, there was no chance you'd make the wrong choice and screw everything up.

She walked through the lobby to the elevator without anybody stopping her. She emerged into the basement, and something was different. It took her a moment to realize that the lights were no longer red.

Peter and Levon sat on the couch, and they looked up guiltily when Sarah arrived. "Yeah," Levon said, "good to see you, Sarah. I've gotta go and, uh, tune up the bass, you know, stuff I have to take care of in a soundproof room. See you." He got off the couch and practically ran down the hall, leaving Sarah and Peter alone.

This wasn't what she wanted.

"Well," Sarah said. "I've got to go get my stuff together too. I have a couple songs to—"

Peter sprang off the couch, and Sarah looked at him carefully for the first time. His hair was a mess, he hadn't shaved (that makes two of us, Sarah thought), his pants had some big gross stain that probably accounted for the sour smell that was wafting toward her. "Wait. Just listen, please, please, Sarah, just listen to me."

Sarah took a deep breath. "No, Peter, no. There's no excuse that you can make, and I don't want—I just don't want to get into it, okay? You want Pamela, you're not who I thought you were, so we move on and just—"

Peter was wild-eyed and practically jumped up and down. "Aaaagh! I do not want Pamela! I don't even know what she told you, but—"

Well, shit. Now she was angry, and she hadn't wanted to get into it, but now they were into it, all right, they were very into it. "She told me that you fucked her, okay? Which you neglected to mention!"

"I did not! That's a lie! She's lying! Just like she lies about everything!"

"At Antioch? You didn't fuck her at Antioch?"

Peter suddenly looked sheepish. "Oh, at Antioch, yeah, but not since then."

"You didn't think that might be important to mention?"

"Why? Was I supposed to give you a list of everybody I had sex with and never spoke to again?"

"Well, I bet that's a pretty long list, but no. You just . . . you went over there and made a pass at her because you still want her!" And now the tears, the tears of humiliation and rejection were back. You ugly little troll, it said, you don't get the guy. You get to pine for the guy and be alone on prom night. You get to be the friend they come to to ask you how to get the good-looking girls. You're a girl, is how they always start their questions, as though this just occurred to them. What can I do to get Lisa, to get Denise, to get Pamela to like me? You know what girls like, right? You are female enough to ask for advice, but not female enough for me to want, right?

And so it was with Peter. All the time she'd thought they were forging some kind of connection, it was just a lie—he was biding his time with her until he could get to Pamela, and he was probably only biding his time with her because Julie the ice queen needed a black guy to really prove to herself that she wasn't her mom.

"I don't still want her! I want you! And I did not go over there to make a pass at her! She made a pass at me!"

Sarah rolled her eyes. "Yeah, sure. Why should I believe you? Why should I believe a word you say?"

"Why should you believe Pammy Finocharrio?"

Sarah was getting ready to yell, but she just looked at him. "Who's that?"

"That's an Italian girl from Cherry Hill, New Jersey, who pretends to be some kind of Chicana folk princess. That's the liar that you've believed about everything! How can you believe her and not me?" He was starting to cry now, and though it did not make her want to take him back, it did make Sarah pity him. He was dirty and smelly and red-faced and crying, and he looked kind of like a lost little boy. "She lies about everything! She lies about who she is! How can you believe her? You don't have any idea who she is! And we . . . after everything we . . . I mean, I guess I'm stupid, but I thought . . ."

"You thought you could get Pamela back, and once you found out you couldn't, you had to fall back on Plan B," Sarah said. No matter what Peter said, she knew that that was the truth. She wasn't beautiful and talented, and she'd never get a guy, at least not a guy worth having.

Still, she wondered if Peter was right. Was Pamela really somebody else? And if she pretended to be somebody she wasn't, did that mean she'd lied about Peter?

"Goddammit, no! I could have had her, and I turned her down because I wanted you! And I guess that was a dumb choice, because you don't . . . I obviously didn't mean to you what you meant to me, so I guess I was just dumb."

Peter wiped his nose on his sleeve, and the elevator opened, and Julie walked out.

"Good morning," she said. "Peter, I spoke with Clark, and your request has been granted. The remainder of your contract will be honored whenever the project ends. Of course, you'll be expected to be available for overdubs, and our friend Captain Sunshine has gotten wind of the project and would like at least two new songs per week, so we'll be expecting the staff here to contribute on that front as well. So—hey, did you sleep in a Dumpster or something?"

Peter managed a smile. "I may have. I'm sorry, Julie. I . . ."

"You should have trusted me. I told you I would go to bat for you."

"I know," Peter said quietly. "I've just been all screwed up, and it's hard to trust anybody when Pammy Finocharrio is in the middle of everything, and—"

Sarah looked from Peter to Julie and back again. "Will one of you tell me what the hell is going on here?" she shouted.

At the same time, Julie said, "Who is Pammy Finocharrio?"

"You know her as Sanchez," Peter said to Julie, then turned to Sarah and said, "Pammy got shitcanned and Julie's in charge now, and Clark wants all the rest of the songs yesterday."

Sarah didn't know what to say. "She . . . what?"

"Clark's under pressure from his old man and decided he actually wanted us to get some work done instead of exploring the interior of our rectums—hey, grammar lady, is that recta? Recti?"

Julie smiled. "I believe either rectums or recta is acceptable," she said.

"Okay then, I'm gonna go with recta. Anyway, so Clark Payson decided that if he wanted us to do something other than explore our own recta, he was going to have to put somebody else in charge."

Was that why Pamela had kicked her out? Maybe she'd gotten fired and just needed some time alone. Well, that was understandable. She was embarrassed and angry and she wanted to be alone. Maybe Sarah had been too hard on her. "So . . . so you're the one who locked me out last night?"

Julie looked kind of sheepish. "Well, I was trying to lock Peter out, since he was on strike or something. Sorry about that. And I'm sorry . . . I feel awful about what I said to you, Sarah. I'm . . . the thing I hate is that I can't unsay it, and I probably can't convince you that I was trying to hurt you but I didn't really believe what I said. I just—it's hard to turn off the killer instinct sometimes."

"Oh. Well. Thanks." This was where she was supposed to apologize to Julie too, and they'd be friends again. But Julie had made them all look dumb and Sarah had sided with Pamela, who might not have been who she said she was, and who might have tried to steal her boyfriend and then lied about it. Or who had told the truth and taken her in when she was sad and vulnerable. Sarah's head was swimming. "Uh, I'm sorry too. I just . . . I'm really confused. Can we make some music?"

Peter looked angry. "But what about . . . what are . . . do you believe me or not?"

"Christ, Peter, I have no idea what to believe right now. I can't think. Can we just play something?"

"That's what I want to hear," Julie said, turning and heading toward the studio. "Dingo's wife said he left an hour ago, so he should be here soon. Peter, can you go get Levon? And can you—you know what, we're on a tight schedule, but if I'm going to be spending all day with you in an enclosed space, I'm gonna need you to shower and change. Can you do that in ten minutes?"

Peter looked flustered. "Yeah, but . . . Okay." He looked at Sarah and spat out, "Fine," then stomped down the hall. Sarah looked at Julie.

"I—" she began, but Julie cut her off.

"Don't ask me. I have no idea. The only thing I can say is get a dog. It's a really easy relationship to understand."

"Yeah," Sarah said, shaking her head. "Well. Let me get my guitar. Oh, and by the way, thank you for locking me out. I slept in a hotel and it was delicious."

"Anytime," Julie said, and she went to the studio.

Sarah went down the hall to get her guitar, though she probably shouldn't even bother. She wasn't here for her guitar playing. She was here for her voice.

They gathered in the studio and ran through a couple of new songs. Dingo arrived and smiled broadly seeing them all in the studio making music. "Fantastic!" he said. "Let's get some work done! Boss lady, what's the agenda for the day?"

Sarah could see Julie puffing up when Dingo called her boss lady. It was annoying. "Well, I guess we should record whatever we have today, which is what, four songs ready to go?" Peter and Dingo nodded. "And then it's off to write. I'd like to get two new songs from everybody by this time tomorrow, and then hopefully we can put them all on tape by tomorrow night."

"Let's get to it!" Dingo said. He sat behind the drum kit and picked up the new songs as quickly as ever. Sarah felt left out because she was the only one who didn't have anything new to add here. "Nothing Civil About War," Peter's new song, was actually a beautiful, sad song about war. It was better than "Gonna Kill Me Some Cong" or any of his old antiwar songs. Had Pamela's influence brought out this depth in Peter's work, or had he been legitimately heartbroken about Sarah and channeled that into his work?

Either way, it was a great song. And she liked Levon's "Some Light on the Subject" too. Both of those songs were recorded by noon, and after a bathroom break Peter taught them "A New Deal." He begged Julie to record "Tuskegee Syphilis Experiment Got Me Down," and Julie just told him to shut up.

"Did you really write that song, or did you just come up with the title?" Sarah asked.

"Oh, I wrote it," Peter said. He began playing a blues riff and sang, "Sittin' in Tuskegee / with my syphilis at stage three / yeah my government made me crazy / syphilis experiment got me down."

Sarah smiled, and Julie yelled, "Please, Peter, we've gotta get two more songs down today!"

As she said this, Pamela suddenly materialized in the studio. "What do you mean?" she said. "Who told you to record today? None of—your work isn't ready yet, and I don't appreciate *your*"—she gave Julie a pointed look—"going behind my back and trying to further your own career at the expense of the project. David!" she bellowed, and Dingo slowly emerged from the booth.

"Hey, Pamela," he said.

Sarah, cringing, wanted to run away, but she didn't want to be the first one to break the silence. She, like everyone else, was looking at Julie. Well, if you're the boss now, then you deal with this, Sarah thought.

She expected Julie to use her razor tongue to cut Pamela to ribbons, and she was surprised when Julie said, softly, "Uh, Pamela, I'm not going behind your back. Clark . . . I assumed he would have spoken to you. He, uh . . . Clark asked me to take over the project."

Pamela looked at Julie incredulously. "I . . . there must be some mistake. David!"

Dingo looked like he was having a root canal. "Um. Yeah."

"Is this true? Did you hear this from Clark's mouth?"

"Uh. Yeah, Pamela, I did."

Pamela turned red and looked like she was going to scream, but then she took a deep breath, and said, calmly. "All right then. David, will you please collect the master tapes we recorded, and we'll take our leave."

Dingo shifted his bulk from foot to foot. He shoved his hands into his pockets and looked at the ground. "I . . . I can't do that, Pamela."

"Why on earth not?"

"Because Clark has the masters."

"Clark what! How did he get *my* master tapes?"

"Well, I . . . uh, I mean, technically, they are actually his master tapes. I mean, everybody on the tapes is an ATN employee. It was recorded at ATN. Hell, the actual tape itself was bought by ATN. I mean, they're really his, pretty much any way you look at it."

Pamela clenched her fists and spoke very quietly. "You didn't answer my question, David. Who gave him the tapes?"

Dingo looked like he would really like to disappear into the wall. "I did," he whispered.

She whirled on all of them. "So. Betrayed. Betrayed by every single one of you. And why? Why? What did I do to deserve this from you? Is it because"—she wheeled on Dingo—"because I plucked you from your bar bands and got you a real job as a touring musician? Because I gave you the job that allowed you to get your pathetic little house in *New Jersey*?" she said, her voice dripping with scorn. Dingo stared at his shoes.

"I wouldn't think Pammy Finocharrio from Cherry Hill would be so shitty about Jersey," Peter said.

If he expected stunned silence from Pamela, he was disappointed. "Oh, yes, Peter. Well done. I took a stage name. God, you think you know everything, and you know nothing. What does my stage name prove? It may interest you to know that your overweight drummer friend is not actually named after a wild dog. My name doesn't change anything. I took a bunch of marginally talented children and tried to nurture whatever tiny seeds of talent existed in them so they would bloom into something wonderful, and they thank me with this . . . this complete betrayal! You'd be nothing without me! None of you would be anything without me!"

"Well, I'd still have my girlfriend," Peter said.

"You never would have met your girlfriend." She turned on Sarah. "Did he win you back with his lies? Did he tell you he didn't kiss me? Because if he did, he's lying. You know you're lying, Peter, you kissed me."

"After you climbed on my lap and grabbed my crotch!" Peter yelled. "You—"

"Grow up, Peter. You're an adult, even if you write songs like a teenager. Nobody forced you to kiss me. That's a choice you made."

Sarah looked from Pamela to Peter, and Pamela whirled around to face Levon. "What about you? Does your girlfriend know who you were fucking last night?" She turned to Julie, whose mouth hung open. "Or does she get off on hearing about your exploits?"

Levon whispered, "Well, she's not my girlfriend."

Sarah felt sick. "Jesus, Pamela, that's a really ugly thing to say."

"Oh, did I offend you? Or do you just need to join this little witch hunt so you can pretend you never—"

"You're pathetic!" Sarah spat.

"Well, you're the one standing there pretending you don't *know* me. Pretending that what happened the other nigh—oh, yes, Sarah, it really happened—pretending you didn't . . ."

"Shut up, Pamela! Just shut up!" Sarah yelled. She looked at Peter, who wouldn't look at her, and she started to cry. Please, she thought, as the tears of anger and humiliation poured out of her, please, Julie, save us.

"Pamela," Julie said, "I'm going to have to get security to remove you if you don't leave here right now."

"Why would I want to spend one more second in the company of such hypocrites? Such failures? Yes, go back to convincing yourselves that I'm the cause of all your problems. That's so much more comfortable than confronting the emptiness in your own souls."

Sarah sniffed and looked up, waiting for Julie to deliver the verbal death blow. What came out instead was a shock. "Pamela,"

Julie said, "you are going to have an emptiness in your mouth where your front teeth used to be if you don't shut the fuck up and get out of my studio."

Everyone stared at Julie in shock. Pamela was the first to recover. "You wouldn't dare."

"You just told me you fucked my boyfriend," Julie said.

Levon piped up with "Do I get a say in this? Jesus! If I knew I had a girlfriend I never would've gone over there." Nobody paid him the slightest attention, and Julie continued.

"Even in Westport people get beaten for that. Of course, we normally hire people to do our dirty work, but I think I'd actually enjoy doing this myself. And I doubt you'd find a witness in this basement who saw anything. So you need to leave right now, or I swear to God I will beat you like the cheap whore you are."

Pamela gave Julie a steely look, then without another word she spun around and walked out.

Sarah wiped her tears away and looked at Julie, who was panting. "I was really hoping she was going to refuse to leave," Julie said.

"Thank you," Sarah said quietly. She meant thank you for getting rid of Pamela, but also thank you for behaving in a way we never expected and drawing everyone's attention away from Pamela revealing that I'm a lesbian.

Or whatever she was. She had sex with a woman and enjoyed it. She had sex with men and enjoyed it. She had no idea what that made her. She had no idea who she was. Ever since she got here it was like she was watching this body move around, this body that was occupied by infatuation with Peter, by enthrallment with Pamela. What was inside? All she knew was that she felt worthless.

And she had to get out of here. Forever. She needed to just put this whole thing behind her right away.

"Well," Julie said, finally breaking the silence. "Let's take ten minutes to get ourselves together and then hit the studio. We still have a ton of work to do."

"I . . . I can't, Julie," Sarah said. She knew she might have let herself in for some verbal or even physical abuse with that comment, but she simply couldn't.

Instead, Julie spoke softly and calmly. "I know how upset you are. I think we're all upset. But we have to work. It's really important."

Sarah stood up and began walking toward the elevator. "No. It isn't. It's cartoons. We're making songs for cartoons. If this never gets done, nobody in the world except for you and Clark is ever going to care. It's just cartoons. And it's not worth this." And she started crying again. "Nothing is worth this. I'm sorry, Julie, I know you still think this is important, but it's really not. Go home and walk Simone—that's important. Dingo's kids are important. None of the rest of it matters at all. It's all bullshit, and I'm . . . I'm just so ashamed that I ever hurt anybody over this bullshit. People shouldn't treat each other like this. Especially not over cartoons. It's over. I'm done. I'm sorry, Julie, I'm sorry, Peter, I'm sorry, everyone. I can't do this anymore. I have to go."

She walked down the hall and picked up her guitar. She looked at her pile of clothes in the corner. She never wanted to wear anything she'd worn here ever again. Carrying her guitar, she walked up the stairwell and into the ATN lobby. The elevator bonged behind her, and she looked back and saw Peter running after her.

"Sarah," he said. "Please don't go. I love you. Please don't go."

It was certainly tempting. Crawl back into the basement and take up the mantle of Peter's Girlfriend again. It had been fun. But she just couldn't do it now.

"How could you possibly love me? There's nothing here to

love. I don't even exist, Peter, I'm just an idea in other people's minds. I have to go away—I'm sorry, I'm sorry. I had fun. But I have to go."

Suddenly Peter was yelling. "Goddammit, no! I have never . . . I've never met anyone like you before, and we had something wonderful, and I'm not going to let it get ruined! I'm not!"

Sarah sighed. "I'm sorry, Peter. I wish you could—there is no one like me. I'm not even like me. And I don't like me. I . . . I can't love anybody, I can't be loved until I figure out who the hell I am."

Peter was crying. "That's bullshit. That's Pamela talking. I know who you are, and I love you! Please don't leave!"

"I'm sorry," Sarah said. There was nothing else to say, so she just turned and walked out of the building, hoping Peter wouldn't follow her. He didn't. When she reached the sidewalk, she hailed a taxi. She hopped in and realized she had no idea where she was going. Away from here was all she knew. Away from here.

"Port Authority," she said to the driver, and the taxi pulled away from the curb and joined the river of traffic that bore Sarah away.

23

THE PLANE REACHED cruising altitude, and Levon put his seat back and closed his eyes. The engines roared, but the ride was smooth, and Levon had a fanciful idea that the machine he was riding in was not an airplane at all, but rather a magical life-changer. He walked on to the plane in New York a professional musician, and he would emerge in Dallas as an engineer.

Somewhere beneath him, there was a truck bearing his clothes on the highway to Texas. Somewhere in the truck, there was a bass guitar that, for a brief time, Levon had used to make a living. By the time he was over Arkansas, the whole thing seemed like a dream. The reason he knew for sure that the whole experience had really happened was that two little white kids two rows back kept singing, in a shrill and distinctly unfunky way, "Funky Solar System."

CAPTAIN SUNSHINE, DRUNK, yelled at Peter again that he was a hack, that he wouldn't sing this piece-of-shit song at a birthday party, let alone on national television. Peter breathed and said nothing. Not that he really cared about Captain Sunshine's opinion of his work in the first place, but he understood that part of the Captain's problem was that he knew Peter had worked on *Pop Goes the Classroom,* and ATN had just cut four minutes out of Captain Sunshine's show to make way for more showings of the *Pop Goes the Classroom* cartoons. The ATN grapevine said they were getting more mail on *Pop Goes the Classroom* than they had on anything since Mister Chuckles had forgotten that his mike was still open and cursed a blue streak back in the live-TV days. Only this time the mail was positive. As *Pop Goes the Classroom* grew more successful, the only recognition that came Peter's way was Captain Sunshine's venomous jealousy. Peter, who had come to terms with the fact that he would never be the New Dylan, was undisturbed by this.

Down in the basement of ATN, where Peter still slept, there was a letter containing his acceptance to the PhD program in American history at Columbia. A few more months, he thought, a few more months of living rent-free and eating only employee cafeteria food, and he'd have enough money to be that rarest of things—a graduate student who lived like a human being. While Captain Sunshine ranted on, Peter already dreamed of his thesis on the impact of patriotic songs on the success of the Revolution. Captain Sunshine finally stormed out of the room, and Peter got to work writing yet another draft of "Jimmy Giraffe's Long, Long Neck."

IT WAS TWO in the morning. Julie was the only person in the control booth, and she sat down to watch *The Richie Stevens and Floppy Variety Hour.* Again. She rolled her eyes as Richie Stevens did his opening ventriloquism act with his dummy, a rabbit named Floppy. This part was horrible, but Richie had it in his contract that he always got to write the monologue. As for the rest of the show, the musicians were competent, the writing was not embarrassing, and the dancers could dance. It wasn't great television—it probably wasn't even good television. It certainly wasn't the job she'd hoped for after she'd pulled Clark Payson's bacon out of the fire with the *Pop Goes the Classroom* project. Every time Julie turned around, ATN was squeezing another showing into the already packed Saturday-morning schedule. Senator Prescott, whose public reaming of Briggs Payson over kids' TV had gotten the whole *Pop Goes the Classroom* ball rolling, had recently praised ATN's responsible use of the public airwaves to educate while entertaining.

And so Julie's career in television was off and running. But she was young and still had dues to pay, so she'd been handed this turkey of a show, already on its second producer. She'd taken a show that was poised to become a famous disaster and turned it into what would probably be a forgettable and, more importantly, inexpensive failure. So her first producing job probably wouldn't be her last. "Come on, sweetie," she said, and Simone raised her head, looked at Julie skeptically, and slowly got to her feet. "Good girl," Julie said. "Let's go home."

THE MAIL CAME just as Sarah had finalized her set list. Or whatever this was. She had five poems that she was going to perform at Chris's art opening, accompanying herself on the Mosrite electric guitar she'd bought. Chris told her she was wonderful, that this was edgy, exciting art, but then she couldn't really trust Chris's opinion because Chris was in love with her. She grabbed the mail that had come through the slot in the front door, and there was her first reaction to her demo tape. She opened the envelope and laughed. Well, maybe next time.

She pinned the letter on the corkboard where all of Chris's rejections from various galleries and exhibits hung. She was proud to be able to add her first one to the board.

Dear Sarah,

    I'm really sorry. I love your songs and really wanted to sign you, but the powers that be—you remember Clark?—have made it clear that we can't be the label that's known for female folksingers, and Pamela is currently occupying the roster spot we've got for that type of music. (She was so pleased with our distribution that she begged me for a three-album deal, which, after what I did to her, I couldn't really refuse.) Which is a shame because you're better. Good luck, kid.

                  Sincerely,
                  David Donovan
                  Vice President for Artists and Repertoire

She supposed at least for now, she'd be keeping the day job at PS 122, where yesterday, when her third-grade class had reached the nines-times tables, eight students had favored her with a spontaneous a cappella rendition of "Nine's Magic Multiples."

DINGO GRITTED HIS teeth. Just a couple more minutes. He hated these parent conferences. Some girl who looked twelve with no kids of her own or else some old crone forty years past childbearing would tell them how Davey was so smart, she couldn't figure out why he didn't do his work, she couldn't figure out why he was so disrespectful. And then there would be a pregnant pause where she would look at Dingo and Cass and not say, *You're obviously horrible parents,* but they would understand her message clear as a bell. And then he and Cass would have a big fight that would consist of her saying you're too hard on him, and him saying you baby him too much. I've seen this movie so many times, Dingo thought. Why do I have to watch it again?

Nevertheless, he went into the classroom, holding Cass's hand, and felt ridiculous sitting his extra-large frame on an undersized chair. Miss Loring shook their hands and said, "Well, I just wanted to let you know that since we started our multiplication unit, Davey has really begun to shine. He knows all the multiplication songs that they show on Saturday morning, and he's just been breezing through the quizzes. I have to tell you, it's just so great to be able to give him attention for something positive."

Well, this wasn't what he was expecting, but he would certainly take it.

"Now, Mr. Donovan, Davey tells me that you were actually involved in making those cartoons?"

Dingo blushed. "I kind of produced the recordings."

"And played all the drum parts," Cass added, smiling.

"Well, I wonder if you'd be willing to come in and talk to the class about it sometime. They're all familiar with the songs—that bicameral one made my civics lesson a breeze—and I'm sure they'd be interested in the behind-the-scenes story of how they were made."

Dingo imagined facing a class full of kids and telling them what went on behind the scenes on the *Pop Goes the Classroom* project. No way in hell. "Well, it really wasn't that interesting," he lied, "just pretty standard recording"—he felt Cass's elbow in his ribs—"uh, but of course I'd be happy to come in and talk to the class."

"That's wonderful," Miss Loring said. "You know, it's not that common for me to find that something on television actually makes my job easier. I just want to thank you. You really did a wonderful thing."

Dingo smiled. "Yeah," he said. "I guess we did."

CAROLYN

AROLYN GAVE ONE last check of the catering table and adjusted one blue glass bottle of water so it sat more symmetrically with the other eleven.

She checked the pastries. They looked just as artfully arranged as they had two minutes ago. Carolyn considered moving the chocolate croissant on the right, but then decided she might as well leave it alone.

The boss's story of *Pop Goes the Classroom* had lasted hours and had concluded next door over drinks, and Carolyn still didn't know if this made her "The Boss's Favorite Protégée" or "The Person Who Heard Too Much When the Boss Was Feeling Vulnerable and Now Must Be Eliminated."

Carolyn looked at her BlackBerry. Nothing from the boss, which she supposed was a relief. Nine oh two. Where was everybody?

Between nine oh five and nine twenty, everyone arrived, greeted Carolyn, and started making a mess of the pastry tray. It occurred to Carolyn that she should have taken a picture of the arrangement so that when the boss made her entrance, she would know that it had once been beautiful.

She looked around the room and had a hard time picturing this bunch of gray-haired (well, the black guy and the really old guy were bald, but everybody else was gray, thick-around-the-middle people being the same bunch of confused young horndogs from the boss's story. And for that matter, the tall old man with the tight T-shirt stretched across his firm, youthful pecs did not seem like he could have been the big biker-looking guy from the story.

Something else was strange—all the old people were smiling, hugging, and laughing, showing pictures of their children and grandchildren.

At nine twenty, the boss arrived, her hair still blond, her core toned from Pilates, and her clothes casual but still reeking of money.

"All right, you slackers! Get to work!" she barked, and the room erupted in laughter.

"Julie!" voices called out, and she was surrounded by people giving her hugs and kisses. Carolyn watched carefully for any hint of tension between the boss and Levon Hayes, but she didn't see any.

"Is Carolyn taking good care of you?" Julie asked, and Carolyn blushed.

"Everything's great, Julie. And the hotel you put us in—my God, that's a nice place," Sarah Stein said.

"I don't know, Julie, you should be careful," Peter Terpin said. "When you were her age, you were already stabbing your boss in the back and taking her job."

Carolyn was afraid that the boss's famous temper would emerge here, but it appeared to have taken the day off. Julie smiled broadly and said, "Well, I hope I'm a better boss than Pamela was."

Everybody looked at Carolyn. "Well?" Peter, who had obviously decided to be the troublemaker, said.

Carolyn decided to bet everything on "Favorite Protégée," and before she knew what was happening she heard herself say, "Well, she hasn't tried to sleep with my boyfriend, if that's what you're asking."

Silence fell on the room, and Carolyn had already mentally updated her résumé in the long seconds it took for laughter to erupt.

"You have time to have a boyfriend? I'm clearly not giving you enough work to do," the boss, Julie, said, with a big smile on her face. "We're all ready to go if you guys will head in to the studio and find yourself a mike to sit by," she added.

The old people began filing into the studio where they would talk while watching *Pop Goes the Classroom,* and the boss—Julie, Carolyn mentally corrected herself—hung back until they were alone in the reception area.

"You're fired," Julie said, and Carolyn was dumbstruck. "I'm kidding, I'm kidding. We'll be fine in here. You've worked really hard, so take the rest of the day off."

This was even more unexpected than getting fired. "I . . . uh . . . okay."

"Go sleep with your boyfriend," Julie said.

"Well, I'll have to find one first."

"Go get on that, will you? I can't very well steal an imaginary boyfriend from you."

"Right. Okay. I'll just make sure everything's all set up here, and then I'll . . . uh . . ."

"Go buy a dog, maybe. It's a good way to meet people. Thanks, Carolyn. It's . . . you're way too young to understand how great it is to see these people, but I really appreciate your getting this all together."

"I . . . you're welcome," Carolyn said, and the boss squeezed her arm and then disappeared into the studio.

Carolyn straightened up what was left of the snacks, made a call to make sure lunch would be delivered on time, and wondered what she was going to do with the rest of her day. She went upstairs and e-mailed her friends, ordered a couple of books, read a couple of blogs, and checked her online personal ad, finding the usual assortment of messages from professors and professorial wannabes twice her age.

She decided to take one look into the studio before she left, just to make sure everything was working okay.

"Hey," she said, poking her head into the booth. "How's it going?"

Kadeem the sound engineer looked up and said, "They all sat around and talked for the first hour. But now—well, you have got to see this." Carolyn walked into the booth and looked into the studio. *Pop Goes the Classroom* cartoons played on the big TV, but nobody was really watching them. Two joints were making circuits around the studio. "That's the boss's weed," Kadeem said, and Carolyn was momentarily hurt that the boss hadn't delegated the purchase to her.

The instruments Carolyn had ordered at Julie's request were all in use. Behind the glass, inaudible, the boss banged away at an upright piano. Peter Terpin and Sarah Stein played guitars, Levon Hayes played bass, and Dingo Donovan played drums.

"You getting anything usable out of this?" Carolyn asked Kadeem.

"It sounds like complete shit," Kadeem said. "You want to listen?"

Carolyn looked at the musicians banging away at their instruments, looks of stoned bliss on their faces, and suddenly felt like listening in would be some kind of violation of privacy.

"No, thanks," Carolyn said. She left the booth and took the elevator up to the lobby and walked out onto the street.

Carolyn walked into the crowd on the sidewalk toward the subway that would bear her back to her apartment in Brooklyn.

And for the rest of the day, and into the night, five people sat in a basement in Manhattan, singing.

ACKNOWLEDGMENTS

Thanks to Suzanne Demarco, Casey and Kylie Nelson, Rowen Halpin, and Cooper Demarco for love, support, and inspiration.

Thanks to Doug Stewart for consistent encouragement, support, and friendship.

Thanks to Bruce Tracy for seeing clearly what needed to be changed, added, and cut out.

Thanks to Trish Cook, Dana Reinhardt, and Kirsten Feldman for early reads and helpful feedback.

Thanks to Betsy Gaines Quammen and Dorothy Shaffer, who got me thinking about mentors in 2005.

ABOUT THE AUTHOR

BRENDAN HALPIN lives in Boston with his wife, Suzanne, and their children. Find him on the Web at www.brendanhalpin.com and at www.myspace.com/brendanhalpin.